Praise for J. R. Campbell

IMPROBABLE REMAINS

THE BIZARRE AND UNCONVENTIONAL
ADVENTURES OF SHERLOCK HOLMES

IMPROBABLE REMAINS

THE BIZARRE AND UNCONVENTIONAL ADVENTURES OF SHERLOCK HOLMES

J. R. Campbell

WEIRD HOUSE

Editor & Publisher, Joe Morey

layout based on design by F.J. Bergmann, and reproduced by
by Cyrus Wraith Walker

ISBN: 978-1-957121-20-8

Weird House Press
Central Point, OR 97502
www.weirdhousepress.com

Grateful acknowledgement to Conan Doyle Estate Ltd. for
permission to use the Sherlock Holmes characters created by
the late Sir Arthur Conan Doyle.

For Kim, for introducing me to so many people I love
For Charles, for introducing me to so many books I love

Publication History

The Missing Coppertop first published in Curious Incidents 2 edited by JR Campbell and Charles Prepolec A Mad for a Mystery Publication.

The Entwined first published in Gaslight Grimoire: Fantastic Tales of Sherlock Holmes edited by JR Campbell and Charles Prepolec Edge Science Fiction and Fantasy Publishing.

Court of Honour first published in A Study in Lavender: Queering Sherlock Holmes edited by Joseph R.G. DeMarco Lethe Press.

Best Laid Plans first published in Gaslight Grotesque: Nightmare Tales of Sherlock Holmes edited by JR Campbell & Charles Prepolec Edge Science Fiction and Fantasy Publishing.

Mr. Other's Children first published in Gaslight Grotesque: Nightmare Tales of Sherlock Holmes edited by JR Campbell & Charles Prepolec Edge Science Fiction and Fantasy Publishing.

Lord Garrett's Skulls first published in The MX Book of New Sherlock Holmes Stories II edited by David Marcum MX Publishing.

Original stories to this book:

The Haunted Inspector
The Oba's Voice
Contaminated Sample
Grimoire
Hero of Baker Street

Table of Contents

Foreword

 uzzah! There is a collection of Jeff's Sherlock Holmes stories! Double huzzah! The time has come when I finally get the honor and privilege of writing nice things about a collection of Jeff's Sherlock Holmes stories.

It's something I've been eagerly expecting to do at any time during the last 20 years, or so, which is, not at all coincidently, about when I'd read one of the first of them. You see, though Jeff and I had already known each other for a decade—we met when he strolled into my mystery-themed bookstore as a publisher's rep in the very early 90s—I had no idea he was a closet writer until we sat down to put together, co-edit and publish a sort of Sherlock Holmes journal. The idea was, perhaps naively, to give something back to the Sherlockian community, which had brought us both a good deal of joy in the form of pastiches, or stories in the style of Sir Arthur Conan Doyle.

I was a keen and active Sherlockian at the time, so began soliciting stories from the online community, which was painfully small in the late 90s, and I can still recall being surprised when Jeff said that if we didn't come up with enough material, he had written a story that might work to fill it out. Well, a shortage of submissions was not a problem, and at the suggestion of our printer, the journal morphed into a perfect-bound micro-press paperback anthology: *Curious Incidents: Being A Collection of the Further Adventures of Sherlock Holmes*, with Jeff's excellent story "The Adventure of the First Mate's Jacket" included. A year later we produced *Curious Incidents*, again with a story from Jeff, "The Missing Coppertop", which opens this present collection. It was at that point that I knew I'd one day be penning this foreword, but there's more to the story. A few years later my tastes had shifted away from the traditional mystery-centric pastiche towards a sort of Holmes-and-horror story-telling hybrid, and Jeff had always been a fan of SF and fantasy, so we pitched a pro-anthology along those lines to a Canadian publisher. It was a distinct shift from our very traditional *Curious Incidents* approach, but again Jeff served up a great story for inclusion, and that anthology became *Gaslight Grimoire: Fantastic Tales of Sherlock Holmes* launching to acclaim at World Fantasy Convention 2008, and spawning a series, some with further stories from Jeff included, that we're still co-editing today.

All well and good, but we're talking about Jeff's work, and he was also busy elsewhere, with Sherlock Holmes stories appearing from publishers as varied as Lethe Press and MX Publishing. Some of those excellent stories are included here, but he's also written a number of entirely new pieces unique to this collection—"Grimoire" is a particular standout for me, with echoes of James and Machen—that absolutely floored me when reading them for the first time today. As an editor familiar with some stories, I can sometimes be a bit blind of the forest for the trees, or more accurately blind of the forester's hand, but reading this collection, this aggregate of stories, was an eye-opener.

Jeff knows his Holmes, but I don't think I've ever truly appreciated the wealth of creativity, imagination and skill he piles into his stories until now. I'm particularly in awe of the imagination on display. This collection does, indeed, embrace all that is "bizarre and outside the conventions and humdrum routine of everyday life."

You're in for a treat, dear readers, enjoy...

—Charles Prepolec, BSI
January 21, 2022

Introduction

by J.R. Campbell

"I know, my dear Watson, that you share my love of all that is bizarre and outside the conventions and humdrum routine of everyday life. You have shown your relish for it by the enthusiasm which has prompted you to chronicle, and, if you will excuse my saying so, to somewhat embellish so many of my own little adventures."

—Sherlock Holmes, The Red-Headed League

herlock Homes is the detective all the world knows, yet, when you actually encounter him in Doyle's stories, he somehow manages to be surprising. Certainly this was my experience with the Great Detective. Despite so many adaptations, in so many types of media, I've been aware of Sherlock Holmes before I ever took a serious interest in his adventures. He took me very much by surprise when my attention belatedly swung in his direction.

I knew he was a genius, everyone knows that, but Doyle

deftly writes exactly how his genius works. So often genius is presented as something magical, something present but unexplainable, but Doyle presents a man who by study, talent and enthusiasm elevates himself above those who share the field with him. He is not without limitations. I appreciate that the first of his cases to appear in The Strand could hardly be considered one of his triumphs but remains one of his most famous adventures. Even in the stories where he is less than successful, his capacity to perceive what others cannot is obvious to the reader.

Now, when films are packed with super-powered heroes, it's worth remembering that Sherlock Holmes' super-powers are enthusiasm, concentration and intellect. And Holmes' partner, Doctor Watson's, lone super-power is the ability to be a truly amazing friend.

Of course, none of these observations are new to the reader who has purchased this offering. The odds of this book being your first introduction to Sherlock Holmes are vanishingly small. Yet, I feel obliged to say a few words for the sake of the innocents who might find these words on a relative's shelf, a library or any of the other improbable ways in which young readers discover their books.

What you, the first reader, is more likely interested in is a sense of the writer throwing these stories your way. In that spirit, like I toss a few of my Sherlockian opinions out there, rapid-fire style. Feel free to agree or disagree as you wish. I think Sherlock, when he is engaged in a case, works best in short form. Sherlock is a story engine, chewing through a novel's worth of story before ignoring his midday meal. I don't think Holmes gets enough credit for his work as a consulting detective, a detective who other detectives visit for assistance with their cases. I understand Watson's preference for stories in which he and Holmes are directly involved but I think these were a sideline and that his consulting work was the basis of Holmes' practice. Though I understand the temptation all too well, I'm generally opposed to origin stories. Did you catch the qualifier there? Generally. I have to admit that Stephen Volk's *Under a Raven's Wing* from PS Publishing is as perfect an origin story as could be imagined. While I can't help but agree with purists who say Arthur Conan Doyle wrote the best Sherlock Homes stories, I cannot imagine limiting my Sherlock Holmes reading, and re-reading, to just those excellent tales. I enjoy Sherlock-adjacent works, such as Steve Hockensmith's *Holmes on the Range*. I think Holmes and Watson can work in any literary genre and I believe Watson is every bit as fascinating a character as Holmes, just not as flashy. How well these opinions present themselves in the stories that follow is for you, the reader, to decide.

My earliest memory of Sherlock Holmes is embarrassing. It happened when I was a wee lad, maybe eight years old, though not yet interested in counting such things. My grandmother, a lover of mystery fiction and an Agatha Christie devotee, asked me who my favourite detective was. At the time this seemed an important and very adult question, but one for which I did not have an important nor adult answer. The name Sherlock Holmes flashed across my thoughts like an echo from the future. I'd read a story, possibly The Red-Headed League, so that answer seemed, if not honest, at least earned. As I recall, I hedged my bets, answering that my favourite television detective was Columbo, a popular choice, but that my favourite book detectives were still Frank and Joe, the Hardy boys, as I had not really read enough mysteries yet. It was an answer that satisfied my grandmother, who valued honesty, but delayed my reading of Sherlock Holmes for far too long. After all, what lad or rebellious young man seeks out the correct books?

I was encouraged to try Sherlock Holmes much later by a friend and, remembering my youthful answer to my Gran, I decided to give it a go. I started with a novel, predictably *A Study in Scarlet*, but like so many others before me found myself hooked about halfway through *The Adventures of Sherlock Holmes*. It was, for me, a revelation about the power of short fiction. I also cherish the fact that my passion for the Sherlock Holmes stories, stories of friendship, was sparked by a friend. From there my experience with Sherlock Holmes expanded into writing, working with Jim French's *Imagination Theater's Further Adventures of Sherlock Holmes* radio plays, and editing the *Gaslight* Sherlock Holmes anthologies, five volumes and counting, with the friend who started it all, Charles Prepolec, whom I've had the pleasure of knowing before his lip was twisted.

And my latest memory of Sherlock Holmes? No points for guessing it was writing this introduction, though there is nothing more deceptive than an obvious fact. It's been a pleasure for me to revisit the stories I've written about Sherlock Holmes, remembering what it was about him that I hoped to pin to the page when I wrote them. I'm grateful for the chance to pull these efforts into a collection and grateful to those who have decided to take a chance reading them. I hope you enjoy them.

—J.R. Campbell

The Missing Coppertop

 one but Sherlock Holmes would have noted the sound, as it was barely audible and singularly unremarkable, but to Holmes it was as unmistakable and welcome as the music of his violin. How many cases began in this manner, with the swing of the door and the creak of the steps leading to his Baker Street lodgings? Too many to count and yet, to Holmes, these mundane noises were a clarion call, trumpets announcing the game's commencement. Holmes turned and listened eagerly, his angular face animated with an almost predatory keenness,

"Odd," Holmes remarked, the midday meal, thoughtfully prepared by Mrs. Hudson for the occasion of my visit, forgotten on the table before him.

I paused, listening, knowing only one sound could silence Holmes so quickly and completely. Despite my attention I heard nothing, prompting me to ask Holmes directly, "What is it?"

"A visitor," Holmes reported, pushing his chair back as he stood. "Surely you heard the door open and close and yet whoever has come lingers upon the landing. The natural inference, given the chill of the season, is that our guest is removing his footwear. Yet the stairs remain curiously silent; either our visitor bears no weight at all or had refused the natural seat offered by our steps. You remember, of course, the dreadful picture Mrs. Hudson insisted on hanging in the landing? The frame produces a distinctive knock when anyone, heavy or light, leans against the wall. I'm certain you've heard that knock a thousand times, yet you've not heard it today. Whoever has come refuses the support of wall or step, opting instead to remove their footwear by bending awkwardly in the narrow space at the base of the stairs. For what reason, I wonder? Ah, here he comes now!" And saying this, Holmes turned to the door and opened it before our visitor could announce himself.

Over the course of my friendship with Sherlock Holmes I had become something of an observer of his methods and I was well aware of his technique for appraising prospective clients. Disregarding the natural impulse to meet a stranger's eyes, Holmes preferred to quickly, but thoroughly, examine the newcomer's boots, trouser-knees, coat-sleeves, hands and fingernails first. No telltale sign was too subtle for Holmes' carefully trained eye and, more often than not, he was able to impress prospective clients with his deductions before they were able to speak a word.

It was with some delight then that I observed Holmes struck speechless by the sight of the visitor waiting behind the door that day. To a man who relied on the subtleties of shirt cuffs and calluses to determine a man's profession, this visitor was a positively overwhelming avalanche of information. If I had been both blind and deaf I could still have identified our visitor as a railway man by the smell of coal dust, machine oil and the lingering musk of good, clean steam hanging thick around him. From the top of his cap down to his trouser-cuffs our guest wore the stiff, heavy work clothes I had often observed about the periphery of rail platforms. Our guest was three or four inches shorter than Holmes, and so solidly built as to be himself reminiscent of a locomotive. Beyond these simple observations I could tell little of our visitor, covered as he was in a patina of coal dust.

"Won't you come in?" I invited the shadow standing before the dumbstruck Holmes. "I assume you've come seeking Mr. Sherlock Holmes?"

"I have," the railway man agreed, stepping into our rooms on unshod feet. Despite the courtesy he'd shown thus far, in removing his footwear and carefully avoiding a smudge to our walls or steps, I couldn't help but chuckle when I considered Mrs. Hudson's reaction should she discover this coal-blackened spectre in her rooms.

"Would you care for something to eat?" I asked, waving my hand towards the ample meal on the table.

"Sorry," our guest replied, looking wistfully at the table and holding up his blackened hands by way of explanation. "I can't, I—"

"Nonsense," Holmes interrupted, regaining himself. "We've very little time. Your superintendent expects you back before your midday break is over, so best to eat while you're able. Watson, pull that wooden stool over from my chemistry bench. You'll not be able to stain it, I assure you, its capacity for stains has already been exceeded. Here," Holmes spread some discarded newspapers over the tabletop. "Eat while you can. Now, I take it the managers of your company do not know you are here and that there would be unfortunate repercussions for you if they did?"

Now it was the railway man who stared at Holmes in open amazement, "However do you know all this?"

"Really sir, it is not difficult to deduce. Your appearance makes it plain you hurried here from your place of work, not even sparing the time to tidy up first. Familiar as I am with the Underground's comings and goings, it is evident your walk from the station was a brisk one indeed. Obviously your intent is to contact me and then, with some luck, return to work before your absence is noted. Clearly you do not wish the company to know of your mission here."

A smile appeared on the railway man's features, startling white in his soot-begrimed face. "You're very quick Mr. Holmes, I tip my hat to you."

"Eat instead," Holmes urged. "It is apparent from the care you've taken not to dirty our lodgings that you are a conscientious man, nor the sort of fellow who regularly sneaks away from his responsibilities as a boiler inspector."

"How—"

"Eat. The brass gauge in your jacket gives away your profession as surely as Doctor Watson's stethoscope does his. Now then, once you are fed, I should like to hear what matter has brought you to me. Leave nothing out, you must trust to our discretion. Both Watson and I will do all we can to safeguard your employment, won't we Watson?"

"Of course, Holmes," I answered, intrigued despite myself.

Our guest ate quickly, taking a sip of tea to wash down his hastily consumed meal and leaving black fingerprints on the cup. He turned to Holmes, his round face arranging itself in an intent expression.

"They told me not to come, warned me that if I contacted the police I'd lose my position, but I had to do something. I mean, it's one of mine, Mr. Holmes, and they've searched all morning and found nothing. Nothing!"

"Start at the beginning," Holmes instructed the shadow.

"The beginning? Well, my name is Warboys, Leslie Warboys, and as you've deduced I'm a boiler inspector. This morning I was to check over one of our Coppertops but, when I arrived, it wasn't there. Someone's stolen it."

"I assume a Coppertop is a steam locomotive?" Holmes asked.

"Oh aye, a Wainwright class D steam locomotive. A four-four-oh. You've likely seen them, heading off to the coast, Dover and Folkestone. It's a handsome engine, no mistake. They're called Coppertops because they've a polished copper dome in the upper works."

"And you're certain it has been stolen?" Holmes asked. "Isn't it possible the engine was returned to service without your knowledge?"

"No sir!" From his tone it was clear Warboys regarded this suggestion as something akin to blasphemy. "No one would be foolish enough to take an engine out of my corner of the shop without my say-so. Besides, if it had been returned to service they'd have found it by now. They've been burning up the telegraph wires searching for that engine. They're certain it's not left London; they've checked every station on every line leading out of the city and no one's seen it. For some reason, my employers take comfort from this, as if knowing the engine is still in London makes it less lost. They can't find it, and that's why I've come. I want you to find it Mr. Holmes. I've not much money to offer ..."

"That's not a consideration, Mr. Warboys, I assure you."

"Why on Earth," I interjected, "would anyone steal a steam locomotive?"

"Indeed, Watson," Holmes nodded in agreement as he reached for his pipe and then the tobacco he kept tucked in the toe of a Persian slipper. "You've cut to the heart of the matter. Any thoughts, Mr. Warboys?"

"Well, it has happened Mr. Holmes. Young men, deep in their cups, see an unattended engine on the tracks and decide to indulge their boyhood dreams of driving a locomotive. Aye, it's happened before."

"Since you are here, I assume you don't believe this

locomotive disappeared in such a manner," Holmes observed, lighting his pipe.

"No sir, I don't," Warboys confirmed. "Though management seems content to believe it. Thing is, if it's mischief, there were four or five other engines in the yard that would have been more convenient to take than my Coppertop. And if some scoundrels did take my Coppertop, it's not likely they'd have hidden it. It should have been found by now."

"Quite valid points," Holmes agreed. "Anything else?"

"Just this, sir, in order to get the Coppertop out of the shop the thieves would have to pass through three locked gates. I examined each gate and none of them show any signs of having been tampered with. I'm no expert on such things but I do know that young men in their cups are more likely to drive an engine through a gate rather than fiddle open their locks. No, someone took that engine."

"Why?" Holmes asked, the question emerging in a cloud of blue smoke.

Warboys spread his arms to indicate his bafflement. I winced to see a fine sprinkle of coal dust descend onto the carpets with every gesture. "I've no idea, sir, no idea at all. It's not as if they could hope to sell it and there's no value to be found in its parts."

"Perhaps your competition wishes to examine it," I ventured, having read in the papers of the sometime fierce rivalry between the two London railway companies.

"There are no secrets in a Coppertop's construction," Warboys pointed out. "There's nothing there they'd need to learn."

"Perhaps they seek to embarrass your company," Holmes mused.

"No sir, I'll not believe that, not even of them. We're all

railway men after all; I can't believe they'd sink to such depths."

"Where does that leave us?" I asked.

"With an interesting problem," Holmes answered, fitting his pipe to his mouth. "Tell me, Mr. Warboys, you believe the thieves took this Coppertop instead of other, more readily accessible locomotives?"

"That's right."

"I want you to think carefully about this Mr. Warboys: Is there anything special about that particular locomotive? Any unusual history or anecdotes associated with it?"

"Can't think of a thing, Mr. Holmes. Sorry."

"The facts are what they are Mr. Warboys, you need not apologise for them. Now, think again: Over the last few weeks, has anyone shown a special interest in that locomotive?"

"Well, no, not really," Warboys answered.

Holmes smiled, examining the coal-blackened man intently. "You hesitated Mr. Warboys," Holmes observed. "You thought of a name and then dismissed it. If I am to help I must have your trust."

"It's nothing, Mr. Holmes, I assure you."

"Quite likely you are correct, however if you wish my assistance you must allow me to judge what is or is not important. The name, Mr. Warboys, please."

"Since you insist Mr. Holmes." The railway man sighed, shaking loose another fine sprinkle of coal dust. "Norris Bodmer is the name I thought of, an engine-driver who retired just last week. He often piloted the missing engine, you see, to Dover and back. Last week, as he was leaving the shop, he made a comment about not spending anymore time with the petulant Wainwright."

"Petulant Wainwright?" I asked.

"He meant the missing Coppertop, it's a Wainwright Class D." Warboys answered helpfully.

"Yes, but petulant?"

"Well, you have to understand these locomotives are complex machines, so complex that they develop personalities of a sort. Now, this Coppertop that was taken is a fine engine but unforgiving. Norris was a good engineer but he had a heavy hand on the throttle, he never really got on with that Coppertop. As I said Mr. Holmes, it's nothing really."

"Perhaps," Holmes admitted. "Still, best to eliminate all possibilities. Where might this Norris Bodmer reside?"

Looking rather uncomfortable, Mr. Warboys answered. "Goldington Street, but—"

"Why, what luck!" Holmes interrupted, returning his pipe to the mantle, "Watson, didn't you tell me you were visiting a patient on Crowndale Road this afternoon? Would it be an imposition to dash around the corner and knock on Mr. Bodmer's door? Just to see if he's enjoying his retirement?"

"No imposition Holmes, I'd be glad to." In truth, I'd no patient on Crowndale Road. Still, I was always willing to assist Holmes in his cases.

"Mr. Warboys, we best return you to your work before they mark your absence. I shall accompany you, I wish to examine these locked gates your locomotive passed through for myself. On the way, perhaps you can tell me what efforts your employers are making to locate their missing engine. Watson, I shall meet with you here once our errands are complete. Lead on, Mr. Warboys, time is not our ally."

§

So it was that I found myself knocking on a stranger's door that afternoon. When no answer was forthcoming I turned to leave. As I did so the door behind me opened. Turning back, I found myself looking at a thin woman with fine, silver hair, a pinched expression and a worn, haggard cast to her features. She looked at me with such timidity, stealing glances behind her, that I felt rather guilty for intruding upon her.

"Mrs. Bodmer?" I asked, tipping my hat.

"Yes?" The small woman's voice was barely more than a whisper. Behind her, visible over her shoulder, stood the figure of a man. "I was hoping I might speak with your husband."

Mrs. Bodmer glanced nervously back into the dark of her home. The figure looked up, his stern, determined gaze focusing on me though he made no effort to close the distance between us.

"Norris Bodmer?" I ventured.

"No," Mrs. Bodmer answered. "This is ..."

"A friend of the family," the man answered gruffly. There was a trace of amusement in his tone, though his did not seem a face much accustomed to expressions of cheer. A high forehead sloping to a heavy brow, a square chin, a full, elaborately trimmed moustache, the solidly built fellow had an air of unshakeable competence about him.

"And you are?" The man inside asked.

"My name is Watson," I answered automatically. "Doctor Watson, Leslie Warboys sent me."

"Is Leslie ill?" Mrs. Bodmer asked.

"Oh, it's nothing serious," I assured her, grateful her mistaken assumption provided me with an excuse for my visit. "He mentioned that your husband was recently retired, I was hoping he might sit with him a while and as I was in the area—"

"Of course," the man nodded. "Unfortunately Norris is not in at the moment; he's gone down to the yards to visit some friends. We'll be certain to pass along your message Doctor Watson, please give Mr. Warboys our regards."

"I'll do that," I answered but the door was already closing as I did.

My errand completed, though I had little to show for my efforts, I returned to Baker Street to make my report to Holmes. Approaching the residence I had once shared with my friend, I was amused to see a trail of blackened boot-prints leading to the door of 221B. Letting myself into the sitting room, I made myself comfortable as I awaited Holmes' return.

"Remarkable," Holmes announced as he crossed the threshold. "I should have brought you with me Watson. I must confess I thoroughly enjoyed Mr. Warboys' tour of the yards."

"Well, I'm relieved you had some luck Holmes. I'm afraid the results of my errand are somewhat less than you'd hoped."

"In truth Watson, I found all as Mr. Warboys described. He's quite right when he suggests the Coppertop was intentionally taken, although for what reason is not yet clear. I wish you'd been there Watson. During the journey Mr. Warboys pointed out each train as it passed, informing me which engines were 'his', that is to say which engines he had inspected. With a glance he was able to tell who drove each train and how that engineer was treating his locomotive."

"He did seem rather possessive of 'his' Coppertop," I observed.

"Indeed," Holmes agreed. "In his corner of the yard he is Zeus, the absolute monarch of his small realm. You know Watson, while I was there he inspected one of his engines. With the front open it was like standing before a blast furnace, yet he walked right in. In fact, he picked up a split piece of wood and tossed it in before him, when I inquired why, he explained that when the wood started to smoke, it was time for him to leave the engine. Without the wood's example, he might cheerfully remain inside the engine until the heat reduced him to ash. Quite an experience, seeing a man so devoted to his work."

Although I didn't answer, I couldn't help but smile as I considered the truth of Holmes' words. How strange to hear such a comment from a man capable of discerning so many types of tobacco ash or the colour of mud unique to each borough of London.

"Enough of my wool-gathering Watson, tell me of your errand. I assume you found Mr. Bodmer resting with his feet up, happy for the stationary earth beneath him?"

"Well, no," I admitted. "I spoke to Mrs. Bodmer and was informed that her husband had gone to the yards to visit with friends. I rather thought you might have seen him there."

"Gone to the yards?" Holmes asked, frowning. "I assure you Watson, Mr. Bodmer has not been seen by his employers since his retirement. I made certain of it. You say you saw his wife?"

"Yes, though she did not seem well and I did not wish to intrude."

"Unwell? Yet her husband left her alone?"

"Not alone, there was another gentleman there with her. Quite a capable looking fellow, a friend of the family I was told."

"Describe him if you will, Watson."

"Really Holmes, he didn't come to the door, I saw him for only a moment." But Holmes was deaf to my pleas. Recalling the scene, I did my best to describe the figure I'd glanced over Mrs. Bodmer's shoulder. "Average height, fair hair, stout but quite fit looking. In his mid-fifties I should say, prominent chin, high forehead, somewhat swarthy I suppose."

"Moustache? Deeply lined face?" Holmes asked.

"Yes, on both counts."

"Watson, did this man carry himself with a military bearing?"

"Really Holmes, I saw him for just an instant. I suppose he may have but if he were in the service he was undoubtedly an officer. Only an officer would trim a moustache so."

"Good heavens Watson," Holmes exclaimed, walking over to his desk and retrieving pen, ink and paper from the clutter there.

"What is it Holmes?"

"Perhaps nothing," Holmes admitted, his pen scratching across the paper. "Yet the description you've given matches an individual whom Inspector Gregson and Scotland Yard have been scouring all London for."

"You think Gregson's case has some bearing on the stolen locomotive?"

Holmes took the note he had written, placed it in an envelope and sealed it with wax. "I distrust coincidence. Watson, I want you to take this message to Gregson, however it is imperative you not be followed. Better the letter go undelivered than risk revealing Gregson's current whereabouts. I trust you recall the necessary precautions?"

"Of course," I assured my friend.

"I should warn you, Gregson will not be pleased to see you," Holmes said, writing an address on the front of the envelope. "His case is of national importance and it has been very trying on him. Should he ask your assistance—"

"I'll do all I can," I said, accepting the message.

"Good man," Holmes thanked me.

"Holmes?" I asked as my friend reached for the door. "May I ask as to the nature of Gregson's case?"

"Blackmail," Holmes answered.

"What would a blackmailer want with a steam locomotive?" I wondered aloud.

"Indeed," Holmes nodded. "The answer to that question

may well be the key that unlocks this entire affair. Good luck Watson, and remember: You must not be followed."

Assuring Holmes I would take every precaution, I preceded him down to the street and flagged a passing cab. Much to the annoyance of my driver, I obeyed Holmes' instructions to avoid any pursuit. Seeing nothing suspicious behind me, I travelled to a street near the address on the envelope and offered my driver a generous tip before crossing the remaining distance on foot. Knocking on the nondescript residence, I was greeted by an unfamiliar and decidedly intimidating face.

""I've a message for Gregson," I informed the hulking brute before me. The frown on his broad face deepened but the name Gregson was apparently familiar. The tall man gestured me inside, looking up and down the street to make certain I had not been followed.

"Wait here." The curt instruction delivered in a manner that left no room for argument. I waited in the hallway, wondering who the large, stern man might be. In short order the familiar flaxen-haired visage of Tobias Gregson appeared from around the corner. As Holmes had predicted the Scotland Yard Inspector was not pleased to see me.

"He's got some nerve, sending you here," Gregson complained. I held out Holmes' message and the Inspector snatched it from my hand, examining the seal before opening it. I noted, with some satisfaction, the way Gregson's frown deepened as he read the hastily written note.

"Confound it," Gregson cursed, folding the note into his pocket. "I can't leave the prisoner alone with Constable Rimbly. Tell Holmes—"

"If it would help, I could stay with the constable until you return." My offer was immediately accepted, with profuse thanks from the Inspector.

"Did you bring your pistol, Doctor?"

"No," I answered, somewhat unnerved by the question. Gregson frowned but then assured me it was unlikely I would need it. I was taken to a small parlour and introduced to Constable Rimbly, the large man who had greeted me at the door, and the prisoner whose name was not spoken. Then, as quickly as he could, Gregson left.

After shaking hands with the constable, I sat and took the opportunity to examine Gregson's prisoner. A slight man, balding, with a weak chin, large ears and deep-set eyes. His dress seemed more suited to a clerk than a blackmailer and his unlined face appeared untroubled by vice. Despite his unimposing appearance, the prisoner was manacled. I must confess I disliked the man on sight, for some reason he seemed more amused than concerned by his predicament.

"Tea, Doctor Watson?" Constable Rimbly offered, the cup seeming very small in the policeman's massive hands. I accepted and found myself answering questions regarding Sherlock Holmes, of whom the constable had heard rumours. The prisoner listened intently to each word I spoke, causing me to speak more guardedly than I might have. The time passed slowly but in due course Gregson returned.

"Well, Doctor," Gregson greeted me. "It was him all right. Mrs. Bodmer is safe, thanks in no small part to your alertness, but our man has eluded us."

"I'm sorry to hear that Inspector," I sympathised, gathering my hat and coat. I returned to Baker Street but Holmes was not there. Leaving him a note, I proceeded home where I managed to enjoy a dinner with my wife before Holmes' messenger found me. Written instructions, in Holmes' familiar hand, bade me to collect Mr. Warboys and to meet Holmes outside Scotland Yard. Remembering Gregson's concern from that afternoon I collected my revolver and ammunition before hailing a cab to carry me to the Warboys domicile.

The railway man had just finished his own supper when I knocked on his door. His wife, an attractive woman with a most welcoming smile, ushered me into the cosy dwelling. I barely recognised Warboys without his covering of coal dust. He readily accepted Holmes' summons, made his apologies to his wife and joined me in the cab.

"Has he found my Coppertop?" Warboys asked as we hurtled towards Scotland Yard.

"I don't believe so," I answered, explaining to him all that had befallen me that afternoon.

§

Holmes was standing alone by the archway leading to Scotland Yard, barely visible in the night's gloom. The streets were empty of traffic as the good people of London had retreated from the chill air.

"Watson," Holmes barked without preamble or greeting. "Whatever did you say to Gregson's prisoner this afternoon?"

"Why, nothing at all, Holmes," I answered, taken aback by Holmes' question and the brisk manner in which it had been asked.

"Nothing?" Holmes scowled.

"I assure you," I answered. "The constable, Rimbly was his name, asked me some questions about you which I answered. The prisoner was listening quite intently so I answered carefully, I don't believe I gave anything away."

"You did not have opportunity to speak with the prisoner alone?" Holmes inquired.

"Certainly not," I answered. "The constable was with me the entire time, he can vouch for the fact that I never spoke directly to the prisoner."

Holmes frowned, evidently displeased by my answer.

"Are we going inside, Holmes?" I asked, conscious of Mr. Warboys' confusion. "It is rather cold tonight."

"Sorry, Watson, Mr. Warboys, I'm afraid duty requires us to spend the night outdoors." Holmes wandered through the archway, moving into the shadows. Warboys and I followed.

"It may interest you to know, Watson, that Scotland Yard officers of all ranks are singing your praises."

"My praises, Holmes?" I asked, confused by his remark,

"Indeed, the Yard's opinion of you has never been higher. Not only did you discover the whereabouts of the fugitive they've searched for all week—"

"Now, Holmes, be fair. When a volley finds the mark, credit belongs to the marksman and not the bullet."

"Quite so," Holmes smiled. "Yet not only did you discover the whereabouts of Gregson's quarry, it seems you also convinced his prisoner of the error of his ways. Suddenly, after a week of Gregson's constant questioning, the prisoner is willing to make a full confession."

"What has that to do with me?" I asked.

"Why, Watson, he claims it was you who convinced him to unburden himself."

"Ridiculous!" I protested. "Constable Rimbly was there the entire time, he can set the record straight."

"He could," Holmes mused. "That he has not is extremely troubling."

We'd wandered behind Scotland Yard to a position overlooking the river. Although the night was overcast and chill enough to make our breath visible, Holmes spread his arms and directed our attention to the barren surroundings.

"This, gentlemen, is the nexus of our investigation," Holmes proclaimed, a note of desperation in his voice. "The pivot about which the elements of this tangled affair turn, the place where I must confess my failure and beg your indulgence."

"I don't understand, Mr. Holmes," Warboys said, echoing my own confusion.

"You came to me with a very simply request, Mr. Warboys," Holmes reminded the railway man. "You wished me to find a steam engine that had been stolen from your care, the missing Coppertop. You see? There," Holmes waved towards the Charing Cross rail bridge. "And there," he pointed down to the embankment, "The tracks of our quarry."

"Very droll, Holmes," I commented. The darkness hid the railway metals but I knew they were there.

"From here, we shall enjoy a superb view of your Coppertop as it approaches."

"Then you've found it?" Warboys asked hopefully.

"Not yet, but I am certain this is your Coppertop's destination."

"How so, Holmes?" I asked.

"Consider your discovery at the Bodmer residence, Watson, Mrs Bodmer fatigued, her husband missing -"

"You're not suggesting Norris Bodmer stole the Coppertop?" Warboys interrupted.

"Rather more serious than that, I'm afraid. Norris Bodmer has been kidnapped. Mrs. Bodmer explained how he was taken last night, abducted by men neither of them recognised. There's no doubt that he was taken to drive the Coppertop, the engine he had piloted so many times before. For as long as he is needed, he will be kept unharmed. However, when the task for which he was taken is complete, when his captors have no further use for him, I fear Mr. Bodmer will be disposed of."

"Poor Norris!" Warboys exclaimed.

"It is in our hands gentlemen," Holmes offered encouragingly. "We may yet prevail."

21

"Who are these villains?" I asked. "Confederates of Gregson's prisoner?"

"Not confederates so much as masters," Holmes answered. "The man you saw at Bodmer's has been seen meeting with Gregson's prisoner many times. Gregson believes, and I agree with him, that the two are part of a much larger conspiracy. A criminal organization which blackmails men of influence in order to shield other, more profitable, criminal pursuits. Whoever these men are, they've proven themselves as ruthless as they are clever. There have already been three attempts to free Gregson's prisoner, indeed it has reached the point where Gregson no longer feels it safe to keep the man in any official confinement and has moved him to the rooms you visited. Only a handful of men know where the prisoner is being held and, it would seem from Constable Rimbly's inexplicable behaviour, those few are too many."

I considered this, remembering the prisoner's smugness when I first approached him, as Holmes continued. "Which brings us here, to Scotland Yard and the Thames embankment. Gregson is bringing his prisoner here to have a confession witnessed and recorded, a confession we know to be a lie. And then there are the railway tracks, a convergence of events too plain to be avoided. Whatever will happen, it will happen here and it will happen tonight, that much is clear. Whoever absconded with Warboys' Coppertop cannot hope to keep it hidden forever ..."

"They've done well so far," Warboys complained.

"A simple matter," Holmes shrugged. "Why did they take the Coppertop? Because it is easily disguised, some paint over the celebrated copper dome atop the boiler and it is no longer a Coppertop but an anonymous engine, at least to the untrained eye. No doubt they took the locomotive to one of the other London yards, disguised it and left it there. At some point however, a trained eye will notice it. It is a gambit sufficient enough to keep the engine hidden for a day or so, but no longer."

"And Norris?"

"I'm sorry, Mr. Warboys, but I believe Mr. Bodmer will cooperate with the thieves, believing Mrs. Bodmer will pay dearly for any disobedience on his part."

"So they mean to use the engine to escape," I surmised.

"Do they?" Holmes grimaced, waving his arms out over the embankment. "There's the river, Watson, surely it would have been simpler to take a boat instead of a steam locomotive? This is my failure, I confess it freely. Why a steam engine? What do they intend to do with it? The answer eludes me and I've run out of time. So, we three must endure the chill of this night, hoping patience and vigilance can make up for my lack of intellect."

Turning to Warboys, Holmes continued. "Not the first time Watson and I have endured such bitter conditions, Mr. Warboys, but I regret you must suffer along with us. Your knowledge of locomotives may prove invaluable however, and I—"

"Say no more, Mr. Holmes," Warboys assured him. "Norris is my friend and that's worth more than a night's warm sleep."

Looking back to the looming bulk of Scotland Yard, the constabulary's command post, I wondered aloud. "Should we inform them of our presence?"

Holmes shook his head. "No doubt Constable Rimbly is the exception and most, if not all, of the police inside are trustworthy, but I'll take no chances. If Gregson arrives I will speak to him. Until then we shall keep our presence here secret."

§

The night passed slowly; I fancied I could feel the chill sweeping in off the cold waters of the Thames. There is a vaguely disquieting stillness that descends over a city in the wee hours, not so much an inactivity but an inert anticipation of the coming day. Such a feeling had just crept up on me when Holmes saw the train approaching along the embankment.

"Not on schedule," Warboys said, checking his pocket watch. "Not at this time of night."

The engine and its tender approached. Somewhat to my surprise it pulled no cars, for passenger or freight. Slowing, it stopped almost directly below us, where a dozen or so men scrambled off the tender. With practised efficiency, they unloaded long beams of heavy lumber that had been piled on the tender.

"What are those?" Warboys asked. Following his gaze, I noticed for the first time a series of posts set into the ground beneath our position. A slender figure scrambled around, attaching lengths of white string to the posts and pulling them taut.

"They seem to have surveyed the area," Holmes observed. As we watched, the men ran the long beams between the wheels of the engine. The tender was uncoupled and rolled a short distance away. Using jacks and levers, they lifted the beams and the engine, twisting it off the tracks.

"They've tinkered with my engine," Warboys growled.

"What do you mean?" Holmes asked.

"See, there by the cab? They've attached some sort of tub. And there, one of them's got a chain attached to something by the crown plate. They may have done more, it's too dark to tell, but—there's Norris!" Warboys whispered excitedly.

As the engine was levered upwards, a figure was revealed in the glow of the engine's fire, dressed in the heavy clothing of railway men. Although it was difficult to tell, it seemed his hands were bound behind his back, securing him inside the engine's cab.

"You see," Holmes said, intent on the activity below us. "It's as if they mean to have the locomotive leap up, as though to fly it up here and drive it through the walls of Scotland Yard. Quite impossible, and yet ..."

"Warboys?" Beside me the railway man had gone ashen, rigid, his eyes wide as he looked down on his missing Coppertop. "Are you all right?"

"That's just what they mean to do, Mr. Holmes," Warboys whispered. "By all that's holy, they mean to use that engine to bring down Scotland Yard!"

As we watched the locomotive twist at an alarming angle, it became apparent they meant to position the heavy engine in alignment with the strings spread between the posts. I had no doubt they would succeed, for they brought to mind the example of the splendid Corps of Royal Engineers I had witnessed at the Afghan frontier.

"I don't understand, Warboys," Holmes frowned. "A locomotive cannot fly."

"No, Mr. Holmes," Warboys explained, quivering with a maniacal energy. "A locomotive can't fly but their boilers can explode. There've been boiler explosions that tore roundhouses apart brick by brick, explosions that threw the engine's boiler over a distance of twenty-five hundred feet. I've heard of a boiler explosion that threw the boiler five hundred feet in the air before it came down on the cars it was pulling, and those were accidents. Don't you see? They mean to cause that engine to explode, they're aiming it at the building. If we let them blow that boiler it will punch a hole through Scotland Yard, make no mistake about it!"

Holmes looked down the embankment then back at the

looming bulk of Scotland Yard. "Surely the distance is too great," he protested.

"No, Mr. Holmes, it's not." Despite his mounting fear, Warboys answer was sure and confident.

Down on the tracks, a man was spooling out a thin chain from the engine's cab to the shelter of a nearby ditch. I fancied I could hear the trickle of running water, as if someone had turned on a tap.

"How does one cause a steam engine's boiler to explode?" Holmes asked.

"If the water in the boiler is drained, it leaves the crown sheet exposed directly to the fire. It'll heat up, white-hot, and if water splashes on it, the water will super-heat and ... Boom!"

Was that the purpose of the chain? To release water onto the Coppertop's crown sheet?

"Warboys, you must warn those inside." It was clear from his tone that Holmes had been convinced of the danger. "Tell them of our predicament. If they refuse to listen, ask to speak to Inspector Gregson or Inspector Lestrade. Understand?"

Warboys nodded, then hurried towards the unsuspecting Scotland Yard.

"You were right Holmes," I observed.

"Not right enough, it would seem," Holmes spat. "It was all there before me but I failed to make the connection. Now, here we are, helpless—Watson, what do you have there?" A smile spread across Holmes' face and a great weight seemed to lift from his shoulders. "Watson, you've brought your revolver!"

"And ample ammunition," I assured him.

He clapped me on the back, as cheerful as if the Lord Mayor had just presented him the keys to the city. "I'll find my way down. Keep a special watch on that scoundrel, don't let him pull that chain."

Quick as a cat, Holmes was gone. I watched the scene below, pistol clutched in my hand. Was it my imagination or was the glow from the engine's furnace brighter? Poor Mr. Bodmer's face was hidden by the locomotive's every-increasing tilt.

"Stop what you're doing!" Holmes voice boomed confidently, seeming to fill the night. "Set down your tools and your weapons! Move away from the engine!"

Confusion rippled through the men like wind through tall grass. They looked at each other, uncertain. I fired a shot into the still air to help persuade them.

Several of the men dropped their tools and raised their hands. One of them called out, "Who's there?"

"My name is Sherlock Holmes." Stepping out of the shadows, Holmes presented himself to the villains below. Seeing him, seeing the way in which he seemed to radiate confidence, I was torn between a desire to applaud his courage and a deep-seated certainty I was about to witness my friend's murder. Sure enough, one of the scoundrels stepped towards him, pulling a knife from the top of his boot. I fired a shot, hitting the knife-wielder high on his leg. He spun and collapsed, his moans a very effective deterrent to the others.

"You there!" Holmes barked. "Set down that chain at once!"

Beneath me, a dark figure, chain in hand, started running towards a nearby ditch. There was no time to consider other options, an explosion would not only have threatened Scotland Yard but killed Holmes, Bodmer and all the others below. I aimed and fired, the figure collapsed in a silent heap.

"Doctor Watson?" The welcome voice of Inspector Gregson sounded behind me. I urged the Inspector to hurry down the embankment to assist Holmes and, as I did so, two figures broke and ran, scuttling off into the shadows. I fired a warning shot, freezing the others, but the escaping villains did not hesitate. Unwilling to kill another man that night, I chose instead to let them get away. By the time they reached the river, Gregson and the constables had arrived at Holmes' side and any further opportunity for escape was gone.

§

Despite the ordeal he had endured, Norris Bodmer remained with his old locomotive and helped Warboys extinguish the fire in the engine's boiler. Officials from Warboy's shop were summoned to set the cooling engine back on the metals. Holmes suggested a letter of commendation might forestall any unfortunate misunderstandings between Mr. Warboys and his company concerning the recovered Coppertop.

"It's all very incredible," Gregson observed as Holmes finished explaining the night's events. "Did they really believe they could direct the locomotive's explosion with enough precision to free the prisoner?"

"To free him?" Holmes shook his head. "No doubt Constable Rimbly's message to your prisoner promised escape but I am certain those plotting tonight's adventure had no intention of freeing anyone. As you say, such an operation would require more precision than anything as unpredictable as a boiler explosion could deliver. No, Inspector, their aim was not to free your prisoner but to silence him. To silence him forever."

"Then the men we arrested—"

"After the explosion they would have combed the wreckage of Scotland Yard searching for your prisoner. Had they found him alive, they would have silenced him themselves. In the chaos and confusion it is not unreasonable to expect such an act to go unnoticed. I assume you found knives on those you arrested?"

"Indeed we did," Gregson confirmed."Scotland Yard is in your debt Mr. Holmes."

Holmes waved off the praise. Safe within a cab, making

our way home after the difficult night, Holmes voiced his unease to me.

"Very nearly a complete debacle, Watson," Holmes berated himself. "Had I been able to anticipate the locomotive's purpose in their plan, I assure you, tonight's events would have proceeded with much less drama. How could I not have seen it? You or Gregson might consider a steam locomotive to be nothing but an engine, what is the American expression? An iron horse? Yet a boiler inspector recognises the dangerous potential of such machines and I should have as well. Of all his company, only Warboys was concerned enough to bring the matter to my attention, how much plainer could it have been?"

"I think you did quite well under the circumstances," I said. "You deduced their intentions, where and when they would strike, and you knew enough to have Warboys brought out."

"And you, old friend," Holmes smiled. "Your marksmanship saved my life tonight."

I nodded modestly, glad to see Holmes relieved.

"A remarkable conspiracy, Watson," Holmes continued. "One I fear will take some time to unravel. Can you imagine the mathematical skill necessary to accurately aim something as unpredictable as a boiler explosion with any degree of confidence? Audacious, cold-blooded, meticulously planned, whoever is behind this conspiracy will make a fascinating study in criminal behaviour. I look forward to discovering his identity."

"You'll get him Holmes."

But Holmes was staring out the cab window, considering his next move in the deadly game just begun.

The Entwined

he strode across the neatly trimmed grass, immune to the charms of the day around her. Spring was in full bloom, the wind rustling the leaves in the trees and carrying the season's fresh scents to the fortunate and unfortunate alike. Her feet were bare as she walked across the lawn; tracing out a path perceived by none but her. She walked with her head bowed. Whether to watch the rise and fall of her hesitant steps or to shelter her frighteningly pale skin from the sun's warmth I could not say but her posture and slack expression telegraphed an utter disinterest in everything and everyone around her. The pleasant English countryside unfurled its full lush glory but, for all the pleasure she took from it, a bleak, arctic wasteland would have served her as well. Slender and pale, her wispy hair tousled by the breeze, she seemed almost insubstantial until she turned her remarkable brown eyes to you. Confronted with the depths of those ravishing eyes a man realized this young woman was meant to be beautiful. In those dark eyes was a promise unfulfilled, a potential thwarted by the insidious affliction from which she suffered.

Dark circles gave her face a hollow-eyed aspect. Next to her pallid skin, even the grey clothes of the asylum appeared bright. Her footsteps, her translucent skin, her painfully thin form all but lost in the asylum clothes, all combined to make the young woman insubstantial. Seeing her I found myself in agreement with the opinions I had read in her case file. The poor creature suffered from nothing which food and rest could not cure, nothing save a flaw in her mental process preventing her from accepting that which her body craved. We followed her unnoticed, despite my friend Sherlock Holmes' attempts to gain her attention.

"Miss Drayson!" Holmes, impatient and frustrated, called once more. He moved to stand directly before her. She lifted her head slowly, careful not to lift her feet from her unseen path as she dealt with this interruption.

"You must be Sherlock Holmes," Catherine Drayson said, offering the detective a shy smile. "I trust you received my letter?"

"Yes," Holmes said impatiently. "However I do not understand what it is you require of me."

Her smile, so small a thing, slipped from her features as she examined my friend. "I thought I had explained myself adequately, Mr. Holmes," she said, a charming childlike lilt in her voice. "I require you to determine whether or not I murdered the men I listed. Obviously this matter is of the utmost importance to me. Until my guilt or innocence is proven I am trapped here. Abandoned. Uncertain which world I am to be a part of..."

Having spoken, she lowered her head and resumed marching along her invisible path. She appeared startled when she encountered Holmes who, unmoving, remained directly before her. Looking up, her expression of concern was replaced by a shy smile. "Mr. Holmes," she greeted him as if meeting him again after a lengthy absence.

"Miss Drayson." Holmes returned the courtesy. "I can assure you: These murders are not of your doing."

"That is wonderful news," she said, bringing her hands

together in delight. Her shy smile expanded into something more substantial. "You must tell me how you were able to determine this. Was the investigation difficult?"

Holmes cast a concerned look at me before returning his attention to the young woman. "It was not difficult at all."

"You mustn't be so modest, Mr. Holmes," Catherine Drayson said.

Holmes, a man seldom accused of modesty, was momentarily nonplussed by this assurance. Nevertheless, he pressed on. "It is quite impossible for you to have committed any murders. You have been confined here in this asylum, under constant observation, for the last twenty-three months. I have reviewed your medical file, Miss Drayson. I have spoken to the doctors and staff charged with your treatment. They assure me you have not left the asylum grounds for almost two years."

Catherine Drayson listened patiently to Holmes as he explained his findings. When he finished she laid her small hand on his forearm in a friendly, familiar gesture obviously intended to lessen the sting of her reply. In her musical, untroubled voice, she chided the detective. "Now really Mr. Holmes, I have no wish to be difficult but I did expect better from you. Reading a medical file to solve such ghastly crimes? And everyone says you are so very clever. If you do not wish to accept my case that is one thing, but to stint on an investigation is quite another. I am relying on you, Mr. Holmes, is that not clear to you? I must know one way or another before I can decide which world I should direct my efforts towards."

It was a rare instance indeed when Holmes cast a look of desperation my way, and I will confess to being somewhat flattered as he did so now. I cleared my throat, drawing Miss Drayson's attention to me. "Excuse me Miss Drayson, but that's the second time you've mentioned different worlds.

May I ask which worlds you are referring to?"

"There is this world," Catherine Drayson said, waving her hand in a dismissive gesture towards the blue skies, the looming asylum and the lush, green woods. "Here I am a daughter to a kind man. A child whom everyone likes and pities at the same time. I fear I am a disappointment to those who know me here although they cling to a fading hope. This world is, I confess, a difficult one for me. Often it is a remarkably lonely and frustrating place. Yet it is not without its attractions."

"I see," I said. "And the other world?"

"In many ways the other world is much like this one," she answered earnestly. "Yet in that world I am different. In that world I have neither friends nor family yet, somehow, I am never alone. It is as if there is another me, a part of myself which is missing in this world. When I am there I know myself to be a fearsome thing, capable of the most vicious violence, yet in that world I am untroubled by my nature. Under the red sun of that world, the only frustration I know comes from my inability to unseat my rider."

"Rider?" I interrupted. "Like a horse?"

"Much more dangerous than a horse." Her words bore a strange flash of bravado, very much at odds with her feminine voice. "The person I am in that world has tasted the flesh of men and gloried in the spilling of their lifeblood. My rider believes I can become great. A beast so fearsome I will carry him beyond the red sun to where all his ambitions might be realized. Although I know such a path will be bloody indeed yet, when I am in that world, I find myself eager for the bloodshed."

"When I look up to the red sun the memories of my life here disgust me. Everything seems so weak and lonely, devoid of purpose or companionship. But when I am here the memories of the other world horrify me, such cruelty and wickedness. You see how I am trapped, don't you? There is a choice to be made. I cannot exist between such extremes. I must be one thing or another. I am not large enough to encompass both. So when my rider commanded me to murder those men, I did so eagerly. I knew it would solve my unendurable riddle."

"Solve it how?" I asked.

"I should think it obvious." Catherine Drayson explained pleasantly, her brown eyes captivating as she spoke to me of murder. "If I have indeed killed men from this world then it proves the other world is more than a delusion. It follows then, having spilled the blood of living men, I no longer belong here. Knowing this I am free to commit myself to the world beneath the red sun. Oh, I admit I shall miss the compassion and independence of my life here but one cannot deny one's nature. Besides, if I am truly a murderer, I cannot harbour any expectations of continued kindness on my behalf. Then again, if Mr. Holmes can prove my innocence, I shall abandon the other world. While I will miss my rider and—how shall I put it?—my savage half, it will be a relief to know such frightening deeds are nothing but a delusion."

"I see," I spoke with a confidence I did not entirely feel.

Holmes' frown deepened as he listened to Miss Drayson's explanation. "These men you claim to have murdered, how did you learn their names?"

The question seemed to puzzle her. For a moment she was silent as she considered her answer. "Yes," she said. "I can see where that might trouble you. In truth I know their names only because I tasted their lives. You see, in the other world, when a creature such as I feeds on their prey we gain a sense of our victims. Perhaps it would be more correct to say we gain a sense of who our victims were, for it is only in the last swallow of blood the knowledge appears. I knew their names because I tasted their names. Can you understand that Mr. Holmes? No, I see you do not but I have no better explanation to offer. However I came to know their names, you must admit I did know them. These men did exist and each of them was recently murdered."

"That has not yet been proven," Holmes said.

"It hasn't?" Catherine Drayson's childlike voice betrayed an adult note of hopefulness. Yet even as it built I could see it fade. "Oh, of course, Mr. Pursey was aboard a ship, wasn't he? I should have recognized that I suppose. The small room with the ocean all about. Have you been able to contact him?"

"Not as of yet," Holmes admitted with ill grace.

"And the other names I gave you?" Miss Drayson asked.

"Mr. Mulchinock has been reported missing," Holmes said. "His fate has not been determined. I should remind you that India is a savage land, full of perils for unwary travellers."

"Those are but two names from my list of five," Catherine Drayson reminded him. "Nor have you disproved my contention they have been murdered. What of the remaining gentlemen on my list?"

Holmes scowled, his expression answering her question more eloquently than words could have. The remaining gentlemen had been murdered and Holmes did not wish to admit it to her. Instead of answering her question, Holmes countered with an argument.

"You could not have murdered any of these men," Holmes insisted. "You were confined here, in the asylum."

"In the other world, Mr. Holmes," Catherine Drayson said earnestly, "I have wings."

"Like an angel, Miss Drayson?" I asked.

She smiled an ironic, humourless smile. "No, Dr. Watson, not in the least like an angel. You see, Mr. Holmes? I doubt the guards who watch over us are prepared for inmates who sprout wings and disappear into other worlds."

Almost against my will I nodded as she said this, feeling she had spoken the simple truth. It was unlikely, after all, asylum guards would be instructed to watch the unimposing Miss Drayson in the event she unfurled hidden wings and flew off to sea with the intent of determining a sailor's name by drinking the last drop of his blood. Still my unthinking nod was noticed by Miss Drayson who graced me with a grateful, pretty smile. Holmes also noticed my reaction, and glowered furiously at me.

"You see Mr. Holmes," Miss Drayson continued. "Your investigation has only just begun. You'll wish to be paid, of course, my father will see to the details. You understand they do not allow us currency in the asylum else I would settle our account now. Oh, and Mr. Holmes, there is one more thing I feel I should mention. I did not include it in my note as I was uncertain how to properly explain such a thing to you but now that you're here, now that you've heard my explanations, perhaps you will understand. The last victim, Mr. Wolfe, as he perished I tasted a fear in his blood, a concern that his friend—Mr. Willingham—was in grave danger. I understood this to mean Mr. Willingham was likely to be my next victim. You understand I know nothing of Mr. Willingham beyond the fact Mr. Wolfe feared for him. I do hope you will be able to prevent his murder. When I am in this world I find thoughts of death and murder most distressing."

"Of course," Holmes agreed, his expression humourless. "Miss Drayson, who told you of these murders?"

Smiling in a friendly manner at Holmes, she answered sweetly. "If you have looked in my file, Mr. Holmes, and spoken to the doctors and staff here, you know I receive no visitors aside from my father. No doubt you will have noticed how newspapers and the like are not permitted within the institution? The staff feels news from the outside world is not helpful to those suffering nervous disorders. If that is all, Mr. Holmes?"

Holmes looked as if he wished to say more but was unable to articulate his questions. Instead he merely tipped his head to the slight girl. "I trust you will have a pleasant day Miss Drayson," he said in farewell.

"And you Mr. Holmes," returning the courtesy with a smile. "A pleasant and productive day."

Holmes stepped aside and, as if a switch had been thrown, Miss Drayson bowed her head and her expression slackened as she resumed her joyless walk along her invisible path. For a moment Holmes and I watched the young woman walk away from us. The detective's hands twitched as he watched her. It seemed to me he was reaching for the pipe and tobacco which he'd unthinkingly left behind in Baker Street. Then Holmes turned and indicated with a tilt of his head that we should be leaving.

"Holmes," I asked when we were in the cab leaving the asylum behind us. "What on Earth was all that about?"

In answer Holmes reached into the pocket of his jacket, pulled out a small, carefully folded note and handed it to me. The stationery was plain, the woman's writing somewhat ornate but easily read.

Dear Mr. Sherlock Holmes,

I am writing to you in hopes of securing your services. Much to my dismay, I have been witness to a series of ghastly murders. I wish for you to investigate the following deaths:

Russell B. Wolfe: Killed in a room overlooking London's Hammersmith Bridge.

David J. Johnson: Killed in a flat with a large brass clock.

Ronald A. Pursey: Killed in a small room with the ocean all around.

Robert W. Elliott: Killed out of doors, on a city street.

Jonathan E. Mulchinock: Killed in a library not his own.

It may make no difference; however, I feel compelled to add that each of these gentlemen's murders occurred quite late at night.

As to the matter of your fee, I have enclosed my father's address and a note to him explaining how very important this matter is to me. You must understand that there are decisions I am compelled to make but, until I know the truth of these crimes, I lack the information necessary to make such choices. Obviously if I am guilty of five murders such knowledge will affect the future I must select for myself.

Appreciatively yours,
Catherine Drayson

I handed the note back to Holmes. "The Elliott murder was a sensation, of course. Anything so ghastly in such a public place attracts the curious. No doubt she read of it in the papers."

"As Miss Drayson correctly pointed out, news of the outside world is not permitted within the confines of the asylum," Holmes reminded me. "Still, what are an institution's rules against the power of gossip? I've no difficulty believing Miss Drayson learned of the unfortunate Mr. Elliot's murder through the careless whispering of the asylum staff."

"And the other names on the list?" I asked.

"Aye, there's the rub," Holmes said. "Mr. Wolfe was found murdered last week in his home and, before you ask Watson, he was killed in a room overlooking Hammersmith bridge. Like the sensational Elliott murder his death was both bloody and violent. Mr. Wolfe was beaten and repeatedly stabbed. Scotland Yard believes someone attacked him with an unusually large sword, possibly a weapon from the Far East. Unfortunately they did not think to allow me the opportunity to examine the body."

"Pity," I remarked.

"Indeed," Holmes agreed. "David Johnson was murdered in the Charing Cross Hotel. His body was found beneath a large brass clock. Like Mr. Wolfe and Mr. Elliot, Mr. Johnson was cut several times with some manner of large weapon. As neither Mr. Johnson nor Mr. Wolfe's deaths were as public as Mr. Elliot's, the newspapers have shown little interest in their cases."

"Then Miss Drayson's observations have been correct," I said. Seeing Holmes' frown, I quickly amended my statement. "At least, she has been correct three out of five times."

"I fear her average is better than that Watson," Holmes admitted. "Mr. Mulchinock has not returned from a trip to the subcontinent. I placed a telegram to the hotel where he was meant to be staying. Although they disavow any knowledge of murder, they assure me the blood in the library has been thoroughly cleaned."

"Leaving just one, what was the name? Pursey?"

"Departed on a lengthy sea voyage six weeks ago," Holmes said. "I've received no word of his murder, nor have I been able to confirm his well-being. If, as Miss Drayson suggests, the gentleman was killed while at sea we will be obliged to wait before receiving word of it. If we disregard Mr. Pursey, whose status can neither be confirmed nor denied, it appears Miss Drayson is correct in all of her descriptions. Each of the known victims was, in fact, killed during the night. Furthermore, with the possible exception of Mr. Pursey, she has arranged the names in chronological order of their deaths. Mr. Wolfe being the most recent murder and Mr. Mulchinock being the first. Strange, is it not?"

"Very strange," I agreed.

"Apparently Miss Drayson is being informed of these murders somehow," Holmes said. "It is possible these deaths are connected. At least three of the deaths were achieved by similar means. Given these circumstances, if we could discover the source by which Miss Drayson learns of the crimes it may well lead us to the perpetrators. Ah, here we are!"

The cab rattled to a stop and Holmes eagerly clambered out. "Where are we Holmes?" I asked as we emerged into the brightness of the day.

"In her time at the asylum Miss Drayson has only received one visitor," Holmes reminded me. "Likewise there is only one person with whom she has exchanged correspondence."

"Her father," I said.

"And we have been invited to discuss the matter of my fee with him," Holmes said, his face alight with a hunter's grin. "Many criminals feel an inexplicable compulsion to confess their crimes. Perhaps this father feels his confessions safely hidden in his daughter's insanity. Let us discover what manner of man this Drayson is."

Confident the answer to his mystery was close to hand Holmes marched purposefully into the Drayson residence. Sharing Holmes' enthusiasm I followed but nothing in the man's home bespoke a murderous nature. Neat and ordered, it seemed a bachelor's residence although here and there photographs and other mementos gave evidence of a happier past. Photographs of a child and her mother were scattered about, the resemblance to Catherine Drayson obvious in the mother's attractive features. Other portraits showed young Catherine at various stages of her childhood, telltales of a doting father.

"Mr. Holmes, is it?" Drayson greeted the detective uncertainly. Despite his immaculate apparel, Mr. Drayson appeared a tired, worn man. His was a thin face with a drooping, grey moustache arranged in a permanent frown. The father's form betrayed the same slenderness as the daughter's, and soulful brown eyes peered at us from behind round, wire-rimmed glasses.

Holmes quickly explained our business, handing over the note Drayson's daughter had prepared. Catherine Drayson's father read the missive carefully and then pulled a chequebook from the drawer of his desk.

"I do not think you fully understand the implications of your daughter's message sir," Holmes said as Drayson readied his pen. "You have not inquired if there is any factual basis to the murders your daughter describes. For all intents and purposes she has confessed to a series of monstrous crimes yet you have not requested any further information from us. You seem remarkably trusting sir, perhaps you've heard my name before?"

"I have not," Drayson said, his pen filling in the cheque as he spoke. "To be honest Mr. Holmes, it makes no difference to me if you are what you say you are or a charlatan. As a father I cannot afford to overlook any action that might result in a betterment of my daughter's condition. In her note she claims you may be able to help her. Your fee, Mr. Holmes? Please."

Holmes stated a figure.

Drayson's eyebrows rose and the father looked over the top of his spectacles at the detective. "Is that all, Mr. Holmes? May I include an incentive, to insure this matter receives your full attention?"

"Unnecessary," Holmes assured the man. "My professional charges are upon a fixed scale. In any instance, a trail of five murdered men cannot help but attract the attention of one such as I."

"There have been murders then?" Drayson inquired as he completed the cheque. "As she describes them?"

"Yes," Holmes answered. "Though how your daughter knows of them is something of a puzzle. Her confinement is such that she should have no knowledge of such brutality. Unless you know some way by which such news might reach her ears?"

"I do not," Drayson assured Holmes as he handed the detective his payment. "Had Catherine been outside the asylum she would have told me of it and I know of no one there who would speak of such things to her."

"Yet she possesses more than a passing knowledge of these deaths," Holmes observed. "I believe someone connected with these murders has spoken to her about them."

"I don't understand," Drayson said without suspicion. "You suspect a member of the staff?"

"No sir," Holmes said bluntly. "I do not."

"Oh," Drayson said, blinking in surprise as the implication of Holmes' statement became apparent. "As far as I know, I am the only visitor my daughter receives."

"That is true," Holmes said with a pointed stubbornness.

"You think I committed these crimes?" Drayson removed his spectacles and cleaned them thoughtfully. "I see the suggestion does not surprise you. Very well, I keep a diary of my appointments and activities. It reaches back several months and the older ones should still be here someplace. My diary should supply a reasonably complete record of my comings and goings. Would that be helpful to you Mr. Holmes? Is there anything else I can provide you with that may prove my innocence?"

Holmes spent the better part of the next two hours interrogating the unfortunate Mr. Drayson about his whereabouts, his daily practices and the sad history of his family. I listened but had nothing to add to the proceedings. To my ear it sounded as if Drayson was exactly as he seemed to be: A man whose life, through no fault of his own, had been marked by tragedy. A father surviving as best he could in the somewhat desperate hope that his daughter's health might be restored. As we left the Drayson residence I saw Holmes' scowl had returned.

"Baker Street." Holmes informed the cabbie curtly. His eyes were distant as he considered the problem before him. As we were dropped before the familiar door of 221B Holmes impatiently pushed past me, hurried up the seventeen steps to where his pipes and rough-cut tobacco waited. By the time I had ascended the stairs pungent smoke was already thickening the atmosphere.

For the remainder of the day Holmes smoked his pipes, the great engine of his brain grinding away at the puzzle. As night approached he removed his ash filled pipe, grimaced and exclaimed, "It won't do, Watson, it simply will not do!"

"Perhaps we should return to the asylum," I suggested. "Interview more of the staff."

"In case I overlooked something significant!" In another man's mouth such a statement might sound reasonable. Holmes spat it like a curse. My friend was not accustomed to doubting his own formidable abilities. Holmes shook his head. "No need for that, Watson, we still have fresh earth to turn. You recall Miss Drayson mentioned a Mr. Willingham."

I nodded. "She suggested he would be the next victim but not how we would find him."

"But she also suggested he might be a close friend of the last victim," Holmes reminded me. "Mr. Wolfe had a business partner, a Theodore Willingham. An interesting coincidence, isn't it? I have the address here. We best leave if we are to arrive before nightfall. And Watson—"

"My service revolver," I finished the thought, already in motion to retrieve the deadly weapon. Holmes allowed himself a small smile as he left to hail a cab.

My old wound ached as we climbed the stairs to Mr.

Willingham's fourth floor lodgings. As I navigated my way upwards it occurred to me that living in the upper reaches of a London residence offered a strange protection. Perhaps Holmes had a formula to calculate the frequency of crimes in proportion to the number of steps between the criminal and his desired felony. At last we stood before the thick oaken door of Mr. Theodore Willingham. I might have hesitated, uncertain as to what welcome we should expect given the improbable tale we carried with us, but Holmes had no such compunction. His determined knock echoed in the cramped confines of the hallway like a series of artillery shots.

The stout door opened fractionally, barely enough to reveal the concerned eye of the occupant. Holmes paused long enough to determine there would be no further introduction unless he initiated it. "My companion and I were hoping to speak to you regarding the unfortunate Mr. Wolfe."

Curiously, Mr. Willingham's response to this was to thrust his hand out into the hallway so that Holmes might shake it. The heavy door opened no further. The distrust gleaming in the watching eye did not lessen. Nor did Mr. Willingham offer a single word in way of greeting.

"Of course," Holmes said, as if the out-thrust hand explained everything. Holmes took the offered hand and shook it briskly and deliberately.

"Thank God," Willingham welcomed us with a desperate sincerity as he withdrew his hand. Holmes cast a self-satisfied look my way. Bringing a finger to his lips, he warned me to silence. While I did not understand the need for my quiet, I knew Holmes well enough to trust he would explain his odd request when the opportunity presented itself. I nodded as Willingham pulled open the heavy door and hurried us inside.

Our host, Willingham, was a tall man of imposing stature. Haunted eyes in a weather-beaten face looked worriedly up and down the hallway. His wide, dashing moustache and the tuft of beard on his chin put me in mind of an adventurer, like a knight from the tales of chivalry beloved by schoolboys across the Empire. Closer inspection revealed a nervousness, an unshakable fright, such as I had witnessed during my military service. Willingham seemed to me a once dashing figure who was now haunted by his intimacy with the battlefield.

As we stepped into the small apartment I was surprised to see a long sword leaning against the wall beside the doorframe. Should our meeting evolve into something less than cordial the weapon was within easy reach.

Our host held out his trembling hand to me but as I reached for it Holmes interrupted. "The Doctor is with me," Holmes said. I did not understand what he meant by the comment but Willingham nodded. Pulling back his hand, he crossed the room to an open liquor cabinet.

"Can I offer you gentlemen something to drink?" Willingham said as he reached for a bottle. An empty tumbler waited on a table. Pouring himself a measure of amber liquid, Willingham looked over the table and out a large window.

"Thank you but no," Holmes said.

Drink in hand, Willingham turned to face us. "I cannot tell you how relieved I am to see you. When Wolfe was murdered I thought myself quite alone. All the members of my detachment are either dead or out of the country."

Holmes shifted in his seat. Looking regretfully to Willingham, he spoke. "We have heard reports suggesting Pursey and Mulchinock have been killed as well."

The colour drained from Willingham's lined face. The tumbler in his hand fell to the floor, forgotten. Fearing the poor man might faint I hurried to his side and guided him into a nearby seat.

"We have not been able to confirm these reports," Holmes

hastened to add. "Obviously, we hope the information is false and both men are well."

"Of course," Willingham said. He raised his hand but discovered his drink gone. Holmes rose and poured the poor devil another. The taste of it seemed to restore the forsaken figure somewhat. "It appears I am the last of the detachment. It will come for me next."

"Most likely," Holmes agreed reluctantly.

"So the Brotherhood sent you to check on me." Willingham made no effort to conceal his bitterness. "To see if I'd break before the end? I've no assurances to offer gentlemen. You may inform them that I know what duty requires of me. My hope is that I will go down fighting, in keeping with the Brotherhood's glorious history, but I'll not pretend to be grateful for the opportunity."

Glancing at the sword leaning by the door, Holmes spoke speculatively. "Perhaps the Doctor and I might—"

"Would you?" An expression of gratitude softened Willingham's face, making him seem younger. As quickly as it appeared, the expression was gone. Willingham's voice was firm.

"No. God bless you for offering but that's exactly what they want. I've no idea how they've breeched the gate but obviously they're seeking out as many of the Brotherhood as they can. They can't beat us there, our fortifications are too strong, but here—at home—we're all vulnerable. No, my detachment may be lost but I've no wish to bring down another. Much as I appreciate your offer I cannot accept. You gentlemen will have to leave."

Holmes frowned. "Is there anything you wish us to report to the Brotherhood?"

Willingham emptied his drink, rolling the spirits over his tongue.

"A deathbed statement? Very well. Tell the Brotherhood

my detachment served with an honour which exceeded our situation. I know how desperately the Elders seek the forbidden knowledge of the *Melvaris*. Tell the brotherhood such partnerships are not meant for men. My situation is hopeless. I cannot defeat the abomination which comes for me. Even so, I would rather die a man than know victory as such a monster. Tell the Brotherhood to remember us as we were: Men who stood together beneath the red sun. We earned our conquest, fighting as comrades. Do not let the Elders corrupt that victory. Remember the courage of men. Do not let them turn brave men into a blasphemy of foreign sorcery. Alone I cannot match a creature of the *Melvaris*, but if we stand together, as men, none can defeat us." Willingham looked out the large window at the lights of London. "How strange to have travelled so far only to learn we had no need of the magic we sought."

Visibly composing himself, Willingham tore his gaze away from the window. Looking at Holmes and I, the man set down his glass. "You should leave now."

Holmes opened his mouth to protest but Willingham strode to the door and took the long sword into his hand. Despite the alcohol he'd consumed the man still appeared quite formidable. "Thank you for coming but you must go if you are to carry my message to the Brotherhood. Farewell."

There was simply no way we could remain. In short order Holmes and I found ourselves in the hallway, the sturdy door closed behind us.

I started for the stairs. Holmes' hand fell on my shoulder, stopping me. With a nod of his head, Holmes indicated we should proceed in the opposite direction. I followed as Holmes walked to the flat next to Willingham's. He tapped lightly on the door and, receiving no answer, pulled a familiar, but illegal, set of tools from his pocket.

"Holmes!" I protested as my friend made short work of the door's lock.

"The apartment is vacant," Holmes explained as he stepped into the dark room beyond. "You did not notice the 'Room to Let' sign downstairs? Come, it serves our purpose to remain close to Mr. Willingham. If he is attacked, as he obviously expects to be, it would be best if we remain near enough to render assistance."

As Holmes predicted, the flat was empty of occupants and furniture. Striding across the empty room Holmes walked up to the tall window, opened it and leaned out. Satisfied with what he saw he pulled himself back in. "Nothing unusual on the street or dangling from Mr. Willingham's window. This flat is empty, leaving the hallway as the only avenue of attack. Unless this killer flits about on angel's wings."

Miss Drayson, I recalled, had insisted her wings were nothing like those of an angel. Refusing to be baited, I asked, "What was all that business in Willingham's? Who did he think we were?"

"Oh yes," Holmes replied, amused. Opening the door to the hallway fractionally, the detective placed a small mirror against the doorframe so he could watch the comings and goings in the hallway unobserved. Seating himself on the floor, settling himself for a long wait, Holmes explained. "You noticed how Willingham refused to speak until I had shaken hands with him?"

"Yes." I recalled the incident.

"Apparently Mr. Willingham belongs to some manner of secret society," Holmes explained. "A club fond of secret handshakes and the like. Having made a study of such things I decided to risk passing myself off as a member, thinking he would be more willing to discuss his situation with a fellow."

"It worked," I said.

"Too well I'm afraid," Holmes confessed. "Having bluffed

my way in, I couldn't very well admit to having no idea what the man was talking about. *Melvaris*? The term is not one I am familiar with, although I suppose it may be the name of some rival society."

"He spoke of their secrets," I remembered.

"Yes," Holmes replied dismissively. "What use is a secret society without secrets? No doubt they have a closet full of all manner of mystical refuse. It makes no difference. Whatever nonsense Willingham said our interview has confirmed two important points. Firstly, there is a definite, if secret, connection between the murdered men. Secondly, Willingham himself believes he will be attacked tonight. All we need do is wait for his attackers. Once we have taken them into custody I am confident they shall lead us to the answers we seek."

"If we can take them into custody," I amended Holmes' statement. Holmes, ever confident, merely shrugged.

We settled in for a long night's watch. Holmes sat by the door, his eyes never wavering from the mirror and its reflection of the hallway. I sat with my back against the wall shared with Willingham's flat, occasionally pressing my ear against the barrier and listening. Willingham seemed to be spending his time pacing back and forth. The hours stretched on and we endured them silently.

Checking my watch, I noticed it was just after three o'clock. Pressing my ear against the wall again, I checked on Willingham once more. My hope was the man had ceased his pacing and retired for the night. Certainly by that point I was wishing the same for myself. Rather than the even tread of a man's stride, however, I heard the unmistakable sound of a deflected sword thrust. Hurried footsteps jostled for position. The battle had begun.

"Holmes!" I leapt to my feet, weariness forgotten.

"There's been no one," Holmes insisted, pressing his

ear against the wall. Hearing the sounds of combat from the other side Holmes uttered a curse and hurried to the window.

I looked to the door and Holmes, seeing my confusion, called for me. "Willingham's door is too thick to breach," Holmes said. "Expecting an attack, he'll have locked it securely. No, the window is our only way. Check your revolver Watson."

Holmes disappeared out the window. I checked my service revolver, it was loaded and ready, and placed it back in my jacket pocket. Reluctantly I followed Holmes out the window. A small, wrought iron balustrade surrounded the small balcony. Climbing over it, Holmes leapt from our window to the next. The space between was not great but the distance to the street below was daunting. Climbing into the brisk, night air I caught a glimpse of Holmes frowning as he kicked in the glass of Willingham's unbroken window.

Summoning my courage, I leapt into the air in pursuit of my friend. Climbing over the metal railing, I was startled by the sound of a loud collision. Heart in my throat I saw Holmes thrown against the windowsill. His head connected loudly against the ledge. Pulling my pistol, I hurried through the broken window.

Holmes lay crumpled on the floor, unconscious. Blood flowed from a wound to his head. Across the room stood Willingham, his clothing dishevelled, bleeding from several wounds. All of this I noticed in a glance for my attention was drawn to the unearthly creature hovering among the overturned furniture in the room's centre.

She'd spoken truly. Her wings bore no resemblance to those of an angel. They were great, curved muscles. Bones sharp as blades over taut, grey skin. Her legs merged together like a serpent's tail. Along her flanks rows of articulated bones emerged like knives. Despite these and other changes,

I knew the face which turned to me. I had looked into the depths of those brown eyes before.

Her new form must, I know, seem hideous as I describe it. Indeed, it was hideous. And yet—there was a grace, a beauty, to the creature. The potential for loveliness I had glimpsed earlier was fulfilled in ways both unexpected and chilling. The Catherine Drayson I'd seen was present but her youthful anatomy had been melded with that of a monstrosity. The flesh of her savage half, for that was how she'd termed it, shared an appalling intimacy with the woman I had met earlier. Her faintly green skin seemed, in places, to roughen into blue-edged scales. Dagger-like teeth crowded her newly grown snout, making it impossible for her to smile. Still the curve of her back, the swell of her breasts, those dark brown eyes, all remained deliriously female. For a moment I simply stared, terrified and captivated, at the apparition before me.

She raised her hands and reached towards me. I saw her fingers had become daggers. Seeing that, I understood Scotland Yard's confusion over the murdered men's cuts. First her hands would pierce my flesh then she would spread her fingers. The resulting wound would seem like a puncture left by an unusually wide sword. Yet, even knowing this, I made no move to defend myself. Catherine Drayson and her savage half stepped towards me. Eagerness shone in her eyes. I waited.

Behind her Willingham swung his sword. The blade was deftly turned aside by the bony edge of one slender wing. Her expression angered. In a quick, powerful twist she turned to face Willingham. She thrust a closed hand at the dishevelled man. He parried the lunge and stumbled backwards. Looking down I saw the revolver still in my hand. Raising the gun, I took aim at the back of the creature's head and squeezed off a round.

Somehow sensing the attack, a wing twitched and

deflected the bullet. Disbelieving, I fired two more rounds but each time the edge of the creature's wing deflected the bullet before it could reach its target. Behind me Holmes lay on the floor, bleeding. Unwilling to leave him undefended, yet powerless against the strange hybrid, I looked about frantically for something, anything, that might serve as a weapon.

Returning the revolver to my jacket pocket, I took hold of the empty bottle Willingham had been drinking from earlier. Breaking the glass against the table allowed me to fashion a crude knife. I watched in sick fascination as the creature battled the swordsman. Despite Willingham's obvious skill, it seemed to me the creature was toying with him. Blocking his escape. Allowing him to strike only where the creature could easily deflect the thrust. Willingham knew it too. Looking over the creature's shoulder he cast me a desperate look.

Unfurling its wings, the creature blocked my view of Willingham. Between the outstretched wings I saw a long, black ridge. Vividly I recalled Miss Drayson describing her savage half. I also remembered her speaking of her rider. Seeing that long, black, snake-like ridge between her shoulders, I was struck with the notion this was the rider she'd spoken of. I did not hesitate. Lunging forward, I plunged the broken glass bottle into the black ridge.

Battered by the surprisingly strong wings I wasn't certain I had found my mark. With a hideous scream, the creature lunged forward and thrust its hands into Willingham. Blood splattered on the floor as those terrible fingers spread within the man. Willingham, his face twisted in agony, threw himself forward. The unexpected action slowed the creature. Rather than pull its hands free, the hybrid lifted Willingham off the ground and drank deeply of the man's flowing blood.

Finding myself on the floor, I reached into my jacket pocket and pulled out my revolver. Black ichor oozed from the wound on the creature's back but the ridge, revealed now as a dangling snake, still held fast to the creature. I fired at it. The wings moved but not quickly enough. The bullets found their mark. The hybrid creature shuddered and screamed. With a savage gesture it pulled its hands free of Willingham, tearing the man in half as it did so. Turning to me, it staggered. The snake fell from its perch. The hybrid creature's wings flapped in a vain, uncoordinated effort to keep itself aloft. It fell to the floor.

I stood. Finding my revolver's ammunition spent, I reloaded. Standing over the twisting, struggling snake I emptied my revolver into it. At last it stopped moving. Was this the *Melvaris* Willingham had spoken of? I turned to the fallen winged creature Catherine Drayson had become and wondered: Was this the secret magic the Brotherhood sought? The ability to entwine the flesh of two distinct beings to form something new? Willingham had been correct. The creature was an abomination, its reptilian creator a blasphemer.

The winged creature turned on its side. It looked up at me with those brown eyes. Fallen, it was still captivating and horrible. Reluctantly, seeing no alternative course of action, I started to reload my revolver again but there was no need. Whatever magic held the creature together was coming undone.

I watched as the two halves pulled free of one another. The shuddering was horrible to witness. Each wailed in sorrow as their unnatural intimacy ended. Somehow the creature they had been was greater than the sum of their individual parts. Each of them knew it. They mourned the loss as they were torn from each other. My eyes remained on Miss Drayson. Uncertain if either of them would survive, I could only give witness to the horrible process of separation.

When it was done they were both gone. There had been a green light, bright enough to make me avert my eyes. When

I looked back both had disappeared. The *Melvaris* remained, as did the savaged body of Willingham. Holmes lay where he had fallen. I hurried to his side.

So it was that Scotland Yard found us—in the centre of a bloody room that stank of gore and spent ammunition. It was indeed fortunate that we were known to the officers of the Yard. Had Holmes and I not been so familiar I do not doubt we would have found ourselves locked in a cell to await charges of murder.

I told the police Willingham had been attacked by a large, foreign-looking man with an uncommonly wide sword. Willingham, I explained, was dead when we entered the room. Upon our arrival the attacker knocked Holmes to the ground, giving me time to draw my revolver and fire six shots into the brute. The assassin screamed and left by way of the window. Rather than give chase, I remained behind to tend to Holmes.

"Watson." Holmes shook his bandaged head as he listened to my tale. "Your aim is slipping."

"So it would appear," I agreed. Holmes listened to the account I gave to Scotland Yard without comment or question. Nor did he make any inquiries as we journeyed back to Baker Street. Very quickly the matter became just another case. Other crimes took Holmes' fancy. A letter of gratitude arrived from the much-improved Catherine Drayson. Another grateful missive from her father informed us of her release from the asylum. Such tokens were nothing new to Holmes and, as was his custom, he ignored them. Holmes quickly put the case behind him. However, as you might suppose, I have thought of the matter often.

It is not my custom to hide the truth from my friends. Sherlock Holmes is dauntless in the face of horrors which chill my blood. Murder and violence, the screams of the innocent and the doings of evil men, all part of Holmes' environment and as natural to him as water to a fish. Yet, as courageous as he undoubtedly is, Holmes is not without his personal demons. He lives a life built upon small but unshakeable truths, upon what is and is not possible. Catherine Drayson and her savage partner disappeared from Willingham's apartment. In Sherlock Holmes' world such things cannot be.

Sometimes I assure myself I acted to protect my friend. When confronted with a horror not of this world, I feared his skills, as a detective, would be rendered useless. Robbed of the very foundations of his courage, how would Holmes react? Such an event could well push him back into the drug usage we had struggled so hard to put behind him. The reality of other worlds, of beings such as the *Melvaris* and their unexplainable magic, seemed a truth which might unravel Holmes. A revelation capable of tainting the detective's skills with doubt, poisoning his future work. At such times I am convinced my response was entirely appropriate and that my actions were those of a loyal friend.

Yet there are other times. Late at night, when sleep is inexplicably elusive, my thoughts stray into the shadowy realms of doubt and I wonder. Were my actions those of a friend or was it simple cowardice? If Holmes had witnessed the truth, had seen the creature sent to kill Willingham, where would he be now? In his own way Holmes has always been a hunter of terrible monsters. A man who exposed secrets. Given the choice would he remain here, solving crimes in London, or would he venture forth to explore that world under the red sun? I find myself reaching for the answer but it eludes me still, eclipsed by another, more troubling question. If Holmes were to leave this world, would I follow?

The Haunted Inspector

he ghastly affair in Lochabar, during which Sherlock Holmes was forced into a public confrontation with an Inspector who insisted the killer was safely in custody despite Holmes' logic indicating the man in custody was an imposter, was unfortunately fresh in the memory not only in London, it seemed the entire Empire had read of the unfortunate incident in newspapers around the globe. The Inspector, waving the paper he felt proved the truth of the cunning murderer's captivity, was for a brief time a symbol of incompetence thanks to the art of clever illustrators. Thank goodness we were able to save the poor young woman, yet the cost was a rushing tide of publicity which Holmes despised. It was hardly surprising that Holmes found himself awash in inquiries from a wide variety of institutions who had never previously considered employing the services of a consulting detective. Holmes, as was his custom, accepted only those cases which aroused his interest and, regardless of the proffered fee, firmly dismissed the rest. Despite our efforts to keep our role in the appalling affair out of the headlines, it appeared the entire Empire was overrun with whispers both of Holmes' brilliance and the local constabulary's stubborn refusal to heed any voice not their own. This had the odd effect of leaving Holmes unusually

occupied, yet bereft of his most faithful employers: the Inspectors of Scotland Yard. Holmes was simultaneously delighted with the diversity of problems presented to him, while simultaneously distressed at his long term prospects without the supply of Lestrade, Gregson and others at Scotland Yard for whom the involvement of the detective was, for the moment, deemed impolitic. Often, over those weeks, I contemplated the possibility our cause would be best served by letting the scribes openly proclaim the role we had played in their headlines, but Holmes frowned profoundly at the suggestion. Dismissing his own anxiety, Holmes insisted the Yard could eventually forgive his competence but headlines of their incompetence would be unpardonable. Among the halls of power, documentation of an act was often a greater sin than the act itself.

I had come to the Baker Street lodgings that evening hoping to hear the conclusion of a Swedish embezzlement case, nor was I disappointed. Holmes considered the entire matter dull and, despite its intriguing beginnings, ultimately uninteresting. Having heard the violent conclusion of the matter, I drained my glass, cleaned my pipe and stood in preparation of departure, when the detective called out to me. "I would be indebted if you could remain a short while. I'm expecting a visitor to discuss a case which, I must admit, I am loathe to accept."

"Oh?" I inquired. How often had I accepted invitations from Holmes for matters that promised a measure of interest? Yet this was the first time I could recall being asked to linger for a matter Holmes deemed unworthy.

Holmes shook his head. "Foolish of me to accept the appointment but you understand the current tensions between myself and the Yard. If you would, I'd ask you to observe the room carefully before our guest arrives."

"I see," I said, though in truth I was not entirely clear as to the purpose of my scrutiny. "Anything in particular to which you would draw my attention?"

"The absence of murder weapons," Holmes answered. My expression must have betrayed my amusement, for Holmes added, "That is, the absence of unfamiliar murder weapons. The Inspector we are expecting has a reputation for placing such items in locations where they will do the Yard the most good."

"You mean to say he tampers with evidence?" Stepping through the chaos that habitually filled the lodgings, my eyes dashed from the clippings piled on the floor to the elaborate tangle on the chemistry table. I saw nothing out of place.

"Naturally," Holmes declared with a wave of his pipe. "The Yard often values expediency over the rules of the game. It is sometimes difficult to fault them for such shortcuts, at least when you are not the villain in the frame, however such actions have always struck me as an admission of failure. Effort and deduction may take a slower path than a conveniently discovered item of evidence, but it has the virtue of being wholly trustworthy."

"I don't quite follow," I admitted. "Are you expecting this Inspector to plant evidence here? In your lodgings?"

"Possibly." Holmes stood suddenly, setting aside his pipe and walking to the door. As he did I heard, belatedly, the arrival of our guest.

"Inspector Lambton," Holmes greeted his visitor as he ascended the steps. "I never expected to see you darken my doorway but I am, as always, pleased to assist the Yard."

Lambton stood almost as tall as Holmes, though less lanky. The muscular Inspector had an almost brutal sense of competence about him, an old dog accustomed to hard roads. Perhaps it was the sneer he turned to Holmes, perhaps it was the stomping of his boots, but I was put in mind of a grizzled veteran I'd known during my military service. Steady and grim, whether under fire or at liberty.

His sunken eyes gave the appearance of a man who had seen much of the world and found very little of it to his liking.

"Not here on Yard business," the Inspector announced as he shrugged out of his heavy coat. "They don't know I'm here and it'd be best to keep it that way, you understand?"

"You may rely on our discretion," Holmes assured the man. Returning to his seat, Holmes gestured to the waiting chair, but Lambton remained standing. "You know of Dr. Watson?"

"I do," Lambton answered, gruff disapproval in his voice. "Though I'd prefer to have spoken to you alone."

"And I prefer the presence of the good doctor," Holmes replied. "From your note I take it there's a matter you wished to consult—"

"No," Lambton interrupted with a slash of his hand. "I've no need of a consultant. As you well know, I'm not Lestrade or one of your other flock of admirers. That's not how I work. You know that."

"Yet here you are," Holmes said, not bothering to disguise a note of triumph.

"Here I am," Lambton agreed, glaring down at the seated Holmes. "There's a matter which I cannot look into myself. A murder."

"Murder?" Holmes' eyebrow rose in surprise. "A homicide which a Scotland Yard Inspector cannot look into? I rather thought that was their *raison d'etre*."

"Being funny, are ya?" The words emerged as a growl. A trembling finger stabbed towards Holmes, then swung in my direction. "I'll have your word on this, both of you, before I say anymore."

"No, Inspector, you will not." Holmes, unperturbed, leaned back in his chair. "I've no doubt you are troubled by something, your manner practically screams agitation. The shake in your hands, your furtive glances between Watson and the door; it is also apparent from your eyes that you've not slept soundly in some time. Enough. This may be your first visit, Inspector, but you know how the game is played. You may trust the Doctor and myself, or you may choose not to. We'll not perform to earn your trust. Leave if you like, or stay and explain what brings you here. The choice is completely yours."

Lambton sighed, considered, and then sat in surrender. From where I was seated I could see his knuckles whiten as they gripped the armrests of the chair. The man was under a terrible strain and, when he looked up and met Holmes' calm gaze, I had the impression of a drowning man frantically reaching for a lifebuoy.

"It's the Allen girl," Lambton admitted.

I wondered if the Scotland Yard Inspector saw as clearly as I did how Holmes started at his utterance. I doubt it. Lambton's gaze had dropped, unable to meet Holmes' scrutiny. Of course, Holmes was not easily startled and, when he was, he took efforts to contain his emotions. Still, I saw his reaction plainly.

"Hann's second victim? They hung him yesterday for it."

"Yes," Lambton said, his eyes firmly fixed on his shoes. "And no. They hung him aright but he didn't kill the Allen girl, just the other one. As if that makes any difference."

"If we are to help you," Holmes replied, "You'd best start from the beginning."

Lambton looked up, meeting Holmes' eyes for the first time. "You know the case?"

Holmes nodded.

"Well, that morning, around nine, I was called to a flat on Cowely Street. When I got there a Superintendent was waiting there with another bloke—"

"Which Superintendent?" Holmes asked.

"Don't matter," Lambton protested. "Not likely the Super aided her to room temperature."

"Even so," Holmes insisted. Lambton, reluctantly, provided a name. Holmes nodded and urged Lambton to describe the other man at the scene.

"Not tall, about five, two. Mustache and door knocker beard. Round face, looked a little Spanish but bleached, like he'd been in town for a while. Dressed and polished, despite the hour. Full kit, looking around like something didn't agree with his nose."

"Was there an odor?" Holmes asked.

"No, nothing; poor thing hadn't been dead long and she was in the next room anyway. The Super nods to the dandy and the tosser checks his watch and leaves without so much as a tip of the hat. I'm taken into the next room, shown the girl. She's stretched out atop the bedcovers, still dressed in her clothes from yesterday, jacket and boots all laced up."

"She'd been arranged there?"

"Sure as I'm sitting here," Lambton agreed. "Not a mark on her otherwise."

"No wounds?"

"Not that I saw," Lambton reported.

"That would change," Holmes prodded, eyes fixed on the reluctant Inspector.

"Super explained they'd nabbed a madman over on Tufton Street, that they'd caught him dead to rights but had doubts the court would see it the same. Since this woman had died of natural causes, and since we had the knife the lads were out looking for, it were a chance to make the charges stick tight. No one gave a toss about the first victim but a pretty thing like this, why, it was just the thing to make our madman swing."

"So what did you do?" Holmes asked. Something in my

friend's tone warned me that he knew the answer already but, for reasons of his own, wished to hear it from Inspector Lambton.

"You think I'm ashamed?" Lambton hissed at Holmes. "I done what the Super asked. That Hann, he was a killer. A madman. I'd have cut the throats of a hundred dead women to get Hann off the street and away from decent folk. Ain't all chemistry and geology out there, I'd have thought you'd known that. You've been in the game long enough. I cut her throat with the knife the Super handed me. Ripped at her clothes, made it look like she'd been set upon. Once he was satisfied, the Super sent me away, left the door ajar and instructed one of the constables to look around. Sure enough, they found her, found the knife, case closed. Hann swings and the world is all the sweeter for his absence."

"Yet here you are," Holmes said, his gaze intent on the Scotland Yard man. "If justice has been served, what is it you wish me to solve?"

"Well," Lambton's defiance was gone. "It's the girl, ain't it? I mean, the Super said she'd died all natural-like but I don't believe it. Fact is, I'm certain she was murdered."

"Really? You suspect the woman did not climb atop her bedcovers in her jacket and boots and simply expire? Tell me everything you noticed about the body as you found it. I've already had reports as to how you left it."

"I don't know what you want of me. She was just … laying there."

"Arms at her sides?" Lambton nodded. "Legs straight, toes of her boots pointed upwards?" Lambton nodded again. "Her coat, completely buttoned up?" Lambton nodded, then corrected himself. "A couple of the bottom buttons were undone."

"Good," Holmes offered before asking, "Were her boots

clean?" Lambton nodded. "On the bottom? Had they been scraped?" Lambton frowned, then shook his head.

"Better. Any jewelry? Rings, bracelets, necklace?" Lambton shook his head. "Were her hands closed or open?"

"Closed, fist-like."

"Tell me about her hair," Holmes continued.

"Very neat," Lambton remembered. "Auburn, lots of hair, it seemed neatly done but when we moved her, well, it fell free. Wasn't fixed up at all." Lambton looked up, meeting Holmes' eye. "It's the dandy man you should be asking about. He's the one who killed her."

"Indeed?" Holmes scoffed. "What makes you say that?"

"Why else would he be there?"

"You were there," Holmes reminded the Inspector. "You didn't kill her. All you did was cut her throat. I can see from your expression there's much you want to tell me about the gentleman. Please," Holmes reached for some paper and a pencil from the side table and handed it to the Inspector. "Indulge yourself. Write as much as you can remember."

That accomplished, with the Inspector passionately filling the empty pages, Holmes reached for his pipe. Sparing me a quick glance, Holmes lit his bowl and leaned back in his chair.

An interval passed without any sound save the scratching of Lambton's pencil and the ticking of the mantle clock. When he finished writing, the Inspector read it over all and made some corrections. Setting down the pencil, Lambton was confronted with Holmes' waiting hand.

Handing over the paper, Lambton spoke. "You're not to be bothering the Superintendent with this, you understand?"

"Just as you are not one of my—how did you put it?— 'flock of admirers', I am not one of your raw constables."

"I'm warning you," Lambton growled, still holding onto the papers. "You don't understand—"

"Do I not?!" Holmes barked back to the Inspector. "Are you suggesting I am unaware of the dangers of confronting a Police Superintendant regarding a crime he concealed? Do you think I cannot comprehend how unpleasant a Scotland Yard Superintendant could make my existence? If there's nothing else Inspector, you are free to leave. The hour grows late. You may be unable to sleep but, I assure you, my sleep is untroubled and peaceful. I shall let you know, discreetly, if I find anything of merit in this case. Until then."

Having spoken his piece, Holmes closed his eyes and drew on his pipe. Lambton, hands balled into fists, thrust himself out of his seat like a whale leaping from the ocean. His snarling mouth opened and I expected a burst of abuse to emerge, but it didn't. Lambton, all fury, looked over Holmes' shoulder and, as if his canteen of rage had been punctured, the Inspector's anger seemed to sink in on itself. He collected his coat, stomped angrily to the door. Looking over his shoulder, his rage reasserting itself, he seemed about to hurl a stinging comment but again something he saw behind the seated Holmes—something invisible to my eye—caused the Inspector to bow his head. With a meekness strange to see in so rough-formed a man, Lambton closed the door softly behind him.

I listened as Lambton's uncertain steps sounded down the stairs, as the outer door opened and closed, it was Holmes' turn to leap angrily to his feet. "Can you believe that man? The gall of it! First he destroys the evidence, then asks me to solve it! Might as well ask me to read a letter he'd just burned. He believes the truth can be bent, twisted into a more convenient shape. Made palatable. I don't often use the word 'heretic' but when I can find no other word—Watson, what on Earth are you doing?"

My hands were deep in the folds of the chair Lambton

had sat in. "Making certain the Inspector did not leave any surprises for us."

"Good thought, Watson. Meticulous. Mustn't let our passions overwhelm our good sense."

Holmes moved to examine the path Lambton had taken on entering and exiting the lodgings.

"The Yard tolerates Lambton's behavior?" I asked. "It seems like madness."

"They not only tolerate it," Holmes answered, his keen eyes searching the familiar environs, "They reward it. Your judgment has been tainted by your familiarity with my methods, I'm afraid. As Lambton's tale reveals, the Yard has use for a man capable of taking shortcuts, a man whose trust in the wisdom of his superiors never wavers. Whether he plants evidence or destroys it, he is kept as busy as any of his fellow Inspectors. Lestrade and Gregson are willing to expend skill and effort to uncover the facts of a case but the Yard has always valued the keeping of peace over justice. A convenient lie often serves them better than a disruptive truth, hence inspectors such as Lambton."

"Perhaps I have been in your company too long," I sighed, "but Lambton's efforts just don't seem cricket."

Holmes' hand found my shoulder.

"Will you take the case?" I asked, reaching for my coat.

"I am not certain," Holmes admitted. "The challenge of it does, I admit, appeal. Also, I confess, my professional pride has been bruised. Gregson brought in the killer Hann. He visited me with concerns about the Allen girl's murder. I dismissed them. It was obvious both victims had been cut with the same knife. Clearly, I should have looked closer. On the other hand, I do not understand why Inspector Lambton has brought this case to me."

"Maybe his conscience bothers him?"

Holmes snorted in derisive laughter. "It is kind of you to

think so but this is hardly the first black deed Lambton has performed on the Yard's behalf."

"But this time he didn't just plant evidence," I reminded Holmes. "He cut that woman. While I don't doubt the man is callous, such an act does leave a mark."

"Perhaps," Holmes conceded. "His obvious lack of sleep certainly argues for a sense of guilt. These are deep waters, Watson, I shall plot my course carefully. Now, it is late and you should be getting to bed. As for me, my pipe awaits."

§

Donning coat and hat, I left the lodgings fully intending to reach home and enjoy a good night's rest. As I marched through the shadows of Baker Street, despite the late hour, I glimpsed the figure of a woman ahead. She glanced at me, her expression forlorn, before stepping away into the gloom of the night. Turning towards home, I very nearly tripped over a figure cowering against the metal railings in front of the lodgings.

Inspector Lambton.

The man had collapsed utterly. His face was wet with weeping, his mouth agape as if he were screaming silently. The palsy in his hands had spread up his arms, which covered his head as if shielding himself from unseen blows. I could tell the man had soiled himself. Lambton's face and trembling body were a singular expression of absolute terror.

I pulled him up, speaking his name over and over in what I hoped was a calming voice. The man was incapable of a single utterance. Taking the man's weight, I tried to assist him, tried to get him to walk, but he was incapable of it. As I stood in the street, weighing the merits of returning for Holmes, a cab rattled along the street. Hailing it, I helped the stricken man inside. Searching Lambton's coat,

I was able to find his address and urged the cabbie to take us there.

As the cab lurched forward, Lambton looked up at me, his eyes wide, and whispered, "You saw her too, didn't you?"

Seeing no other course of action open to me, I paid the cab and took the man inside his home. I cleaned him up, set him trembling into his bed, sat at his bedside until the dawn. Neither of us slept. I tried speaking to him but, until the first rays of sunlight crept through the dirty film of his window, the man was unable to reply.

With the dawn, Lambton sighed and swung his legs from the bed. Some character had returned to his face, a touch of the world weariness I had seen in his features when he'd stomped into Holmes' presence.

"Where do you think you're going?" I asked.

"Work," he grunted, hands rubbing his face.

"Not today," I instructed him. "You are to rest. Doctor's orders."

"I don't think—"

"Look at yourself, man! You're no use to them as you are now, nor will you do yourself any good trying. If it will help, I'll send a note to the Yard. You need rest."

Lambton grunted and, defeated, lay back down. I made myself ready to leave but as my hand fell on the door, Lambton called out from the other room. "Holmes will take my case, won't he, Doctor? If he doesn't, I don't know what will become of me."

"I'll see that he does. Now, you need rest."

Accepting his silence as consent, I faced a day of fatigue. At my practice, I set about writing a note to my wife assuring her I was fine and promising to explain all when I arrived home, a note to Scotland Yard informing them Lambton would be unable to report for duty for several days due to a medical incident and, after some consideration, a note to

Holmes urging him to take on Lambton's case. Those duties complete, I soldiered through the day as best I was able.

§

"A ghost?" Holmes repeated in surprise. "You cannot be serious."

I sighed. Three nights had passed since Lambton's visit to the lodgings, two nights since my note urging him to take Lambton's case, yet it was the first chance I had to discuss matters with Holmes in person. After describing how I had discovered the Inspector, and how I tended to him, Holmes had asked my opinion as to what had stricken Lambton. I answered honestly, both as a man and as a doctor. My answer had taken Holmes by surprise.

"What other meaning can we ascribe to his asking if I'd seen her too? You saw how he acted when he was here, furious one instant, then completely unmanned when he looked over your shoulder. Clearly, he saw something we did not."

Holmes waved his hand in a dismissive gesture.

"I am not suggesting that ghosts are real," I argued wearily. "Simply that Lambton believes he has seen one. What difference does it make if he is confronting a spirit or an affliction of the mind? The effect is the same."

Holmes steepled his fingers before him, leaning back in his chair as he considered my words. "Lambton is mad, that is what you are saying."

"He is on the brink of insanity, certainly. His condition was wretched. The difference between the Lambton who left here and the one I encountered on the street was astounding. Something happened to him, or at least he believes it did. He's aware he will be labeled mad should he admit to seeing the woman haunting him but there's no doubt in my mind he believes himself haunted."

"It would explain what drove him to seek my services," Holmes admitted. "Still, Watson, you have no idea of the dreadful things Lambton has done in his career. How many he has sent to the gallows. Why should this misdeed weigh so heavily on his conscience when he's managed to brush off all his other sins?"

"Who are we to judge how little guilt the man struggles with? I've no doubt the man has done terrible things but, Holmes, surely cutting this woman with a killer's knife is one of the most ghastly? You and I have known the feel of blades against flesh but we were shielded by a noble pursuit of knowledge. Lambton's only protection was the wish to falsely accuse another."

"But, Watson, a ghost?"

"In his mind; Yes. If we are to save the Inspector you will have to end his haunting by uncovering her killer. Have you made any progress?"

Holmes reached for his pipe and slipper. "I had not even decided to accept the case when your note found me. Still, I have not been idle."

"You found the man from that morning?"

"The well-dressed gentleman Lambton is so eager to have me pursue? He is inconsequential, a go-between, nothing more. My investigation has been focused on the Allen woman."

"The victim?"

"Naturally. Consider the scene as Lambton found it: She was laid out neatly, almost fondly, atop her bedcovers. It would have been simplicity itself to undress the corpse and place it under the sheets to give the impression she had expired in her sleep, yet it was not done. Being placed so carefully, so respectfully, indicates she was placed there by someone who knew her. Nothing in Lambton's description gives any indication the well-dressed stranger was familiar with her. His dress indicates his plans had been disrupted by this incident, his ability to speak privately with a Scotland Yard superintendent over a corpse suggests power and influence. A go-between. The real question is: An agent between the Yard and who?

"To find an answer, the most efficient line of investigation is to examine the victim. Who did she know? Where did she come from? How did she spend her days? Simple questions, simply answered by those who knew her. I went to her building, asked around. By all accounts Miss Allen was a kind and caring girl, one who was having some difficulty adapting to life in the metropolis. Originally from outside Worcester, Miss Allen came to London almost a year ago to pursue an employment opportunity in government, one proffered to her by a ministry official of some renown, and of some notoriety as a womanizer."

"So, you've a suspect."

"Only a suspect," Holmes scowled. "Given how eagerly Lambton was to pursue the go-between, I've no doubt the Inspector would consider such information sufficient. Of course, we must hold ourselves to a higher measure. Watson, have you considered what Lambton will do should I complete this investigation? Once I prove my case and unmask the killer, what happens next?"

Frowning, I admitted, "I've not thought that far ahead. My concern has been Lambton and the hope that revealing the truth would be enough to free him from his torment. Are you suggesting he will seek to avenge the young woman's murder himself?"

"Unless an alternative is available," Holmes nodded. "We must proceed cautiously and plan meticulously. We cannot bring this investigation to the Yard, it will never see a courtroom. Without these safeguards the situation could very easily spiral out of control."

"Which is unacceptable." Rubbing my forehead, seeking relief from my headache's dull throb, I considered the knot my friend was attempting to untangle. "Yet if you don't present Lambton a killer, I doubt the man will survive a fortnight."

"Your concern for the man is admirable, Watson, but remember: His past is full of dark and terrible deeds."

"I've not forgotten, yet I refuse to be reduced to a helpless witness. I've no wish to watch and do nothing while the man descends into madness. Given his worsening condition, it would not surprise me if he attempted violence against whoever he deems responsible, whether you complete your investigation or not."

"A fair point."

"Whatever shall we do?" I asked.

"All we can. We must trust our nerve and attempt to reason matters out. Given the unpredictable nature and size of our client, we will have to be doubly cautious. Precautions seem in order, when both our prey and our employer threaten us. Care must be taken." Selecting a stout, metal-capped walking stick, Holmes nodded in my direction. "Forewarned is forearmed. We must control events, not allow Lambton's spirit to pull us into chaos."

§

Holmes required a further two days to make preparations. I called on Lambton in the interval and was distressed at his condition. Why Scotland Yard allowed the man to return to duty, I could not say. It was obvious to me whatever respite the man had enjoyed from my note had been thoroughly spent. For Lambton's part, all he was interested in was Holmes progress. I gave him assurances that Holmes was working on the case and was closing in on Miss Allen's killer. All Lambton need do was await Holmes' instructions and, for pity's sake, rest.

So it was that when the dandy man emerged from Scotland Yard with Lambton close on his polished heels, Holmes was waiting. Walking stick in hand, Holmes beckoned to Lambton. The bedraggled Inspector looked dumbly at the detective, then to his dapper quarry, then back to Holmes. I watched, it seemed a near thing but at last Lambton stumbled towards Holmes.

"Did you see—" Lambton started. Holmes silenced the Inspector with a wave and led him towards a cab. I waited inside with one of the Irregulars, a trustworthy lad who had agreed to serve as Holmes' messenger for the day.

"Of course I saw him," Holmes said, stick in hand. "It was I who summoned him. You are certain it is the same man?"

Lambton nodded. The man's continued decline made his skin sallow, though the bags under his eyes had darkened enough to be bruises. His watery eyes were bloodshot and the twitching of his hands betrayed a worsening palsy.

Reaching the cab's door, Holmes turned to Lambton and held out his hand. "Your knife, if you please?"

"What? I don't—"

Holmes pressed a hand against the man's side, where the hidden blade sat under his jacket. "We have no time for this. The trap has been set but it will only work if we do this the correct way. My way. The knife?"

Reluctantly, Lambton handed the blade over. A nasty length of metal, the blade seemed to gleam with malice as Holmes handed it to the filthy child waiting inside the cab. The boy's lip twisted in a smile as he examined the blade. Lambton climbed in the cab after Holmes, turning anxiously to look out the window. "I can't see 'im, Mr. Holmes."

"Not to worry." Holmes signaled the cabbie with his

walking cane against the roof. "I know where he is bound. Now, Lambton, there is to be an understanding between us before we proceed. This remains my case and it will proceed in my way. Do we have an understanding?"

Lambton grimaced but nodded.

"Have you any other weapons on your person?"

"No," Lambton answered, his eyes searching through the window. "I don't see 'im ..."

"Calm yourself. He's in that carriage up there. When we arrive, you will follow my instructions. I've set a neat trap, and it would be a shame to waste it, but if you cannot control yourself I will have no other choice. I must warn you that if this gambit fails, we are unlikely to get another opportunity. Have I your word?"

"You've my word," Lambton said. "What have you done?"

"I placed a piece of evidence into police custody on behalf of the Foreign Office. A diary believed to be the property of Miss Allen. In truth, she had kept such a diary. I found it in the possession of a young girl who lived in her building. It seems Miss Allen had passed it to the child, with her own writing cut out, a day before her murder. Miss Allen explained that her employer felt it improper for someone working for government to indulge in such writings. As her employer was also her lover, she felt she had no choice but to rid herself of it."

Lambton, struggling as he was under the weight of his fatigue and the ghost, blinked in confusion. "I don't understand, what's this diary got to do with the dandy man?"

Tapping his walking stick impatiently on the floor of the cab, Holmes explained. "The 'dandy man', as you call him, is employed by the Ministry and was sent by his superiors to redirect police attention from the crime. It is in that capacity he has been dispatched to the Yard to examine reports of an unexpected diary being placed in evidence."

"Where is he taking the diary?" I asked.

"There are two possibilities; I don't expect the agent to carry it as far as King Charles Street, but it is a possibility. If so, he will—ah, no, see how the carriage turns? There is a private residence ahead better suited to their clandestine purposes. Our aims are better served by their secrecy. Now, Inspector, I remind you that I have your pledge of obedience. This is my investigation, and you will not act against my wishes. With your trust, I believe I can bring this affair to a conclusion acceptable to us both but, should you act rashly, matters could go astray."

"I understand," Lambton growled. His attention was focused on the carriage ahead as it pulled to a stop before a luxurious home. The dapper man stepped out and strode purposefully to the door, a package tucked under his arm as he tipped his hat to the elderly servant who opened the door. Our cab, to Lambton's consternation, proceeded past the house and up the street. We pulled to street side a convenient distance from the home. Holmes led the way out of our waiting cab, walking back to better see the front of the home.

"What now, Holmes?" Lambton asked impatiently.

"We wait," Holmes said, consulting his watch. "At least half an hour. Watson and I will reconnoiter while you stay here and mark anyone arriving or departing." Turning to the lad, Holmes added, "Do not give him back his knife."

Holmes and I set off, strolling along the street. Once we were out of earshot of the cab, Holmes waved to the residence. "A property owned by the Thurlow brothers, both of whom are highly placed in Her Majesty's service. Both brothers are committed bachelors, though for different reasons. Edward sees no reason for marriage when a quick trip to the countryside and the promise of worthwhile employment will allow him to coerce affection from those unfortunates he ensnares. Edgar, though seemingly kinder in disposition, suffers from an inability to contradict his more forceful brother. An unfortunate state of affairs for those young women drawn to the city by Edward's promises but neither brother is interested in changing."

"I've no doubt they are both scoundrels," I argued, "but the villains you describe seem incapable of so passionate a crime as murder."

"Quite so, Watson," Holmes nodded. "Neither of the Thurlow brothers can be accused of an excess of passion but the Inspector's description of her corpse indicated she did not die of violence. I suspect poison but, as her cadaver was not tested for such, we lack proof. This was a cold and calculated affair, however I have enough information to suggest a theory."

"Consider the strange act of Miss Allen handing her diary to the child in her building, combined with the fact that she was employed by the Thurlow brothers, both of whom hold sensitive positions in Her Majesty's government. I suspect she witnessed an event, something she likely did not understand the significance of at the time, which her employers felt they could not risk coming to light. I confirmed with my brother, Mycroft, that the Thurlow brothers, whom you correctly labeled scoundrels, are in a position to profit from their work. A diary, something documenting their misdeeds, was evidence they could not allow to exist. Alone in London, oppressed by her employers, the woman certainly had need of some measure of comfort, yet in the end she surrendered the diary at the insistence of the Thurlows. It seems likely to me the brothers were unaware of her compliance and, in their ignorance, poisoned the young woman to protect themselves."

I could not help but sigh. "A pity it cannot be proven."

Holmes shook his head. "Even if we had the means to

convict, we could not bring this case to the Yard. Not after they solved it so readily and hung the perpetrator. Still, we are not without resources and the game is not yet played out."

Having finished our examination of the Thurlow domicile, we returned to Inspector Lambton and the small lad serving as the big man's watchdog. As we approached the boy opened his tattered jacket to show he still had Lambton's knife. Holmes nodded. An encouraging sign that the Inspector was holding true to his promise as it was unlikely the child could have kept Lambton from retrieving his property if he wished. For that matter, despite the Inspector's questionable health, I doubt I could have kept the blade from him if he desired it with the fervor I had seen him exhibit during our short acquaintance.

"The fella we followed," Lambton growled. "He's left."

"Good," Holmes answered. "Empty-handed?"

"Yes," Lambton admitted. "We should bust our way inside afore anyone else scarpers."

"That's exactly what we will do," Holmes consulted his watch again. "In about twenty minutes."

"Why wait?"

"Because I deem it prudent," Holmes answered.

§

We waited in silence for a time, an odd collection of gentlemen lurking in the street. Yet London was full of such and we did not draw notice. After a time, Lambton looked at Holmes with a slight expression of wonder on his rough features. "You planted evidence, Holmes."

Holmes nodded but added, "There is, however, a distinction between our methods. I planted evidence with the police rather than with someone suspected of criminality.

While I made certain they were made aware of the evidence, nothing I did would compel an innocent to a guilty act."

"Still," Lambton noted, "you surprise me."

"Let us hope our quarry is as easily impressed."

Another carriage stopped in front of the home and discharged a bald, rather heavyset, whiskered gentleman who rushed from the carriage to the front door and quickly disappeared inside.

"Edward?" I asked.

"His brother Edgar," Holmes answered. "Edward waits within. Ground floor, second room on the west side, I observed him through the window."

Lambton shuffled on his feet, his hands clenching and unclenching. "We should —"

"Patience, Lambton," Holmes commanded. "We wait. A trap sprung early is no trap at all."

After an additional ten minutes, Holmes pulled out his watch and, with an air of indifference, checked the time. Tucking the watch back in his pocket, he turned to our young compatriot. "You know your assignment?"

The lad nodded. Holmes turned to Lambton and I. "Shall we, gentlemen?"

We strode purposefully across the street, up to the front door which Holmes pushed through without knocking. Down the hallway the elderly servant we'd seen from the street barked an admonishment. We ignored it. Holmes led the way, directing the servant rudely to one side with his walking stick. We entered the office Holmes had seen from the street. The heavyset, balding man, Edgar, looked up with a startled expression. His brother Edward, seated behind an expansive desk, was thinner and more polished than his brother. His surprise at our arrival manifested itself in annoyance. It was apparent at a glance that the two men, despite their dissimilar physiques, were brothers.

"Who the devil do you think you are?!" The seated brother exclaimed.

The elderly servant pulled at my arm and exclaimed, "I am sorry, sir, they just barged in—"

Into the cacophony, Lambton's exclamation silenced us all. "You!" The big man bellowed, his arm raised and an accusatory finger shaking at the seated brother. "You killed her, you bastard! See how she looks at you!"

Lambton, all fury and rage, stepped forward. From his expression I had not the slightest doubt he intended to rend the seated man limb from limb but Holmes, first to recover from the startlement which froze all in the room, thrust his walking stick between the looming Inspector's legs. Lambton fell on the desk with a great clatter, sliding from there onto the floor. He jerked himself up, only to find his assent halted by the tip of Holmes' walking stick.

"Watson," Holmes called out. Belatedly, I pulled my service revolver from my pocket and trained it on the fallen Inspector. The elderly servant, seeing the weapon, released my arm and stepped away. Lambton glared at me but it was clear he understood the disadvantage of his position.

"You gave me your word, Inspector," Holmes reminded Lambton. "I will hold you to it."

Edgar, seated by the door, his demeanor thoroughly shaken, managed to squeak out, "Inspector?"

"Introductions seem to be in order," Holmes agreed, withdrawing his walking stick from Lambton's chest. "I am Sherlock Holmes. Dr. Watson, Inspector Lambton of Scotland Yard, may I introduce Edgar and Edward Thurlow. The employers of the late Miss Allen and, of course, her killers."

Behind me the elderly servant gasped. "Perhaps," I suggested to Holmes, "this would best be discussed in private."

"It is all the same to me," Holmes proclaimed. "I am willing to speak all I know to whoever will listen, including, should I be granted the chance, a judge and a jury."

Edgar, huddled in his chair, managed a sob. Behind his desk, his expression pale, Edward seemed unable to divert himself from under the violent glare Lambton directed his way. Nevertheless, he managed a wave to dismiss the elderly servant. I followed the elderly man into the hallway, muttered some instructions to him, then returned to the room. The situation seemed less volatile than before, so I slipped my revolver back into my pocket. For a moment, no one seemed capable of speech save Holmes who was waiting patiently and quietly.

"We've heard of Miss Allen, of course," Edward said, a tremor in his voice as a result of Lambton's continued attention. "She was, as you say, in our service—"

Holmes barked, a sharp, bitter laugh. I heard Lambton growl.

"M-my understanding," the besieged man carried on, "is that her killer was arrested, tried and put to death."

"Yes," Holmes admitted. "Yet all of us in this room know Hann was not her killer. You killed her, feeding her poison, then had your brother Edgar escort the dying woman to her home. Edgar watched her suffer the indignities of the convulsions and, when she finally stilled, restored her as best he could. You always took such care not to be seen by those in her building, but it would still have been a risk for you to be recognized there, so Edgar took her home. It must be delightful to have a brother so willing to clean up your messes. I must confess that when I contacted my own brother regarding my suspicions of your activities, he expressed a keen interest in hearing more. I am meeting him later at his club."

"Your brother is Mycroft Holmes, *the* Mycroft Holmes?"

"Just so," Holmes agreed.

Blinking, Edward seemed to slump forward. "I don't know what this is about, Mr. Holmes. As I said, Miss Allen's killer has faced justice and I —"

We heard the front door open, as I had instructed the elderly servant, and the clatter of hobnailed boots filled the hallway.

"Ah," Holmes smiled. "The police, right on time."

Edward exchanged a panicked look with his brother but, finding no solace in Edgar's cowering expression, he turned to Holmes. "You cannot have us arrested for a murder another man was hanged for!"

"If you saw how she looks at you both," Lambton growled. The brothers blanched again, visibly shrinking from the muscular Inspector.

Holmes' smile widened. "You're right, of course. Despite your guilt, we cannot have you arrested for murder. We must settle for a charge of treason."

"Treason?" Edward gasped. Lestrade entered the room, brandishing a pair of darbies and backed by a pair of burly constables.

"Exactly," Holmes explained. "There on your desk. I signed that diary into police evidence on behalf of the Foreign Office myself just yesterday. I could not be certain of its providence yet that doesn't explain why it is sitting on your desk. I trust you signed it out in accordance with government procedure? No? What a shame. Unfamiliar as I am with your professional responsibilities I was unable to theorize with regards to what motive you might have for pilfering it, so I was forced to consult with my brother. He had a surprising amount of insight, assuring me that if the diary was removed without proper authorization the government's only possible reaction would be a charge of treason. His office will be auditing your activities. Perhaps it is a misunderstanding that will be quickly cleared up. Then again ..."

Lestrade had the two brothers, neither quite able to stand, handcuffed and assisted out of the room. Lestrade tipped his hat to Lambton, then picked up the diary on the desk. "Should I expect a visit from the Special Branch over this?"

"Likely," Holmes acknowledged. "Not to worry though, there's nothing secret in the diary. I expect Special Branch will want to conduct the investigation themselves. That said, the Thurlows have at least one friend within the Yard. If you could let him know I have no wish to testify in court, I would be grateful. Were I forced to testify I would be obliged to be unstinting in my testimony. Is my meaning plain?"

"Indeed it is Holmes," Lestrade assured the detective. "I'll see it doesn't come to that."

"That would be best," Holmes agreed. "Well, I have an appointment to keep with my brother. Inspector Lambton, you know my address? Excellent, I shall await the payment of my standard fee. In the interim, perhaps you should introduce the Thurlow brothers to your unseen friend. Perhaps she'll be more interested in their company than yours. At least, that is my hope."

Lambton nodded, observing, "You've a nasty streak, Holmes."

"I try," Holmes admitted.

Court of Honour

rs. Nyland sat in the chair by the fireplace, hands folded in her lap, as she desperately struggled to hold back tears. I stood with my arm on the mantle, forcing myself to meet the poor woman's gaze directly. My association with the consulting detective Sherlock Holmes left me remarkably well-informed on the subject of delivering convincing testimony and I was determined to convey the unpleasant news with as much sincerity as the circumstances allowed. Holmes sat in the far corner of his Baker Street lodgings, scrutinising my performance with a calculating expression on his lean features.

"Dr. Watson, are you certain?" Dark eyes in a pale, heart-shaped face looked beseechingly up at me, seeking some relief from the harsh truths I had spoken to her. A slender, fragile woman, she seemed to me ill-prepared for the words duty compelled me to speak. Still, as Holmes had been so quick to point out, she deserved the truth.

"Quite certain," I said. "You mustn't forget the secret drawer in his nightstand. None of those we spoke with were aware of the locked drawer's existence. The key was hidden within the workings of your brother's pocket watch. It may have escaped our notice had you not informed us of his fascination with complex mechanisms. I am sorry Mrs. Nyland, but the arsenic was locked in that drawer, concealed from all save your brother. It is our opinion that your brother poisoned himself."

"But the doctors said it was cholera."

"The symptoms are similar," I explained. "Both cause death by kidney failure. Had Holmes not discovered the depleted bottle of arsenic, cholera would have been my diagnosis as well."

Hiding dark eyes behind her gloved hand, Mrs. Nyland took a moment to compose herself. I waited, ignoring Holmes' intense gaze, anxious for this ordeal to be over. Mrs. Nyland's brother, Adam Bellamy, had poisoned himself over the course of four days, ingesting carefully measured doses of arsenic in the hope his death would be considered natural. Bellamy's sister refused to accept the explanation her brother had arranged, asking Holmes to investigate the circumstances surrounding his demise. Holmes accepted the case and discovered, in the nightstand by Bellamy's deathbed, a hidden drawer. The secrets contained within the drawer were such that I took the unusual step of presenting Holmes' findings to Mrs. Nyland myself.

"I knew it wasn't cholera," Mrs. Nyland insisted as she dabbed at the tears on her face. "Adam was too protective of his health. I knew it must be something else, knew something happened to him, but I never suspected this. It makes even less sense than the doctor's suggestion. Have you any idea – any idea at all – why he would do such a thing?"

Holmes shifted in his seat, the focus of his gaze growing even more intense. I hesitated to answer, wanting to select my words with care. Mrs. Nyland filled the quiet, her grief making my brief silence unbearable.

"My brother was a mild-tempered man, Dr. Watson, and

I know as well as anyone his guarded disposition. Adam was not given to outbursts or emotional excesses. He kept to himself, never taking a wife, content with the company of his few friends. I know there were times when he struggled, times when I wished he could find comfort in another. Someone with whom he could share his confidences, someone who meant as much to him as my late husband meant to me. I tried to be there for him. I thought our friendship could—"

"You must not blame yourself, Mrs. Nyland. If our investigation proved anything, it was the high regard in which your brother held you. Nothing we found suggests you contributed in any way to your brother's death."

"Then – why?" Her grief was so raw, the sincerity of her question so heartfelt, I struggled to find the words to answer her need.

"Mrs. Nyland, did you request a post-mortem examination of your brother?"

"What?" She shook her head. "No, it did not occur to me at the time. I doubted the doctor's findings but I'd seen his body. It was obvious no violence had been done to him."

"Yes, of course," I said. "It's possible, however, a closer examination would have revealed some sort of illness. As a physician, I have had to inform patients of the fatal maladies they have contracted. As you would expect, such news is a dreadful shock and different men react to the news in different ways. Many seek some way of exerting control over their situations. Rather than suffering through their afflications, they chose to end their lives by their own hand. You understand they are drawn to such desperate actions for a variety of reasons. It can restore a sense of control while, at the same time, sparing their loved ones a long, painful, and – you must forgive me for speaking so bluntly – financially draining illness. You mentioned your brother took precautions regarding his health. Sometimes such men mistakenly feel responsible for succumbing to their illness. A ridiculous notion, but one I have observed in some of my patients. Such guilt can contribute to such decisions."

Mrs. Nyland looked thoughtfully at the empty fireplace, considering my explanation.

"But Adam's doctor said nothing to me about—"

"Nor would he," I interrupted. "Medical men often find themselves in difficult situations of this sort. Our training is strict and unrelenting. We are forbidden from revealing matters discussed in confidence – even with the patient's families. Among my profession it is considered a matter of honour. If your brother instructed his doctor not to discuss his illness with you, then the doctor had no choice but to keep such information secret. Oftentimes such confidentiality is contrary to the physician's better judgement but a doctor's first duty is always to his patient."

"Oh, I see." Mrs. Nyland considered my words for a long moment before nodding. "I must admit that does sound rather like my brother. He often worried about being a disappointment to me, as if such a thing were even possible. And he was always very conscientious regarding his finances."

"Perhaps if we exhumed your brother's body, we might discover the exact nature of his illness." It was a careful suggestion, offered with seeming reluctance.

A look of distaste contorted Mrs. Nyland's pleasant features. "Oh no, Dr. Watson, I shouldn't think that is necessary. My brother has suffered enough."

"Of course," I answered solemnly, hoping to disguise my relief.

Mrs. Nyland took a deep breath, composing herself. It was obvious to me that our appointment was at an end and it seemed I had reached the conclusion of the terrible ordeal. I felt as I imagine a tightrope walker must as he nears the end of his slow, careful journey.

"Thank you gentlemen," Mrs. Nyland said. "Your assistance has meant a great deal to me. You have lived up to your reputation, Mr. Holmes."

Sitting in his corner, Holmes acknowledged the compliment with a slight nod.

Mrs. Nyland stood, gathering her things and making ready to leave. "And Dr. Watson, you've been so very kind to me. My gratitude seems so small a thing next to the compassion you've shown."

Escorting her to the door, I replied. "Not at all, Mrs. Nyland."

She stopped in the doorway, turning to me. "Oh, gentlemen, I almost forgot. In my brother's secret drawer, were there any documents? I only ask because he'd spoken to me of amending his will."

I stumbled, searching for, but failing to find, an acceptable response to her innocent question.

Holmes rose from his seat and approached Mrs. Nyland as she waited in the doorway. "What exactly did your brother say?"

"Well, he mentioned that he had visited our estate in Brighton with a friend who was much taken with the place. He asked if I would be offended if he altered his will to allow his friend – I did not catch the man's name – the estate's guest house."

"And what was your answer?" Holmes asked.

"Of course I had no objection. My late husband left me well-cared for financially and any friend of Adam's is, naturally, a friend of mine. I bring it up now because I visited Adam's solicitor yesterday and he made no mention of any such bequest. I had been looking forward to meeting one of Adam's friends but, well, I suppose it doesn't really matter."

"Nevertheless, I shall make enquiries," Holmes assured the widow.

"You've already done so much," Mrs. Nyland protested.

"It is nothing," Holmes assured her. "I shall contact you with my findings."

"Thank you ever so much, Mr. Holmes." She turned to me. "And you as well, Dr. Watson."

And then she was gone. As the door closed I walked over to the chair by the fireplace, collapsed into it and filled my pipe with rough-cut tobacco. Holmes stood by the door, waiting until he heard Mrs. Nyland descend each of the seventeen steps and exit to the street before risking speech.

"Well, Watson," Holmes said. "A masterful performance! I feel I should report your new-found abilities to my brother Mycroft. The Empire's diplomatic corps have need of men with such skills!"

"Holmes ..." I said wearily, forlornly hoping to divert his inevitable reaction.

"Truly, Watson, I stand in awe. You spoke not a single lie and yet managed to conceal the truth of her brother's death completely. When you suggested she might disinter her brother's body, I was positively breathless! Such a gambit! And it worked exactly as you hoped, ensuring she would make no further inquiry into the state of her brother's health. How can she? To do so she must chose between forcing a physician to break his solemn oath or dragging her brother's corpse back into the light of day. Well-played, Watson, you've an unexpected flair for deception!"

I lit my pipe as Holmes took his customary place in the chair next to mine. His elbows rested on his thighs as he leaned forward to better observe my reactions. "There was," Holmes continued, "one moment, when Mrs. Nyland asked about her brother's will, when you faltered. Oh, I doubt she noticed anything but I saw the lie rise to your lips – and your unwillingness to utter it. Still, you prevailed. I suppose congratulations are in order."

I sighed, exhaling a cloud of smoke. "But?"

"As impressive as your performance was, I fail to perceive its purpose. Surely it would have been simpler to tell Mrs. Nyland the truth – the full truth – concerning her brother's death. I would not have thought such casual deception was in your nature."

"Casual?"

"All men lie," Holmes said as he reached for his pipe. "Deception is part of our nature. Some lie out of habit, others out of compulsion. Honest men lie only under duress, when deception seems the lesser evil. Others lie when the truth might lead to some unpleasantness or inconvenience. Now, I know you are not a habitual liar, nor do I perceive any duress which might result in your extraordinary performance for Mrs. Nyland. Unless, perhaps you feel compelled to protect Dr. Jenkins and the others?"

"Nothing of the sort, I assure you."

Holmes lit his pipe. "I know you have no affiliation with the school in question. Still, I suppose you may harbor a misguided impulse to protect the reputation of the institution."

"No."

Holmes leaned back and spread his arms. "Where does this leave us? You concealed the truth from Mrs. Nyland to avoid – what? Embarrassment? Scandal? Unpleasantness?"

"Has it occurred to you that Bellamy endured an agonizing death to prevent his sister from learning his secret?" My tone was more confrontational than I intended but the ordeal with Mrs. Nyland left me exhausted.

"Of course it has," Holmes answered easily. "You know

my feelings on the subject. The dead are entitled to their secrets only until they interfere with those still living. Had Bellamy wished his secrets protected, he should have remained alive to guard them himself."

I shook my head, though in truth I had anticipated this answer, "Even so," I argued, "I find I cannot so quickly dismiss such determination from my thoughts. Bellamy's death was horrible, yet remember how neatly the arsenic bottle was returned to its hiding place? How carefully the bottle was stoppered? The drawer locked and the key returned to its ingenious hiding place. I admit I was struck by the resolve he evidenced. Everyone we spoke to insisted he was a good man. Bellamy will be missed by many."

"What of it?" Holmes asked, a trace of exasperation in his tone. "It is not a detective's function to pass judgement on the dead. Whether he was a good man or otherwise, it makes no difference to my investigation."

"Are you not concerned that revealing the circumstances leading to Bellamy's death could create a scandal capable of overshadowing the good he accomplished in life?"

"No, not in the least," Holmes said. "I have no intention of revealing the results of my investigation to newspapers or gossips, only to my client. In any event, I have no fear of scandal. Such concerns plague men of other occupations, not mine."

"Fair enough," I conceded.

"Come now, Watson," Holmes said sharply. "You seem to have developed a fondness for this particular brand of deception. While I do not doubt your concern for Bellamy's reputation is genuine, it is not your primary motive. Why this elaborate charade? Why paper over so large a falsehood with so many little truths?"

I leaned forward, ready to take Holmes into my confidence. "What do you believe Mrs. Nyland would have done if she'd learned the entire truth concerning her brother's death?"

"I have no crystal ball," Holmes protested. "I am a detective, not a fortune teller."

"Who is hiding small truths now?" I asked. "It will be helpful to know if your estimation of the woman matches my own."

"Very well," Holmes relented. "She would be quite shocked, I suppose, necessitating a period of retreat and contemplation. When sufficiently recovered, she would seek a confrontation with those who brought about her brother's demise."

"And in your professional opinion, would she receive any satisfaction from this confrontation?"

"It is unlikely," Holmes conceded. "You must remember: No laws have been broken."

"Surely there must be some legal recourse?" Unfortunately, I suspected the answer but I wanted to be certain. Holmes' knowledge of the law was far more extensive than my own.

Holmes shook his head. "You have heard my opinion on this matter before. You seek justice, a quality the law is not always equipped to deliver. Contrary to public perception, the law is a blunt instrument. Law is not a product of justice, rather it is an amalgamation of popular opinion. Given the circumstances surrounding this case, I see no legal path by which Mrs. Nyland might find satisfaction."

"As I feared," I replied. "Weeks, maybe months, wasted while Mrs. Nyland composes herself. And in the end the matter would be thrown back in her face without resolution. She deserves better than that."

"Very gallant, Watson," Holmes said. "Though I fail to see how keeping Mrs. Nyland ignorant of the truth is any improvement. Mrs. Nyland's attempt to gather some measure of justice for her brother may not be successful but there is a nobility to the effort. She is not without resources—"

"When you say 'resources' you mean yourself, do you not?" I asked. "You would offer your professional services to Mrs. Nyland should she seek your assistance?"

"Of course," Holmes admitted. "Being outside the law, such a case would be uniquely suited to my talents."

"I thought as much," I said, not without a trace of smugness. "You and I are in complete agreement in this matter. The reason I kept the truth from Mrs. Nyland is simple: I wished to avoid delay. Holmes, I wish to hire you myself."

Holmes leaned forward in his chair, his features betraying a rare look of surprise. "I beg your pardon?"

"Rather than wait for Mrs. Nyland to ask for your assistance to bring those who wronged her brother to justice, I will hire you to accomplish the same task sooner rather than later. The central problem seems to be what form this justice should take, as you say the courts will be of no assistance. Ideally these villains would be hauled before the courts where your evidence would condemn them to prison or worse. Under these circumstances, well, we are left to our own devices."

"Do go on." Amusement was evident in Holmes' voice as he spoke. "You have obviously directed considerable effort towards a solution."

"Bellamy's will," I said, not without pride. "The entire sorry affair started when Bellamy amended his will. It seems only proper the same document bring it to a finish. I propose we see to it that Bellamy's last will and testament be enforced."

"Oh, well done, Watson!" Holmes said with a genuine smile. "Your solution is elegant and simple. If I recall the terms of Bellamy's will correctly, his lover stands to inherit a good portion of his estate, including control of Bellamy's business holdings. You would release Bellamy's lover from the financial shackles placed on him by his tyrannical family. With a single stroke you undo all Bellamy's enemies sought to accomplish. Jenkins, Schrader, Gillis, and—of course –the elder Birling himself, each of them would see their efforts thwarted. Unfortunately, Watson – clever as your plan is—without the intervention of the courts, it is quite impossible.

"Why?" I asked. "We have a copy of the will. You took it from the secret drawer in Bellamy's nightstand."

"Having a document is not enough," Holmes said. "Schrader was Bellamy's solicitor. All he need do is disavow knowledge of the amended will and your scheme is undone."

I smiled, remembering the document which had lain beside the amended will in Bellamy's hidden drawer. "You have not heard the rest of my plan."

As I explained the details of what I hoped to accomplish, I took a keen pleasure in watching a smile creep onto my friend's lean face.

§

Seemingly unaffected by the thousands of students' feet that had marched over its cold, hard surface, the sound of our footfalls echoed sharp as gunshots. Holmes and I had recently visited the student chapel as part of our investigation and, being hurried, had neither the time nor the inclination to examine the dark, highly-polished wood pews or the timbers of the vaulted ceiling. However our guest, Mr. Eric Birling, looked about him with a mixture of remembered awe and fresh curiosity in his expression. The last light of the day was surrendering to night, the shadows within the chapel were deep and sharp. I followed Holmes up the central aisle in order to help him move a large table. We had discussed the setup, scouted the location, but in our sudden hurry to arrive before the others we hadn't time to inform Mr. Birling of our plans. During the long cab ride out to the school, composing the necessary letters had completely occupied our attention. As I moved the table to block the aisle, cutting off access to the front of the chapel, I called to our guest.

"Mr. Birling? Over here, please."

He looked up, startled from his contemplation of the chapel's unforgiving surfaces. Even in sunlight the chapel seemed austere, in the weak moonlight seeping through the windows the interior seemed pitiless. Finding me in the darkness, he walked hurriedly down the aisle.

"I have always hated this place," Birling said as he passed me. Although the words were not spoken loudly, they echoed in the hollow space like an accusation. Setting the heavy table in place, I joined Birling by the raised area of the stage.

"You are certain we are permitted to be here?" Birling asked. "I do not understand what this place has to do with Adam's death?"

"You have been quite patient with us," I acknowledged. "I am sorry to have to ask you to wait further but there are preparations that must be made. It is imperative that you not be seen. We will place you up in the corner seat there. You see? Completely invisible in shadows. As long as you make no sound, you will not be discovered. You are here as a witness, nothing more. Regardless of what you hear you must remain silent. Do you understand?"

"Not really," the man said. A rueful smile lifted his features, dark eyes sought my own. Until this moment Eric Birling had been something of an enigma, always an essential part of our plan but more an agenda item than an individual. A handsome man but not startlingly so, more than anything else I had been struck by his ordinariness. Foolish, I knew, but all the same I had, perhaps unconsciously, expected Adam Bellamy's lover to be in some way extraordinary in appearance. When Holmes and I called upon Birling, I had been momentarily nonplussed to see such a solid, respectable looking fellow answer. Time was of the essence, our gambit had worked better than we anticipated and necessity forced us to forego the explanations Birling deserved. Instead it fell to me to compel Birling to accompany us. A task which proved surprisingly simple once I informed him our errand concerned the death of Adam Bellamy.

Meeting Birling's gaze, seeing determination, grief and chaos contained there, I realised—somewhat to my surprise—that I admired the fellow. The mere mention of his lover's name was enough to pull Birling out of the safety of his home.

"What do you know about a court of honour?" I asked, ushering Birling up to the stage.

Birling laughed humourlessly. "How odd you should ask that question here, of all places. When I was a student here the head-boys would bring students accused of infractions to what they called a court of honour. It was considered good exercise for students who might grow into barristers, solicitors and the like."

I nodded in understanding, the explanation was much as the current headmaster had explained it. I glanced at Holmes, who was hurriedly arranging four chairs behind the long table. I found another chair and carried it to the darkened corner.

"There is disapproval in your voice," I remarked to Birling.

"The honour of boys," Birling said with venom in his

voice. "Little more than ritualised bullying. A tyranny carried out in full view of the staff. I felt I did not so much graduate this place as escape it."

"Adam Bellamy also attended this school, did he not?" I asked, knowing the answer.

"He did," Birling confirmed. "Adam graduated in the same class as my Uncle Arthur."

From where he was arranging envelopes and candles on the long table, Holmes spoke up. "Mr. Birling, you should take your seat now."

"What has all this to do with Adam's death?" Birling demanded, his voice wary.

"A week before his death Adam Bellamy received a summons," I explained. "Written on this school's letterhead, it demanded he appear in this chapel or risk the punishment of the court of honour. It was signed by four of classmates. Walter Gillis, Randall Jenkins, Gregory Schrader and—"

"Arthur Birling." There was no question in Eric's voice as he completed my sentence.

"Yes," I confirmed his suspicion. Holmes renewed his warning. "Mr. Birling, I must insist you take your place now. We do not wish to endanger you but should you be seen—"

Birling nodded sadly. Removing his coat, he retreated into the dark corner.

"Watson," Holmes called for my help.

I joined Holmes; together we lifted a small but heavily-made table up onto the stage. From the dark corner came the heavy voice of Eric Birling. "Adam did not die of cholera, did he?"

"No, I'm afraid he did not," I answered. "Although it was arranged that his death should appear so. Had things gone the way I planned, there would have been more time to explain this properly—"

"But circumstances did not allow it," Holmes interrupted. With brisk, efficient movements Holmes lit the four large candles he'd placed on the long table. Rather than dispelling the shadows of the empty chapel the feeble lights seemed to make the shadows' darkness deeper. The flickering candles blurred the shadows' edges. "Those who summoned Adam Bellamy to this place have themselves been summoned."

"My uncle will not like that." No amusement tainted Eric Birling's voice. The simple phrase echoed in the empty chapel like a warning.

"His reaction was surprisingly violent," Holmes said calmly. "Rather than wait for the appointed time, he set out to gather his fellows. Apparently he believes there is some advantage could be gained by arriving before those who summoned him. Small matter though it is, Watson and I are determined to deny them any advantage. Are you comfortable, Mr. Birling? I do not think it will be long before —"

From behind him came the distinct sound of the outside doors being thrust open. Footsteps echoed on the narthex's stone floor, voices broke the stillness of the sombre surroundings. Angry, impatient and offended, the men rolled into the place like a wave. Holmes and I fell silent, taking our seats in the darkness. I felt fortunate to have finished our preparations in time, yet still wished we had been able to give Birling more explanation regarding what was to come.

"—intolerable, I tell you!" A loud flustered voice wheezed.

"Yes," an exasperated man agreed half-heartedly. "But who?"

"We shall find out!" The loud voice boomed, making the statement sound like a curse. "We will wait for them here and when they arrive, we shall—"

There was a sudden silence as the footsteps stopped

and the voices were stilled. The new arrivals had reached the chapel's large, open doors. Beyond the doorway, they warily examined the table, chairs and four waiting candles. For a moment they hesitated, open-mouthed and amazed.

"What the devil is this!" The loud voice was now identified as belonging to the corpulent Arthur Birling, uncle of the Eric Birling concealed in the shadowed corner. The two of them made an interesting comparison, sharing many facial characteristics. Yet where the thin nose and high cheekbones of Eric Birling's features gave him a noble, leonine aspect, on his uncle the same structure appeared blunt and axe-like. Arthur Birling entered the chapel like a locomotive, his considerable girth charging up the aisle as if unstoppable. Dark hair escaped the edges of his hat, giving his angry features a savage demeanour. He carried, I noted with professional detachment, a walking stick although his gait was unimpaired. An affectation or a weapon?

Following in the wake of Birling came the other, more reluctant conspirators. On Birling's heels came Schrader. Tall and thin, the solicitor removed his hat upon entering the chapel. Looking left and right into the darkness, it seemed he expected a horde of demons to leap from the shadows. Following some distance behind the solicitor came Gillis, his dull eyes downcast. Finally Dr. Jenkins, no more willing than Gillis but with a spark of wary intelligence in his eyes. Removing his cap, the doctor ran a nervous hand over the smooth crown of his head.

"Who is here?" Arthur Birling demanded of the darkness. "I demand you show yourself immediately!"

Ignoring the large man's outburst, Holmes waited to strike his match until Birling marched up to the long table blocking the aisle. Then, with a lazy gesture, Holmes struck the match and brought the flame to the candle before him.

Still holding the lit match in his hand, Holmes spoke. "That's far enough, gentlemen. Take your seats."

With a wave, Holmes extinguished the match. The dull light of his candle barely served to illuminate his sharp features but in the flickering light the detective seemed calm, almost bored. Though I knew better, it seemed to my eyes Holmes had presided over a thousand such courts. Certainly his confident indifference to those lined up before him produced a marked effect in the conspirators. Meekly they examined the table.

Only Birling stood his ground. "Listen here, what is—"

"Surely this is all familiar to you?" Holmes said, his voice loud enough to interrupt Birling but still maintaining its unexcited tone. "Not a month has passed since you summoned a similar 'court of honour' for Adam Bellamy. Gentlemen, under each candle you will find an envelope with your name written on it. Please take your seats, gentlemen. You may wish to wait before opening your envelopes but – and believe me when I tell you this – under no circumstances should you allow any eyes but your own to read the letter bearing your name."

Birling attempted to squeeze his bulk between the heavy table and the first pew. "That's quite enough! I see no reason why we should be forced to listen to you! When I get up there, you'll wish—"

The time had come for me to strike my match and light my candle. Birling, still trying to negotiate passage around the heavy table, stopped at the sight of me. As he judged the intent in my eyes, I could see his resolve falter. There was a loud scrape as Gillis pulled out his chair and took his seat. The others paused, waiting to see which direction Birling would take before committing themselves. For his part, Birling seemed poised on the balance point, uncertain himself what he would do.

"You've no right to be here," Birling growled, indignation in every syllable.

"No more than you had," Holmes argued. "You have three choices before you. One: you could continue up here and attack us. While I won't deny the idea has a certain appeal, you should harbour no illusions regarding your chances of surviving such a course of action."

Birling's lip curled into a sneer. "You don't frighten ..."

My service revolver made a loud sound as I set it on the table beside the candle. Although Birling was the focus of my attention, I saw Jenkins pale at the sight of the weapon.

"Second," Holmes continued as if there had been no interruption, "you may leave. No one will stop you. Of course, should you ignore our little court you risk punishment. Third: you may take a seat. Decide now and stop wasting our time."

Birling cast a glance at his fellows but found no comfort there. Jenkins took his seat while Schrader looked at the envelope bearing his name as if it were a serpent coiled to strike. Reluctantly, Birling retreated to the accused side of the table.

"First, gentlemen, let me congratulate you on your eagerness to answer our summons," Holmes said. "The sooner such unpleasantness has begun, the sooner it is finished. Now, as was stated in the summons, you have been called before this court to answer for the murder of your classmate, Adam Bellamy."

"We did not nothing wrong," Birling spoke defiantly.

"Indeed?" Holmes considered Birling's statement. "You summoned Bellamy to this chapel to face accusations from your court of honour. The four of you instructed Bellamy as to the method of suicide you determined would be most effective. Had Bellamy refused, you threatened to take it upon yourselves to reveal his secrets. Bellamy is dead because of your actions. Do you deny any of this?"

Schrader cleared his throat before speaking. "You cannot prove any of this."

"Can I not?" Holmes smiled cruelly. "You asked for my name before, I feel you should know it now. I am Sherlock Holmes. Perhaps, Mr. Schrader, as a member of the legal profession, you have heard my name before? In any event, this is not a court of law but a court of honour. The rules of evidence are somewhat different here, wouldn't you agree?"

It was apparent from Schrader's panicked expression that he was aware of Holmes' reputation. The soliticitor's wide eyes darted from Holmes to the letter before him, then dropped downwards. His hands came up, covering his face, and his shoulders shook.

"Do any of you wish to protest your innocence?" Holmes inquired. "Mr. Schrader, did you not rush to report the provisions Adam Bellamy made in his will to Arthur Birling? Specifically the provisions regarding Mr. Birling's nephew, Eric Birling? Dr. Jenkins, when Mr. Birling questioned you regarding how to arrange an accidental death, did you pretend such conversation was idle speculation? And, Mr. Gillis, don't imagine I am unaware of the purchase you made on the court of honour's behalf. And Mr. Birling, creator and chief justice of the court of honour. Your schoolmates had to be dragged to this place, blackmailed and bullied, but their reluctance did not slow you. Gentlemen, you are so quiet. Nothing to say? Very well, let us proceed."

Holmes looked over the accused at their table; only Birling, seething and furious, was able to meet his cool gaze. "It is the judgement of this court that each one of you is guilty of causing the death of Adam Bellamy. The court will forego punishment, provided each of you respect Adam Bellamy's last will and testament."

"What?" Schrader objected. "Bellamy's sister was at my office just the other day; we read through the will and—"

"Not that will," Holmes interrupted. "You will respect Bellamy's amended will, the one granting a portion of his estate to Eric Birling."

"Outrageous!" The senior Birling cried, knocking his chair backwards as he stood to face Holmes. "I will not allow it!"

"That is your choice," Holmes spoke as if the matter made no difference to him. "Then the punishment of the court falls on each of you."

Nodding, Birling turned and, walking stick in hand, started marching down the chapel aisle in triumph. Still seated at the table, Gillis and Jenkins shared a look of dismay while Schrader, wiping tears from his eyes, looked up at Holmes.

"What sort of punishment?" Jenkins asked timidly.

"These envelopes," Schrader's voice was a whisper. "What's in them?"

"The envelopes contain your punishment," Holmes answered. Birling paused partway down the aisle, looking back over his shoulder and glaring at Holmes. "Defying the court will, naturally, cost each of you your honour. Before I summoned you here, I indulged myself with an investigation into each of your lives. I was hoping to discover some scandal, some indiscretion, capable of causing each of you some inconvenience. The letters within your envelopes summarise the results of my inquires, as well as a detailed description of how, exactly, I intend to use all I uncovered. Blackmail, gentlemen, the same tool you employed against Bellamy. When I began my investigation I expected it would be difficult and time-consuming to uncover anything useful to my purpose, you being such upstanding gentlemen. Imagine my surprise! You recall I cautioned each of you to protect the contents of your letters from your classmates. I had no wish to expose any of you to the risk of further blackmail. Now, of course, there is no need for such secrecy. Everything listed in the letters will be a matter of public record shortly. Gentlemen, I cannot say it has been a pleasure but I do feel I owe you a debt of professional gratitude. In my career as a detective, I have encountered a wide variety of murderers. I thought I had seen killers of every stripe, but you gentlemen introduced me to an entirely different, entirely loathsome, form of homicide."

"Wait!" Jenkins stood, casting panicked looks at his fellows. Gillis had already opened his envelope, his eyes widened as he read the letter. Schrader simply stared at his sealed envelope. Jenkins turned to Birling, who stood frozen in the aisle.

"For God's sake, Birling!" Jenkins implored his classmate. "We need to discuss this."

"There is nothing to discuss," Birling insisted. "He is bluffing."

Gillis responded to Birling's assertion with a sharp bark of humourless laughter.

"He has nothing on me," Birling continued. "I will not release my nephew to depravity simply because this man claims to know something."

"At least look at your letter," Jenkins begged.

"There is no need," Holmes informed the doctor. "He already knows what is written there. A daughter, born out of wedlock and abandoned by her father."

"Which is not against the law!" Birling shouted at Holmes. "You cannot bring charges against me for that!"

"Quite true," Holmes agreed. "But you forget, this is not a court of law but of honour. Allow me to explain how this court operates. You married well, Mr. Birling, very fortunate considering how your business dealings suffered under your stewardship. I will ensure your wife learns of your neglected daughter. Furthermore I will make certain others of her circle also learn of the matter. I will provide your wife, and her family, ample scandal to force your departure from her side, and her wealth, should that be their desire. In my estimation, your wife does not seem—"

"You leave her out of this!" Birling bellowed, his walking stick raised over his head.

Holmes did not rise from his chair. Leaning forward, closer to the weak light of the candle, Holmes spoke his words sharply. "You beg this court's mercy? The same court you used to murder Bellamy? I will show you exactly the mercy you showed him. The court simply follows your precedent. Do I make myself clear, Mr. Birling? If you wish to speak with your fellow accused, you may do so. Be warned the court grows weary of your theatrics. This travesty has gone on too long already. Decide your fates."

As if pressing against a wind only he could feel, Birling walked back to the table and snatched up his letter. He tore open the envelope and unfolded the letter. Even in the dim, flickering light it was clear how his hand shook. For a moment I thought he would swoon and I wondered – in a curious, detached way – if he would fall. I made no move to help him. By his actions, Birling had placed himself beyond my compassion.

"Damn you!" Birling barked.

"You've decided then?" Holmes asked. "Do you accept the will of this court?"

An exchange of frightened glances, but Birling's defeat was clear in his stance. "We do," Birling surrendered, to the relief of the others. Turning, he threw his walking stick into the shadows. I knew as well as Holmes how much the large man wished to hurl his weapon at the detective. My hand reached for my service revolver, but there was no need to raise it. Birling's expression, his slumped shoulders, and shuffling step left no doubt that the fight had been drained from Arthur Birling.

"There will be no further summons, gentlemen. If word of any interference in the execution of Bellamy's will, or any attempts to meddle in Eric Birling's affairs, reach my ears I will act swiftly. Likewise, I trust you understand that the evenings you've spent writing summonses and convening secret trials are at an end? Very good. The court grants you liberty to leave."

They rose. Schrader tucked his still unopened letter into his jacket pocket, Birling held his crumpled in his fist. They had entered together, but they walked away without speaking or even meeting one another's gaze. I sat on the stage, watching them leave, filled with grim satisfaction. My plan had worked as I had hoped, yet in the end it had accomplished very little. For what it was worth, Bellamy's last will, the last will and testament which triggered the chain of events ending in his murder, would be grudgingly respected. Yet Bellamy himself was still dead, his secrets, and the valour displayed in his death, were buried with him.

Behind me, I heard the scrape of a chair as Eric Birling stood. He walked over to me. The candlelight revealing tears on his handsome face. I was not surprised.

"I didn't know," Eric Birling whispered. "Adam's death is my fault. He died because he loved me."

"Nonsense!" Holmes angrily interrupted. "In no way did you contribute to Bellamy's murder. Such talk is utter foolishness."

"Holmes is quite correct," I added, more softly. "He usually is."

"Why did you do this?" Eric Birling asked, his hand

waving at the grim court. "Did you even know Adam? I don't mean to seem ungrateful – without you I would never have learned the truth nor won freedom from my family – but why would you, someone like—"

I looked at the man in confusion. "Yes?"

"Come now, Watson," Holmes scolded me. "Surely you are not yet so removed from society you fail to recognize why Adam Bellamy chose death over revelation? My apologies, Mr. Birling, I assure you Watson meant no offence. It is just that, like myself, he has seen more of the evils of the world than most. While we do not mean to diminish your difficulties, such scandals seem very small indeed once you have looked into the eyes of a murdered innocent. You have lost a dear friend and you have our condolences."

"Well said, Holmes," I agreed. "If we have helped, Mr. Birling, it has been our privilege. I do hope you will visit Mr. Bellamy's sister, Mrs. Elizabeth Nyland. Here is her card. I know she would find comfort in meeting another who mourns her brother. How much you reveal to her is a matter for your discretion, however, for what it is worth, she seems a trustworthy and compassionate woman who loved her brother dearly."

The Best Laid Plans

 lay shrouded in darkness, alone in my bed, chasing the elusive balm of sleep. The glances and whispers are finished for another day but the weight of the accusation behind them still sits heavily upon me. It is a stone whose crushing mass I cannot escape nor, if I am to be perfectly frank, can I endure it much longer. Each night I feel a little more of myself slip over into the abyss, with each whisper another part of my soul is dashed into the cold, churning waters. Despite my predicament I cannot find within myself the anger with which I might combat their accusations. They are correct but—and here lies the root of the matter— they do not—cannot—understand. There are times when I long for such understanding. Lonely, late night fantasies in which such an unburdening of my soul produces a new acceptance—even a degree of admiration—from my comrades. Watson always appears in these waking dreams, listening to my words with the same intent manner with which he always listened to *him*. In the end there is shock mingled with determination; I've never met a man able to express determination as well as the doctor. Something in

the set of his jaw, the folds of his eyes, I don't know. At the sleepless dream's end I feel Watson clap my shoulder and I know he understands – and yes, even forgives – me. Laying there, wrapped in dirty linens and shadows, I weep with relief but in the dream I simply stand there, stoic, accepting his redemption as my due.

When the light of a new day creeps in my window, as I stare down the gauntlet of another stage in my ordeal, I feel that redemption disappear. Burned away like the morning fog. Watson has no redemption for me. It has been nearly three years since last I saw the man, not since the death of his friend Sherlock Holmes.

Not since the death which forms the crushing stone, the fall of the great detective which all and sundry believe to be the result of my negligence. My mistake.

I hear the bird then and know it to be the dreadful raven of that night. She is near.

Revulsion overcomes me, knowing the bird is looking with those cursed eyes through my window. Her harbinger. It is late and whatever tasks she busies herself with are complete. I do not wish to know. Embarrassing for a Scotland Yard Detective Inspector to admit, but I know I lack the courage to face such truths, just as I lack the ability to turn her out when she makes her way into my bed. Cold comfort is comfort still and I no longer lack the fortitude to deny myself even that which I know to destroy my soul. Still, my story belongs as much to her as to any of the others. The night we met, the night of my annihilation, the night which has endured three years worth of sunrises and nightfalls, is something the two of us share together. I wait, dreading her arrival but eager as well. Anxious for her cold touch and the slither of her tongue.

All professions have their legends, incredible tales which can only be appreciated by those who practice within their unique trade. Scotland Yard is the same, indeed the Yard thrives on such mythology. No one who has passed through the arch leading to headquarters has forgotten that night. Holmes had sent us a package, a tidy little bundle wrapped in a blue envelope, held together with a black ribbon. Within were instructions, sheets and sheets of them written in his precise hand, each page carefully arranged and meticulously dated. Every officer of the Yard, including several who had been called out of retirement for this night, knew what the distinctive envelope contained. Even now I cannot help but marvel at the genius of the man, the audacity of the plan he presented to us. The best work of the best detective ever, carefully laid out in such a way as to ensure complete success. The day we had all waited for had at last arrived. Old scores and grudges nursed over years were at last to be reconciled. It was the day we were to take down the spider, the last day of freedom for the Napoleon of crime, the day and night in which – provided we obeyed our instructions – Professor Moriarty and those who followed his banner were to be brought to justice.

Precisely at two o'clock in the afternoon we began. I was part of the first arrests, the opening moves in a gambit designed to draw the old spider out from the safety of his hiding holes. Holmes listed the officers to be engaged, the detectives whose careers had inspired special attention from the master criminal himself. There was pride in such a selection. Patterson was in charge of the entire endeavor, Holmes was aware of the Yard's politics; he studied it just as he had educated himself in so many other fields, but those of us who had earned the unflattering notice of the Professor were not forgotten. Gregson, Jones, Bradstreet and myself, all figured prominently in Holmes' great plan.

The first arrests went well, exactly as planned. As the day faded more arrests were made, more prisoners streaming into our gaols, efficiently followed by the paperwork tracking each one. There would be no mistakes. We were well into our harvest by sundown and by midnight our efforts were taking on the aspect of legend. Not a one of us felt anything but satisfaction, pride and confidence. Following Holmes we were unstoppable.

Midnight found me in one of the underground lairs the Professor seemed to favor for his darkest deeds. I had read Holmes' instructions for this raid and puzzled over the number in the lower left corner. A small, seemingly random notation reading fifty-six percent. Written in another's hand it would have been meaningless, a bit of ink-stained flotsam which had crept onto the immaculate, crisp surface of the paper. It being Holmes' hand indicated it was deliberate, a puzzle which I might, or might not, unravel at the scene. With this small riddle in my mind I lead a squad of men under the earth and discovered a palace. A sewer which seemed more a rich man's private railway car than a cave, the gas lamps casting a warm glow over the polished brass and wood of the chamber.

And there he stood, the spider himself. Three other well dressed gentlemen clustered about him, planets orbiting a dark star. All turned when the door opened and I announced our arrival. For just an instant I was granted the distinct pleasure of seeing the Professor's features twist in a grimace of honest surprise. Perhaps the only honest emotion to ever flicker across those brooding features.

Holmes was many things, but he was not one given to poetry. Yet when he described Moriarty to me his description was unusual for the master detective. Normally Holmes' descriptions were straight to the point, five foot four, slightly overweight, auburn hair, fair skin, walks with a limp, scar on the palm of the right hand, wears his moustache in this style, parts his hair on the left, right or middle, purchases his shoes from this or that shop. Yet practicality failed Holmes when he spoke of the Professor.

"You will know him, Lestrade," Holmes assured me. "When you see him, you will know him. The evil mind contained within that balding head shines a malicious light through his sunken eyes. He is tall, thin, a man who appears incapable of enjoying the vices he provides to others. You will know him and you will instantaneously dislike him. Were you unprepared you would doubt your reaction; it would seem too visceral to be trusted and your mind would seek some escape from feelings so strong. But you are ready and surely you know enough of the Professor to know he is worthy of your loathing."

As he so often was, Holmes was correct. I saw that thin, joyless man twitch in surprise and felt instant satisfaction. It lasted only a heartbeat before the Professor's surprise shifted into an ugly sneer. He reached out and pulled a lever, obviously expecting something to happen. We had been warned by Holmes' pen and the escape Moriarty sought was blocked.

One of the Professor's guests tried for a door at the far end of the room but found it locked as well. The Professor's scowl deepened frightfully. He reached under his frock coat and I pushed my squad back as the spider's revolver emerged. A shot came my way, deafening in the enclosed room. Pungent smoke clouded the atmosphere but I could still see the Professor, watch as he turned the weapon on the first of his three companions. I don't believe the Professor's guest saw the pistol swing towards him. He remained unaware of the threat even as the bullet entered his skull. Behind me one of the squad gasped in surprise. I moved forward but was forced to duck as the revolver swung again in my direction. I felt that bullet as it passed my ear and witnessed the next shot impact the wall behind me.

Looking up I saw the Professor turn the weapon towards another of his guests, but this man, having seen the fate of the Professor's other guest, jumped away as the Professor fired at him. It was only a partial escape. Twisting out of the bullet's trajectory caused his foot to slip on a section of floor made slick by the lifeblood escaping the Professor's first victim. He fell.

The Professor had loosed five shots. Only one shot remained. Seeing the Professor lunge at his fallen guest I expected to hear the fatal shot sound. Instead I heard a gasping sound and the splash of blood as it landed on the floor. The Professor stood, knife in one hand, pistol in the other. Madness shone in his evil eyes as he flung the knife in my direction. I managed to dodge the weapon even as the Professor raised his pistol, turned the barrel to his own chest and pulled the trigger.

The old spider fell backwards. Blood splattered and dripped from the wall behind where he had stood, giving evidence of his final shot's accuracy. He was dead. Dead by his own hand. Seeing the grave was his only escape he had hesitated only long enough to murder two of his three companions. The third companion was motionless, his fine clothes stained with a volume of blood which only moments before would have been unimaginable.

We took him easily, the man was too shocked to resist. I searched the room, taking what evidence seemed important, remembering Holmes' instructions to secure a label to each item I took. What secrets had the Professor's companions been killed to preserve? I couldn't begin to guess, that was work for tomorrow. Tonight it was enough to bear the body of our vanquished foe back into the moonlight. Had I a pike I would gladly have impaled the Professor's head upon it and sing songs of triumph all the way back to headquarters. At this point the meaning of Holmes' strange notation, the fifty-six percent he had scribbled in the margin, became clear. By Holmes' reckoning there had been—at the time he had calculated the odds—a fifty-six percent chance the Professor would be waiting in this hole at the time the raid was scheduled.

And the great detective had placed the honor of those favorable odds with me. I was flattered. Given all that happened that night I can only look back on the hours following the Professor's death with wonder. Was that me, walking through the night with such confidence? Me, seeing the respect in all those who turned my way? Surely it was someone else who took that body to the morgue and waited while the police surgeon pronounced what we all knew. Never had I felt so powerful, so accomplished, so confident. Yet that confidence was to shatter so quickly and all I had achieved that night would be stolen from me. In ways I could not even imagine, in a manner I still cannot understand, everything I felt then would curdle, sour and sicken.

I swear this though: Moriarty was dead. In this there was no trickery. I breathed the commingled scents of gunpowder and spilt blood, I saw the wound in his chest that had ruined his fine coat, I carried his still body. The 'Napoleon of Crime' was no more.

After the Spider's fall there still remained more work to be done. The final stage of Holmes' great plan for the night. Small, petty criminals to be rounded up, convictions for literally thousands of felonies would be based on the evidence we collected before sunrise. Never one to let an opportunity go unexploited Holmes had plans for raids into dozens of establishments, rounding up hundreds more before the night was through.

As the clock struck three I found myself again descending into the nether world of London, a squad at my back and villains before me. Again I was guided beneath the earth by Holmes' pen, though by this time his instructions were less certain. Perhaps an opium den, perhaps a brothel, perhaps nothing more than a meeting place for the Professor's favorites, we had no idea what lay hidden down there but we were determined to find out.

The size of the chamber was curious; I remember looking forward to discussing the matter with Holmes when he returned. Had the Professor commanded the chambers excavated or were they the remnants of some forgotten civil project? Flickering gaslight flames cast a warm, almost friendly light on the brickwork, tables ... and the cages below. For a moment – just a moment – all seemed, well, normal isn't the correct word, nor does natural fit. Let me just say that all appeared to belong to the same world I had known outside the chamber, the world where a man was a man and the laws of nature were immutable. I was so very wrong...

The bird was the first thing I noticed. It sat unhappily in its cage. Its dark feathers gave it a distinguished mien but there was something odd about the shape of its head. The skull was too large for a raven's body, too round and then there were its eyes... My stomach seemed to fall as I noticed the eyes; a cold sweat dampened my clothing and suddenly my mouth felt dry. The raven looked at me with the hazel eyes of child – a human child. Understanding gleamed in those depths, a sad intelligence I found profoundly unsettling in such a humble creature.

Jenkins, a reliable old sergeant, stood at my side. The rest of the squad waited in the passage behind us. I waved to Jenkins, who in turn signaled the others to wait where they were. Stepping up to the cage I opened a hatch there and reached in to pull out the bird for closer examination. Pecking at my hand, digging its beak painfully into the soft flesh between my thumb and forefinger, the creature escaped my grasp with a flutter and was gone. Disappearing into the shadows above, camouflaged by its sable feathers, I thought – hoped – I would never see such a creature again. I cannot stress enough how disturbed I was by those child's eyes and the tortured intelligence I saw within them.

Yet the raven's cage was only the first of many. Beside it stood the bars of a cell, a woman locked within. She was turned away from me, as if hiding some shame from my sight. Her hair was red, her form generously female beneath an unremarkable dress. I called to her, but she did not answer, did not turn. Looking about I saw a key hanging from a hook set in the brick wall, out of the woman's reach. It seemed the sort of action Moriarty would take, allowing his prisoner to see the key to freedom but placing it just out of reach. I took the key and, voicing assurances to the captive, I unlocked her cage.

Even as I pulled open the cage door I knew I had made an error. This place was no simple brothel, no illicit meeting hall, but something profoundly more disturbing. Opening the cage door required unusual force and I heard something shift behind the walls. One of the Professor's traps had been sprung. Jenkins, who was looking over a railing into the main chamber below, called out softly:

"Oh my Lord."

I followed his gaze. Below us were cells like the one I had unlocked, cages containing what seemed to be people and beasts. Yet the line where the animal nature began and that of man ended was horribly blurred and indistinct. There were traces of chemicals in the air, strange scents such as I had never smelled before, and I confess I wanted desperately to deny the scene before me. It was as if the flesh of men were clay to be shaped into whatever form the master of the hellish place sought. Men blended with animals, men combined with machines, I saw what seemed to be a short, fat man of extremely pale complexion with what appeared to be a strong box imbedded in his chest. A young girl covered in a fox's red fur, her small pointed teeth snapping at us from between the bars of her cell, a naked man whose head had been replaced by leathery wings, a walrus pulling itself along with two muscular arms. Even as I watched I saw the water begin to flow, a great tide which would drown them all. Even if we could get down there, even if we had keys to open the cages, would we have had the nerve to release those tortured souls? Insanity waited down there, as clear as their warped forms, their misery and madness were even more apparent. As their flesh had been broken so too had their minds been shattered, and in all honesty, who could blame them? One quick glance was all it took to see that they had suffered beyond what even the stoutest of our race could hope to endure. The rushing water would cleanse this place even as it extinguished the burning gaslights.

There was not much time.

I stood in the entrance to the cell, blocking the escape of the woman within. I turned, dazed by what I had seen, and noted for the first time her true nature. Her skin was pale green, lightly scaled like that of a reptile. Her yellow eyes were inhuman but there was a cold gleam of awareness from within them. Slits dilated where a nose should have been. Her lipless mouth was open and the sharp points of her teeth glistened whitely as a forked tongue tasted the air. Her sensuous form writhed curiously as I stared at the tumble of red hair which swept back from her brow. Watching her I wondered if she had once been a woman who had the aspect of the reptile forced upon her or if it had been the other way around. I knew not, nor did it really matter.

She had been placed at the entrance as a trap and I had fallen for it completely. Upon entering such a place what man could resist freeing what seemed a helpless woman? My gallantry had let loose the waters which extinguished the lights in the place. Jenkins stood by the railing, his eyes focused on horrors too numerous to recount. I stood before the reptile woman, knowing her fangs could well be my end. We stood thus for a heartbeat, maybe two or three. As the moment lengthened and it became clear the woman was not going to strike at me, I called to Jenkins.

"We need to get out of this place, now, before we are all drowned."

His eyes wide and haunted, Jenkins looked at me as if not understanding. I repeated my instructions and he blinked, glanced at the rising water below, then turned and fled, screaming his fear into the tunnel before him.

"Out! Out!" I called to the squad, their ashen faces turned to follow their fleeing sergeant. The retreat was not an orderly one, they practically fell over one another in their rush to return to the surface. I stepped forward to follow and then hesitated.

Turning back, I extended a hand towards the creature in the cage. Her gaze fell on my hand and then flicked to my face.

"Come on," I urged. "It's not safe here."

In retrospect it was a foolish thing to say. That chamber had never been safe. Still, the woman stepped forward, refusing my hand, but following. More lights went out with a hiss; the chill of the rushing water filled the chamber as we departed together. I moved through the dark passage, followed by the sound of rushing water and her footsteps. At some point she left me. Once I became cognizant of her absence I hesitated, calling into the darkness for her, but heard nothing except the echo of my own voice. I had climbed out of danger, but I was anxious for the open air and the sight of stars above me. I left.

The squad waited for me on the street, their hands helping to pull me up and out of the hole. Sergeant Jenkins was gone, though one of the squad assured me, he had made his way up to street level. Good lads, all of them. They asked me what I had seen down there, what had affected the solid Jenkins so profoundly. I looked down into the darkness of the hole, straining for a glimpse of her, but gave them no answer.

I ordered them back to headquarters. The night was almost through but they would need to check-in so that they could be properly paid. Looking up at the stars I thought I saw a flutter of dark feathers and shuddered. They asked me where I was going. I explained that I would look for Jenkins. They were satisfied by my lie and left me to my own devices.

Knowing Jenkins was long gone I hurried on to the morgue. An anger had taken root, enflaming my mind with a rage such as I had never felt before. Holmes had no idea what had awaited us in that subterranean chamber, but he had known enough. Whatever those horrors had been they belonged to the Professor. Even knowing the old Spider was dead did nothing to soothe the rage burning within me. I went to the morgue.

His body lay naked on a metal gurney. The police surgeon's examination was complete. Laid out naked there was little doubt as to what had killed the old villain. Powder burns on his hands offered further clarification. I stepped up to the table, fists clenched, my thoughts enduring spasms within the prison of my skull. At some point in that long night I had taken a knife from one of those I had arrested, an unremarkable length of sharpened metal. I felt it in my jacket pocket and I reached for it. With quickness, and a savagery I had not known I was capable of, I plunged the blade into the dead man's neck.

Pulling out the blade, I struck again in nearly the same spot.

Moriarty's eyes sprang open and looked at me dully. I fell back, leaving the length of the blade still embedded in the Spider's throat. No one in my work can afford to be unfamiliar with the ways of the dead. Eyelids might pull open but the eyes within did not move in death. The Professor's chill flesh was devoid of life yet some other power infused it. Alone in the morgue I watched as the Professor sat up, swung his legs over the gurney's edge and stood. His head twitched and oscillated briefly from side to side. I swear the knife was still fatally embedded in his throat yet it did not seem to trouble him. Without a sound, the dead man walked past me and out of the room.

I am not ashamed to say I huddled in the darkness for an instant, unmanned by my fear. Crouching there I felt the edge of my sanity and the beginning of the abyss which lay beyond. Dark as that drowned chamber, chill as the river in December, mad as Jenkins screaming in the night, such a future waited for me unless I remained still in the shadows. My mind wanted no part of any further happenings this night.

Yet, regaining some purpose, I stood and trailed after the dead Professor. Outside I saw the door of a dark carriage close. With a flick of the reins the horse moved off. Unless the Professor, naked and breathless, had called for a cab it seemed there were those willing to submit to his will even after his death. I searched the ground but there was no sign of the knife I had used.

Above me I heard the flutter of feathers and shuddered deeply, but I saw nothing in the darkness. The carriage was gone too quickly to follow, even had I been able to summon a cab at this ungodly hour.

Baffled and wearier than I had ever been, I stumbled home and fell into my bed. Sleep eluded me but the inactivity was a balm to my bruised thoughts. Sometime the next day—or was it the day following?—I dressed and returned to Headquarters.

People spoke to me but nothing they said could penetrate the bubble surrounding me. While I've no doubt I responded correctly, my mind had not yet fully returned. The first news I remember hearing was that Jenkins' body had been found. He had run and run until, finding himself at a set of railway tracks, he had decided to charge an oncoming locomotive. It had ended his life quickly, although not pleasantly. Within the privacy of my thoughts I saluted the old soldier, well aware his sanity had died before the train had found him.

Slowly my awareness started to return and I realized those around me were puzzled by the disappearance of Moriarty's corpse. Theories were bantered back and forth over the purpose his confederates might have for so grisly a trophy. Shaking my head I listened, but did not speak. My thoughts were not fit for sharing. I remember wanting to send a telegram to Holmes but no one knew where he was. The great detective had vanished, taking with him the only man who might have had an inkling as to his whereabouts. I was helpless, but not conscious of the danger. Moriarty was dead. I believed this limited the damage he might inflict. How wrong I was.

Watson's telegram arrived, delivering unwelcome news like cannon fire. None could believe the words or doubt the speaker. Holmes dead. Killed by the Professor. All our good work undone. Watson was returning to London. He demanded answers but we had none to give. In the absence of understanding there grew rumors, speculation and gossip.

Their conclusions are solid, their reasoning sound. Obviously if the Professor followed Holmes to the continent then the Professor had not been killed here in London. Someone must have made an error, somehow the old spider cheated death by pulling the wool over someone's eyes.

My eyes.
    My error.
        My guilt.

Oh yes, and my madness. Should I speak to them? Explain it all? Make them understand that death is not the end we think it? That the flesh of men can be corrupted? Shall I speak of the raven I hear following me or of the sights which drove Jenkins to his suicide? In my mind's eye I can see Moriarty walking up that faraway path, slight and grey as the grave, his wounds concealed beneath an expensive shirt and high collar. I can see his dull eyes fixing on Holmes and I wonder if Holmes – ever the genius, ever the detective – understood what it was he faced on that precipice. I like to think he did. That the signs of Moriarty's death would be immediately visible to Holmes, the master of noting such minutiae as is held in trouser cuffs and ashes. It offers me comfort to believe that no matter what the others think that Holmes himself, in his final moments, knew me to be blameless in his death.

The night following the telegram's arrival at Scotland Yard I heard the bird at my window. I was not myself, having surrendered to the grief, shame and terror of my situation. Even so I heard its arrival, felt the power of its gaze. Later she came to me. Silently settling her form beside mine, allowing herself to feel the heat of my body. I knew what she wanted but I demurred and she, for her part, allowed me my resistance.

Then Watson returned to London. We spoke and we parted. That night I found I had no resistance to offer. Not then, not now.

I feel her presence in the room and I wish for ... I know not what. If there is a way out of this prison I cannot see it. What wouldn't I give to have things the way they were before I'd ever heard the Professor's name? What wouldn't I give to enjoy the friendship of such men as Watson and Holmes once more? Yet, if I am to be saved, better men than I will need to accomplish it.

She is here again. I feel her slide beneath the blanket once more. I shiver as she presses herself against me. My prayers spin unheeded into the cold night sky and all the while the bird watches me with those cursed eyes.

Mr. Other's Children

n evening chill seeped in the open window of my friend Sherlock Holmes' lodgings. Tendrils of brisk December air, smeared with a jaundiced pea-souper, reached delicate, probing tendrils into the still atmosphere of the room. Sitting by the fire I studied the miasma with a fatigued fascination that was equal parts horror and apathy. The recent passing of my wife, which I shall not detail here, had sapped my spirit and drained my vitality. I watched the reaching, yellowed fog much as a shipwrecked sailor watches the ocean lapping against the desolate stones which chance marooned him on. A fate I dared not guess at awaited me out there. The respite I'd found among the familiar confines of 221B Baker Street could not last forever. Like the shipwrecked sailor my destiny waited out there. An inescapable fact I knew but lacked the courage to face. I knew that fog, knew better than most the terrible things hiding in its murk. Knew the greasy caress of it against my face, the wet cough of those it sickened, the cool, damp smell of coal which filled your nostrils and lingered on your coat. As I watched I fancied it was reaching for me, thwarted only by the fire's expiring heat. Among the gathering shadows I waited, almost in a trance, dreading the fog's cold touch but anxious for an end to the terrible waiting.

By his chemistry bench Holmes' lanky form unfolded itself from the bubbling experiment occupying his attention. Carefully setting his equipment aside, he reached for his hat and coat. Holmes turned to me. "It seems my presence is required. I do not know how long I shall be but you are—of course—welcome to stay."

"Where are you …," but I heard it then, the sound carrying from the open window, an approaching horse and carriage, being driven too quickly. "There is a chance they are not coming for you," I remarked petulantly.

A faint smile tugged the corners of Holmes' lips. "A chance," he admitted. "Though you will admit the odds favour my involvement."

Listening closely, I said "It doesn't sound like a police carriage."

"Well done Watson," Holmes remarked. "A hansom I should think. Had it been Scotland Yard I would not have retrieved my coat. As you know, the police are quite adept at bringing relevant evidence to my attention. No, the approaching hansom carries a client requiring my skills some distance from Baker Street. Best to meet them outside. It will save time."

"I'll come with you." My words surprised both Holmes and myself. Still, I dreaded the thought of spending the evening watching the fog creep ever closer. I stood, walked to the window and shut it firmly.

"Very good Watson," Holmes said as I retrieved my coat. We reached the bottom of the stairs as the hansom came to a somewhat dramatic stop before us. Within the cab was a handsome woman of middle years. Her face was streaked with tears and her wide, frightened eyes betrayed a frantic desperation. She began to fumble with the cab door. Holmes stepped across and calmly opened it for her.

Breathlessly, the woman asked, "Are you—".

"I am Sherlock Holmes, and this is my associate, Doctor Watson. I believe you were looking for us?"

"Oh yes Mr. Holmes," the woman said, bringing a linen to her eyes. "It's my husband, I believe you know him. Inspector Bradstreet?"

"Indeed," Holmes remarked. "I know your husband well, as does Doctor Watson."

It was true. I did recall the detective. Tall and stout, Inspector Bradstreet cut an imposing figure to those on the wrong side of the law. I considered Bradstreet among the best Scotland Yard could offer. Always grateful for the consulting detective's assistance, the Inspector watched Holmes' demonstrations of deduction with the same amused fascination as a child watching a stage magician."Mr. Holmes." Mrs. Bradstreet spoke in an urgent whisper, her hand trembling violently. "I fear my husband means to end his life unless you can find him!"

Holmes climbed into the cab. I followed, seating myself next to the distraught woman. Mrs. Bradstreet directed the cabbie to take her home with all possible haste.

Holmes frowned. "I must tell you frankly, your husband does not seem the sort to harm himself."

"He told me he meant to," Mrs. Bradstreet said, panic in her voice. "All through dinner he was unusually quiet but afterwards he told me quite plainly he was going to end his life. He said he was sorry but he needed to explain this to me because his body would never be found. He didn't want me to cling to false hope. He said he'd always loved me and hoped I would remarry, attach myself to a better man. I told him he was frightening me but he just walked out the door. I ran after him but he'd already disappeared. I didn't know what to do, where to look for him, but my husband spoke of you often. He told me you were the best detective in London and I knew you were my only hope. Please Mr. Holmes, you must find him!"

Holmes nodded. I could see the problem had already engaged the engine of his intellect. "What of Scotland Yard? Have you sought their assistance?"

"No, Mr. Holmes," Mrs. Bradstreet answered. "I dare not. If my husband does return he would never forgive me for speaking to his colleagues of such weakness."

"I see," Holmes said. "Why do you suppose your husband presumed his body would never be found?"

"My husband is a proud man," Mrs. Bradstreet explained. "If he really means to do this, he will not wish Scotland Yard to know of it. Ever. He's worked so hard to achieve his position, he's so proud to serve as a detective. To lose face before his fellows would be, for him, worse than death."

"Do you know what caused your husband to speak of suicide?" Holmes inquired. "Was he behaving strangely recently? Had something upset him?"

"No, nothing of the kind," Mrs. Bradstreet insisted. "He was fine this morning. When he arrived home this evening he was quiet. There was, I could tell, something occupying his thoughts but he was often so. You'll think me foolish for saying this but before today there has been nothing in his manner to suggest he was in any way troubled. Had he not spoken to me as he did I would not have suspected anything. He might have walked out the door and I would never have known what happened to him."

"We shall certainly do all we can," I assured the weeping woman.

"Did your husband take anything with him?" Holmes asked.

"What do you mean?" Mrs. Bradstreet seemed confused by the question.

"A weapon? Chemicals? Anything at all."

"No, nothing like that," Mrs. Bradstreet remembered.

"He put on his coat and gloves. I remember because he doesn't usually wear gloves but I don't see what this has to do with—"

Our hansom pulled up before a modest home and Holmes lead us out of the cab. Mrs. Bradstreet hurriedly thrust a handful of uncounted coins towards the driver. Holmes guided her away, helping her up the steps and inside. The cabbie, obviously embarrassed to have his gallantry so richly rewarded, caught my eye. As I walked to his side the cabbie counted out his fee and returned the balance to me. Taking the money I followed Holmes and Mrs. Bradstreet into the house, placing the returned money on a table near the door.

"You went outside and looked for him," said Holmes, returning to the doorway. "Show me exactly how."

Mrs. Bradstreet did as she was told, looking first eastwards and then to the west.

Holmes nodded. "I must ask you to wait here. Your husband might have a change of heart and return. If he does, he must find you. Do you understand?"

Mrs. Bradstreet nodded. To my ears Holmes' instructions sounded somewhat convenient but if Mrs. Bradstreet sensed this she gave no sign. Holmes returned to the street, pulling the door closed behind him.

"An interesting problem, is it not Watson?" Holmes asked, his eyes burning with intensity. "We know Bradstreet to be an intelligent, capable man, well aware of the procedures the police would use to track him. Time is on Bradstreet's side but we must play the hand we are dealt."

"How could Bradstreet have disappeared so quickly?" I asked.

"There," Holmes pointed, "Behind the drain pipe."

It was a small recess but, looking closer, I recognised that it was adequate to hide a man of Bradstreet's build.

"What do you suggest Watson?" Holmes asked.

I started walking. "Having hidden himself so quickly he obviously knew she would be looking for him. He wouldn't risk stepping in front of their home again."

"Correct," Holmes said. "What else can we deduce?"

"Nothing," I confessed.

"The gloves Watson, the gloves! You must have noted Mrs. Bradstreet saying her husband wore his gloves. Did that not strike you as odd?"

"It is December," I reminded Holmes.

"Yet the weather is not harsh. Neither you nor I bothered with gloves. It is unusual and therefore informative."

"You know what it means?" I asked.

"Obviously that he is planning something which will require the use of his hands," Holmes said. "More importantly, the gloves indicate he departed with a scheme already in mind. If we accept Mrs. Bradstreet's claim that her husband was untroubled this morning it follows he conceived this plan sometime today, likely as he walked home from work. You notice the direction we are taking?"

"I do," I said, admiring Holmes' skill, "Towards B Division headquarters, Bradstreet's path to work."

"Remember Mrs. Bradstreet's assertion that her husband would not wish his body found. Obviously he cannot simply jump into the river or leap from a great height. To accomplish his goal he must discover a location where a body might remain undiscovered."

I nodded, considering Holmes' words. "Might he attempt a method of suicide that would render his corpse—," I paused, searching for the correct word "—anonymous?"

"A worthy but misguided thought," Holmes said. "You saw the empty table by the door. Had Bradstreet wished his corpse to remain unidentified he would have discarded his wedding ring, pocket watch, any items of a personal nature. Since he did not we can deduce his intention: he means for his corpse never to be found. Knowing this we must retrace his path as quickly as we dare, trusting we will notice whatever circumstance lead the Inspector to believe he could conceal his remains."

With nothing more than Holmes' vague theory and his unassailable confidence we walked briskly through the fog-shrouded streets. I must confess I was less certain than Holmes. With a man's life at stake I felt a tremor of doubt with each step. What if I missed a vital clue? Even so I could not deny that in a curious way the activity roused me, stirred me from the fearsome melancholy which had gripped me so completely. Friendships, it seemed, followed patterns and inevitably my association with Holmes drew me into the shadowed realms of betrayal and death. A landscape bearing the scars of greed and deception and littered with the remains of the murdered. Accompanied by Holmes' sharp reason such morbid trappings became familiar, almost welcome.

My eyes passed easily over the site, the wooden barriers and the excavated earth standing vigil over the deep hole. I almost walked by, had it not been for Holmes' advice regarding Bradstreet's expectation of using his gloved hands I would not have recognized the potential for burial. I gestured for Holmes attention and together we walked past the barricades and looked down into the pit.

Bradstreet worked silently in the darkness. His gloved hands gripped a shovel left by one of the workmen, shifting the cold earth with determined efficiency. The Inspector had dug himself a neat little grave under the building's foundation. A mound of dirt was balanced precariously behind timbers placed there for the purpose. Twine ran from the timbers down into the hidden excavation, cleverly placed so that a single determined pull might release the piled earth and fill in the grave. I was struck by both the arrangement's ingenuity and the horridness of the death it promised. To dig your own grave, lie in it and pull a string to entomb yourself—I shuddered. Had I claimed the landscape of human misery familiar? It seemed there were always new horrors waiting to be discovered.

"I must congratulate you on your inventiveness," Holmes spoke down into the darkness. "Had your wife not come to me with such haste I doubt we would have been able to find you in time."

In the darkness of the hole I sensed Bradstreet pause at his work and, for an instant, consider his options. It felt to me as if Bradstreet might still leap into the grave and carry out his plan but—once the instant passed—I saw his shoulders slump in defeat.

"I'll not go back," said Bradstreet, his voice heavier than I'd ever heard it. "I'll not endanger her."

"There is much to discuss," Holmes replied, "Too much for this conversation to be shouted up and down this pit. Let us take you to Baker Street where we might speak plainly. Agreed?"

Bradstreet looked to Holmes, then to me. "Agreed," he answered, placing his gloved hand in my mine and allowing me to pull him from the grave. Bradstreet's clothing was, as might be expected, filthy but he brushed himself off as best he could.

"We must at least pass by your home Bradstreet," I argued. "Your wife is in a dreadful state. I doubt she'll be able to rest until she has seen you alive with her own eyes."

Bradstreet looked ready to object but, dropping his gaze, he agreed. Holmes hailed a cab, and in short order we were stopped outside the Bradstreet residence. Mrs. Bradstreet looked gratefully into the cab at her husband. The Inspector refused to acknowledge her, refused even to look her way. Mrs. Bradstreet was in a dire state but, after offering what assurances we could, we took her husband to Baker Street.

§

"Now Bradstreet," Holmes said as we settled into our customary places. "What is all this about? What has brought you to such a state?"

Bradstreet, his expression haggard, looked at Holmes and opened his mouth as if to speak. The words seemed to catch in his throat and all that emerged was a strangled sob. Dropping his face into his hands the Scotland Yard detective wept openly.

We tried to console him, well—in honesty I attempted to console him as Holmes waited and watched. After a time Bradstreet managed to contain his distress and somewhat compose himself.

"Now Bradstreet," Holmes attempted again. "Really, you know you cannot keep secrets from me. Would it not be better to simply tell me what has happened?"

"I—I can't Mr. Holmes," Bradstreet said.

"Can't?" Holmes asked.

Bradstreet shook his head. "I know what I must do but —"

"Now then," I spoke sternly. "We'll have no more of such talk. You cannot still be contemplating anything as ghastly as suicide. Holmes and I found you and we intend to help you out of your predicament."

Bradstreet looked up doubtfully.

Holmes spoke up. "You question my abilities? Still? After all the crimes we have solved together?"

"It's not you I doubt," Bradstreet said. "My situation, my predicament as you called it, is a prison with but one escape."

"No doubt it appears so to you," Holmes conceded. "Prison walls always seem thickest to those within their embrace. Watson and I are free. From the outside we might spot some flaw, some weak point, to enable your escape."

Bradstreet looked into the red glow of the fireplace. "If only that were true—"

"Then it is settled." Holmes waved his hand as if the entire matter were ended.

"No, Mr. Holmes." Bradstreet shook his head sadly.

"Come now," Holmes urged. "What have you to lose?"

"The last thing I still retain," Bradstreet said, "Courage."

"Nonsense," Holmes scoffed. "In the time I have known you, you've made many foolish errors. At times you've been lazy, on other occasions reluctant to pursue matters to their logical if unpleasant conclusions, but you've never been a coward."

Bradstreet shook his head. "You're being kind."

"Am I?" Holmes asked, leaning back in his chair and studying Bradstreet carefully.

Bradstreet looked up and met Holmes' gaze. Weary as the Scotland Yard man was, a smile tugged at his lips. "Well, you're not a fellow given to acts of charity, Mr. Holmes, I'll give you that."

"Quite so," Holmes agreed. "I see things as they are. Now, if you are determined not to speak to us of your troubles—"

Bradstreet shook his head glumly.

"Then your stubbornness leaves us no alternative but this: You will remain here for the next five days, during which time we must have your promise that you will not attempt to injure yourself. Should Mrs. Hudson discover your corpse in these lodgings she may well make good on her threats to evict me and we cannot have that. In exchange for your promise, I offer a promise of my own. If after five days I have not found a path to your deliverance then you shall have my silence. I shall not share the particulars of my investigation, or of your self-murder, to anyone. Is this satisfactory?"

Bradstreet considered the proposal for a moment, but I knew he would agree. He nodded, his weary expression resigned in the red glow cast by the fire.

"Excellent," Holmes said. "After all the cases we've worked together I at last have you as my client. Gentlemen, I suggest we get some rest, the hour is late."

I saw Bradstreet to my old room and laid out some bedclothes for him. His exhaustion was such he swayed on his feet. When I returned to the drawing room to retrieve my jacket and cap I saw Holmes in his dressing gown, seated on the floor by the fire, his pipe already lit.

"Holmes," I said as I shrugged into my coat. "You will—"

"Of course," Holmes said.

Thus assured I left Baker Street for my own empty house. My thoughts were troubled, as they so often had been of late, but exhaustion overtook me. I slept better than I had for many nights.

§

I received word from Holmes early the next evening. A curt note instructing me to meet him on a street corner in a somewhat disreputable part of town. Hesitating, I opened the desk drawer where I keep my old service revolver. Remembering the despair I'd seen in Bradstreet's eyes I loaded the weapon and placed it in my pocket. Thus comforted, I hurried to the address Holmes had provided. As the fading light of the day lengthened the city's shadows I found my friend observing the comings and goings of a hotel across the street. As I approached, Holmes pointed to the windows of the hotel.

"Second floor, third window from the right," Holmes said by way of greeting. "Tell me what you see."

"Drawn curtains," I answered. "How is Bradstreet?"

Frowning, Holmes ignored my question. "You are not observing. Look closer, do you notice anything strange?"

Reluctantly I turned and studied the window again. "I see the curtains are tightly closed. They appear to be pinned shut. Nothing unusual about the curtains, no bloodstains or other signs of mischief. That particular set of curtains are the only ones closed, is that what you want me to notice?"

"No," Holmes answered. "How can you be certain the curtains are not stained? Might they not be stained on the inward facing?"

"No," I answered. "The light behind the curtains is bright enough I would see any stains regardless of— Oh. I see."

Holmes nodded. "An unusual intensity of light, don't you think?"

"What do you think is causing it?" I asked.

"I have no idea," Holmes admitted. "To be honest I cannot be entirely certain that room is our destination, although it is always wise to note the unusual. Often it plays a part in an investigation, directly or indirectly."

"Bradstreet?" I repeated my question.

"Oh, he's well enough. He remains in Baker Street, laid out in bed, no doubt contemplating new methods of self-destruction. After he retired I examined his belongings. I found this hidden in his billfold." Reaching into his pocket Holmes withdrew a key. "I recognize it as one belonging to this establishment. The number indicates it opens a second floor room. Curious, isn't it?"

"Is that why we're here?" I asked.

"Partially," Holmes admitted. "I also went to report to B division that Bradstreet's illness would require an absence of five days or more. I told his comrades such was your opinion."

"You spoke truly," I agreed, "though it would have been courteous to ask me my opinion before presenting it."

Holmes waved off my chastisement, as I knew he would. "Furthermore, I informed the officers of B Division you wished to know Bradstreet's movements for the day in order to pinpoint a cause for his poor health. It is quite remarkable Watson, but the police are as simple to interrogate as anyone else. Their own experience of the art completely disappears as soon as questions are put to them."

"What did you learn?" I asked.

"Mrs. Bradstreet's account of her husband's behaviour matches neatly with those of his fellows. If he was suffering in any way the detectives he works with failed to notice it. By all accounts Bradstreet's behaviour that morning was entirely normal."

"And in the afternoon?" I asked.

"Exactly," Holmes nodded. "In the afternoon Bradstreet went to speak to some of his informants. Although nothing was spoken aloud, his fellow officers seemed of the opinion these 'informants' were unlikely to be the source of Bradstreet's illness. As you might expect none of those present admitted to knowing the identity of Bradstreet's appointment. Interestingly however, they switched from the plural to the singular when referring to Bradstreet's afternoon errand."

"What of it?" I asked.

"Each of them seemed fully aware of the identity of Bradstreet's appointment," Holmes explained. "None of them were concerned this informant was the cause of Bradstreet's absence, certainly they asked no questions regarding such a possibility. One of the officers suggested Bradstreet met with this particular informant weekly. What does that suggest to you?"

I shifted uncomfortably, not meeting Holmes' gaze. An

image of the handsome Mrs. Bradstreet rose in my mind. Stubbornly I replied, "I don't know."

"A woman," Holmes explained. "Such arrangements are not uncommon between members of the Yard and those they police. I admit I'd not suspected Bradstreet as being prone to such unfaithfulness but there it is."

"Still only a theory." The protest sounded weak to my own ears.

"Quite so," waving Bradstreet's key. Holmes gestured to the hotel, "Shall we put the matter to the test?"

§

Reluctantly I followed Holmes across the street. We entered the hotel and, without stopping at the front desk, proceeded directly to the second floor. Walking down the hallway Holmes checked the number on the key and smiled. "Second floor, third window from the right," he informed me, "Just as I suspected."

I nodded as Holmes opened the door. Bright light filled the room, a queer light seeming somehow to be simultaneously both white and green. Custom crystal lenses covered the hotel's gaslights; glowing an almost blinding white. Looking down at my hands, the walls and the wooden floor, I discovered the light reflecting from these surfaces seemed green-tinged. Looking at Holmes I noticed he seemed suddenly ill, his skin grey in the unnatural light. My hands reflected the same unhealthy hue. Blinking in the strange illumination, I looked about the room.

There was little to see. A desk and chair beneath the pinned curtains, a dresser and a bed. Spread atop the bed lay a woman, fully dressed, her head at the bed's foot. She lay face upwards, eyes closed, her left arm stretched over her head while her right lay limp at her side. Such was the quality of illumination that I hurried to the unconscious woman's side believing her to be dead. Reaching the bedside I observed the rise and fall of her chest. Touching her neck I felt a pulse, strong and regular.

The woman did not waken. She did not even stir.

My eyes travelled over the woman's body, observing her as Holmes would. She was not a wealthy woman, the state of her clothing indicated she had been living rough for some time. She was young, her form slender but generous, large eyes in a narrow, appealing, pixie-like face, a wealth of golden hair spread over the bed. Even in the strange light of this place it was obvious why Bradstreet was attracted to the woman. Looking down on her I felt the stir of my own desire. I looked away, shaking my head. Holmes had been correct when he assumed the worst of Bradstreet. Disappointed, I walked to where Holmes was searching the dresser drawers.

"Nothing but a scarf, half a bottle of gin and this," Holmes passed me a worn envelope containing a letter. Pulling the letter's folded paper from its envelope I was confronted with the familiar handwriting of Inspector Bradstreet. The missive stated that any officer arresting this woman should contact him directly.

"Well." I abandoned my defence of the Scotland Yard man's virtue.

"Yes," Holmes replied, accepting his victory modestly. Looking around he moved on to the next item of interest, the girl. "Seems likely the woman has been here for a couple weeks at least."

"How do you deduce that?" I asked.

Holmes nodded to the waste bin in the corner. Several empty bottles of gin filled the container.

"She's been here long enough that the staff no longer concern themselves with her," Holmes reported. Waving to the footprints visible in the dust by the door he added, "No one has entered or exited this room today except for us."

"That's strange," I said.

"Hardly," Holmes said. "Staff in an establishment such as this are quick to learn what corners can be safely cut."

"The bed is made," I pointed out.

"But the linen is not fresh," Holmes observed. "And look here, on her boot. Dried mud, from just outside."

"Not surprising," I remarked.

"But see how dry it is," Holmes pointed out. "It would take several hours for the mud to dry so completely. She has remained motionless all that time."

"How can you be certain of that?" I asked. In answer, Holmes tapped a finger against the woman's boot. The slight touch caused the mud to fall from its perch onto the bed linens.

I nodded, once again impressed by Holmes abilities, but the detective had already moved on. "Her fingers are stained with ink. There's no paper discarded in the waste bin. Check under the mattress, see if you can find anything there."

I looked but found nothing.

"Where there's ink, there's a pen," Holmes remarked. "Where there's a pen, there's paper."

"Perhaps she mailed a letter," I suggested. "Shall I wake her and ask?"

"Not just yet," Holmes said moving towards the desk. "I would prefer to complete my examination of the room without her interference."

Pulling open a desk drawer Holmes looked inside but found nothing. Sliding the drawer completely free of the desk revealed a journal. It had been hidden behind the back of the drawer, held in place by two small tacks and a length of twine. Journal in hand Holmes pulled out the delicate looking desk chair, sat in it and started flipping through the journal pages.

"Holmes, really," I chided him. "You have no respect for privacy."

"One of my many shortcomings," Holmes said. In a louder voice, Holmes addressed the unconscious woman on the bed. "If you have any objection to my reading this journal you'd best speak now."

The woman on the bed did not stir. Holmes continued reading. Pulling some hotel stationary from the desk he began making notes.

"Is it in code?" I asked.

"Not precisely," Holmes said. "Although a combination of deteriorating penmanship and a general lack of experience regarding the written word make it seem so. I shall report my findings when I finish. See if you can do something about this abominable light, will you?"

Setting about my task I removed the crystal coverings from the light fixtures. They were of strange design, lighter than any crystal I had handled before. Inexplicably the light appeared to dim as I removed them, as if the coverings somehow increased the light produced by the lamps. A silly notion, I confess, yet a difficult one to shake. With the crystal lens removed the room's illumination returned to its normal, somewhat dim level. Holmes unfastened one of the pins holding the curtains shut, using the last light of the day to better see the journal pages.

Stacking the crystal lenses beside the door I took the only seat remaining in the room, on the edge of the young woman's bed. In the new light she seemed flushed. With a physician's reflex I laid a hand on her forehead to check her temperature. It was normal. Holmes glanced over to see if I'd woken her but, again, the young woman showed no signs of waking.

"Well," Holmes said, placing the journal back in its hiding place before folding his notes and putting them in his pocket. "A curious if somewhat sordid tale but nothing in it offers an explanation of Bradstreet's behaviour. The last entry is days old and utterly incomprehensible."

"I'm listening," I said.

"According to the journal the young lady, she refers to herself as Sarah, was approached just over three weeks ago by a man who asked her to call him 'Mr. Other'. For her part Sarah saw nothing strange in a man withholding his name from her, indeed it was one of many aspects of this stranger she seems to have found amusing. Apparently Mr. Other approached her on the street one night, wearing a long coat, a wide brimmed hat, dark glasses and a long scarf wound around the lower part of his face. These obvious attempts to disguise his appearance intrigued Sarah. She found him strange, somewhat mysterious; she uses the word 'otherworldly' when describing him. Mr. Other made her a business proposition. In exchange for exclusive use of her he would provide a month's lodgings, food and drink. Needless to say this arrangement delighted Sarah, not only from a fiscal perspective but because it provided her an opportunity to pierce his disguise."

"Do you have any idea who she thought this mysterious stranger might be?" The question troubled me.

"Not really," Holmes admitted. "At first she seems to be under the impression her employer was royal but she abandons that thought after spending some time with him. According to the journal she never saw Mr. Other's face. Her first night here he came to visit but seemed content to examine her in a manner more medical than lustful. He did not remove his coat, hat or scarf. His dark spectacles remained on his face during their encounter and he wore gloves. Apparently satisfied with the results of this examination he presented Sarah with the journal and instructed her to remain in this room until he returned. In her boredom she fills several journal pages with speculation regarding Mr. Other, none of which is particularly well reasoned. After an absence of two days he returned to fulfil the contract of their employment."

"Surely she noticed something that might be a clue to his identity," I remarked.

"Actually no," Holmes said. "Her journal is surprisingly explicit regarding their encounter. Theirs was an unusual joining in many ways, their intimacy was not—how shall I put this?—Conventional. Sarah was not required to undress, Mr. Other did not remove his trousers in order to—I see this discussion is making you uncomfortable. As a physician I would have expected you to be less inhibited regarding such matters."

"You are not a medical man," I pointed out.

"To the rationalist," Holmes replied, "all things are what they are. Neither embarrassment nor social niceties alter the facts of what occurred. At any rate, it seems Sarah, who admits to consuming a generous amount of gin that night, lost consciousness at the conclusion of their business and did not see Mr. Other leave. He returned the next evening with gifts, informing her that she would bear him many fine children. Sarah remained silent on that point, well aware that an intimacy such as they had shared does not result in pregnancy. Following her employer's instructions she remained in her room during the day, becoming increasingly restless. In the journal she contemplates the possibility her employer is disfigured in some horrible way. Her penmanship deteriorates and her thoughts become disjointed. It is apparent she became extremely bored, save for her weekly visit from Inspector Bradstreet."

Frowning, I asked, "Didn't you suggest Bradstreet

visited only yesterday? Does she not write of that encounter?"

"She does not," Holmes said. "But it is possible. In the last journal entries her handwriting degenerates past the point of legibility."

"What of Mr. Other? Did he return?"

"Yes, periodically, although none of his subsequent visits seem to have been intimate."

"Does she write of these strange lenses or the light they produce?"

Holmes shook his head. "No. If we wish more information it seems we must talk to the author. Sarah has been most obligingly disinterested in our investigation so far but if we are to continue we need to wake her. Watson, if you would be so kind?"

I stood, leaning over the unconscious woman. Grasping her shoulder with my hand I shook her gently.

"Sarah?"

There was no response. I repeated my actions, shaking her more firmly.

"Sarah?"

Placing both my hands on her shoulders I shook her again but the woman still did not respond. Beneath my hands the woman was warm but not fevered and, despite my attempts to wake her, soundless and utterly lax. Her eyes did not open, her peaceful expression remained untroubled, my actions did not so much as alter her rate of respiration. Sarah was completely unresponsive.

"Is she ill?" Holmes asked, rising from his seat and coming closer to the bed.

"She seems well enough," I reported. "Her colour is good. She's neither fevered nor chilled. Her pulse is strong and regular."

Fearing the lady was under the influence of some

chemical or narcotic, I leaned over the unconscious woman and pulled open her eyelid. She looked up at me without awareness, without acknowledgment, the lovely blue of her iris startling against the virgin white of her sclera. Her pupil did not contract as I exposed it to light but as I watched—I shudder to think of it even now.

In the black depths of her pupil something moved.

It was small, just the sharp point of a tail belonging to a small worm or insect. It turned, the segmented carapace uncurling its ghastly length as if in greeting. Startled, I staggered backwards, my heart pounding against my ribs. I thudded against the wall but, drenched in a cold sweat, I scarcely noticed. Looking up I found a horror mirroring my own in my Holmes' expression. He'd seen it as well. My hand went instinctively into my jacket pocket, grasping the reassuring weight of the revolver there. I opened my mouth to speak but found myself incapable of forming words.

Shaking his head, blinking, Holmes sought to regain his capacity for language just as I did. Noticing something in the woman's golden hair, Holmes found his voice. "Watson, she seems to be bleeding from her scalp."

Pulling my hand from the revolver I stepped forward, my physician's instincts overcoming my natural revulsion. Stepping around the bed I came timidly to where I could see her scalp, the tumble of lovely golden tresses spoiled by the bright red stain of blood.

"The wound was not there a moment ago," Holmes said, stepping to my side. "I don't—"

Something moved beneath the fall of golden hair, something small and sickly white in colour. It emerged with a rush of blood, somehow delicate in its repulsiveness. Tentatively it pulled itself free of the unconscious woman's skull and eased itself onto the bed. I shuddered violently, feeling terror's horrid electricity tremble my body.

143

Another tendril emerged from beneath the woman's blood-soaked hair. Then another, and another, lifting, probing, and testing the freedom into which they emerged.

It wasn't by overcoming my fear that I found myself in motion, rather it was as if fear itself guided me. Finding myself several steps away from the bed I looked about for a tool appropriate to my revulsion. The pistol was in my hand but I returned it to my jacket pocket. It would not serve me here, the horror before me presented too small a target. Seizing the chair Holmes had sat in, I lifted and struck it against the desk violently enough to shatter it. In my hand the chair had transformed itself into a cudgel. Stepping forward I approached the creatures emerging from the broken skull of the once lovely woman.

With the chair-leg cudgel I knocked the first of the squirming, crawling things to the floor. Once there, I clubbed it with all the force I could muster. Beside me I heard Holmes seize a length of broken chair and repeat my actions. Once I was certain the creature was dead, once I had smashed it beyond all recognition, I turned back to the bed where more of the foul things were emerging. The horror I felt did not allow me to cease my attack upon these terrible worms until each and every one was as crushed as that first. Panting, I looked around the room and heard for the first time the panicked knocking on the door.

It was a horrid site, one rivalling even the Whitechapel case in terms of horror. The woman Sarah lay on the bed, blood flowing from her crown, pooling on the mattress and dripping through to the floor. The remains of several dozen worm creatures were smeared on the floorboards, releasing into the atmosphere a sharp alkaline stench. The broken remnants of the chair littered the room. In the midst of this scene stood Holmes and I, each drenched in sweat, wide-eyed and grey with fear, panting like dogs as we clasped our cudgels.

Holmes, club still in hand, walked to the door and opened it. Outside stood a number of frightened people and I fear Holmes' appearance did nothing to calm them. In a clear, reassuring voice, he spoke. "There has been an accident. Would one of you be so kind as to fetch Scotland Yard? Thank you."

He closed the door as I staggered to the window. With the chemical stink of the crushed worm creatures in my nose I was desperate for a breath of fresh air. London air would have to suffice. I pulled apart the curtains and opened the window. Night had descended, filling the streets with shadows. As I opened the window I saw in the street below a figure in a long, dark coat. The wide-brimmed hat was tilted up towards the window, the lower part of his face covered beneath the windings of a long scarf and his eyes hidden behind dark lenses.

Mr. Other. Seeing me at the window the figure straightened suddenly, raising gloved fists in the air. It looked up at me and I felt the full force of its hate and impotent rage. As I watched it seemed to me the upraised arms straightened to an inhuman length. The body beneath the coat shuddered in a manner no being with a spine could duplicate. Startled and frightened I stepped back from the window.

Looking over my shoulder I saw Holmes examining the once beautiful Sarah. Her crimes were undoubtedly numerous but no one deserved a fate such as she had suffered. Holmes looked up and glanced my way, his expression eloquent enough. The woman was dead. Defiant, I stepped back to the window.

Mr. Other was still there, glaring up at me. Dropping my cudgel I reached back into my jacket pocket and drew out my service revolver. On the street below Mr. Other saw my motion and turned to flee. I fired quickly, my view obscured by the discharge. The figure below continued to run towards the dark of an alley. I fired again and saw the fabric of his coat tear. As the bullet struck, the figure appeared to dissolve, falling from its man shape into the crawling form of a hundred large worms. The creatures hit the pavement below and quickly slithered into a sewer opening. The clothing it – they – had been wearing was carried with the migration.

Blinking in surprise, trembling in rage and shock, I was unaware of Holmes at my elbow until he spoke my name.

"Mr. Other," I explained. "On the street below. I –," The words were tangled in my throat. Holmes stepped forward and looked down at the empty street.

"He escaped?" Holmes' brow furrowed as he spoke.

"No. He— Holmes, it was extraordinary," I said. "He was not a man at all."

On the street below two patrol constables appeared and hurried towards our hotel, lead by a concerned looking man.

"It may be best if we kept the details of Mr. Other to ourselves until we are able to speak privately," Holmes said. "Agreed?"

I nodded, returning the revolver to my jacket pocket. Holmes stepped back to the door, opening it as the anxious constables arrived. Holmes told them everything that had happened in the room, explaining the gunfire by suggesting one of the creatures had tried to escape through the open window. By the time the coroner and the detectives of B Division arrived we had told our story many times. Several hours passed before we were allowed to leave but, due to Holmes' reputation with the officers of B Division, we eventually found ourselves alone in a cab returning to Baker Street.

§

Reluctantly I explained what I had seen, what I thought I had seen. Even though I had witnessed the figure disperse with my own eyes I found myself plagued by doubt. The dark street, the quickness with which events had unfolded and the emotional stress I'd endured of late, I recognised in my account legitimate cause for disbelief.

Once I had finished speaking Holmes turned to the window and looked out in the fog-shrouded darkness of the great city. For a moment he didn't speak but considered my testimony, the passing streetlights casting shadows over the lean planes of his face. I expected him to voice the natural doubt I had heard reflected in my words but Holmes' thoughts seldom trod the same path as mine.

"Have you considered the unusual illumination in the room?" Holmes asked, as if this were the obvious conclusion to my own account. "The strange crystals which fit over the lamps trouble me. It would be easier to assume that shaking the girl woke the creatures within but it is equally plausible to conclude their awakening resulted from the normal light entering the eye. Perhaps the strange light cast by the crystals inhibited this reaction; I can think of no other purpose for the presence of the lenses. Can you?"

"No," I admitted.

"And it is safe to assume Bradstreet reacted as we did," Holmes continued. "Finding the girl, attempting to wake her, pulling open her eye and making the same ghastly discovery we did. Remembering the intimacy they had shared, finding her in so dreadful a condition, the natural assumption would be to assume he was infected as well. Unwilling to confess his infidelity to his wife, and equally unwilling to risk spreading the infection to her, he chose instead to end his life. I am confident that is the cause of his suicide attempt."

I nodded. "Bradstreet isn't the type of man to seek advice about his indiscretions."

Holmes leaned forward, anxious to hear my next words. "And do you have advice for him?"

"I do," I answered. "As a physician I would inform him the chances of him being infected are low. Isolation at the police hospital would serve him better than annihilation. Thanks to the journal Sarah kept we know how long it takes for symptoms to appear. I would say a three week hospital stay should suffice. If Bradstreet shows no symptoms after that period he should be free to resume his life. Nor does the Inspector need to confess his failing to anyone further. I know the truth and will be happy to oversee his case myself."

"Meticulously reasoned." High praise indeed from the detective. "Then our duty to the Inspector and his wife is complete. As for the Other matter—"

"Yes?" I asked, curious to see.

"It requires vigilance – on both our parts," Holmes admitted. "Naturally I will see to it the police destroy the crystals we recovered from the hotel room. You will need to be alert to any medical reports concerning cases such as the unfortunate Sarah's. I will watch for any criminal matters which may cast light on this Mr. Other. At this point I must confess I know of nothing which seems related, however I shall make inquiries."

"Inquiries?" I asked.

"Sewer workers and such," Holmes explained. "I must confess that in many ways this Mr. Other may prove easier to deal with than the villains we've encountered in the past. Although he has attempted to disguise his true nature his motivation seems straight-forward enough."

"Children," I completed the thought.

"Exactly," Holmes said. "Men commit crimes for greed or revenge, motives which they will go to great lengths to disguise even from themselves. Mr. Other, whatever else he might be, practices a simple, honest villainy. Though I will confess to a degree of shock regarding his nature, in many ways such a creature is easier to confront than the many human villains we have battled in the past." In Holmes' words I found an odd comfort. If Mr. Other ventured again into the world of men we would be ready. Looking out the cab's window into the swirl of fog and shadow I felt—surprisingly—better than I had just the evening before. Sitting in Holmes' Baker Street lodgings I had felt my grief keenly and – I must confess – a degree of uncertainty regarding my place in the new and lonely world into which I found myself unexpectedly thrust. Now, with the Bradstreet case closed, I was reminded of where I belonged. No longer would I wait for the leprous fog to enfold me in its oily embrace; such was not my place. Rather I was content to search the foul murk by Holmes' side. In defense of those like Inspector Bradstreet or the forlorn Sarah whose body even now was being transported to a cold table where scalpels waited to search her flesh for answers. Should my courage weaken again I need only recall the upraised fists of the nefarious Mr. Other and my role is recalled to me.

Lord Garnett's Skulls

t the urgent command of the cab's occupant, the horse skidded to a stop in the busy London street. A familiar voice called my name in an impatient tone I had learned to endure. My morning walk interrupted, I turned to see my good friend Sherlock Holmes holding the cab door open and beckoning me to join him. It was, as Holmes correctly anticipated, an invitation my somewhat latent sense of adventure compelled me to accept. My well-intentioned schedule for the day forgotten I leapt aboard the cab and fell into my seat as the driver urged his horse onwards.

"Holmes?"

Recognising the intent of my barely uttered question, Holmes explained the urgency of our trip. "We are bound for Lord Garnett's."

"Young Cambers' case?" I asked, remembering the youthful, thin-faced Detective Sergeant who had visited Baker Street last evening. Cambers had struck me as rather slight for the rough and tumble of police work and every thought, every emotion, experienced by the earnest, young detective seemed to parade across the thin, handsome features of his open face. Perhaps it was simply the contrast to Holmes' aquiline but often stoic face which misinformed my first impression of the Detective Sergeant for it soon emerged that young Cambers had already made quite a name for himself. He'd solved a difficult and gruesome matter in Bedford and, as a result, Scotland Yard offered him an opportunity to practise his trade in London. Having caught the attention of his superiors the young man was anxious to advance his career—however a difficult theft blocked his upward path. Having heard his new colleagues at the Yard speaking of the Baker Street consulting detective, Cambers ventured forth to request Holmes' insight into a rather macabre theft from Lord Garnett's London stately home.

"Apparently there has been a new and disturbing development," Holmes informed me. "How much of Cambers' investigation do you recall?"

"To be honest Holmes, I did not consider the matter important," I admitted. "Certainly the nature of the theft was unusual but, really, it seemed of no great consequence. I understand Cambers' desire to impress his Lordship—he is an ambitious young man—but I'm surprised to see you in such a hurry over so trifling a matter."

Holmes, amused by some private thought, looked out the window. Turning to me he said, "Indulge me."

"Very well." I proceeded to recite the facts of the case. Lord Garnett had recently returned from an inspection of his North Borneo holdings and, fancying himself a man of science, hosted a dinner party to which several prominent patrons and scientists had been invited. The highlight of the evening was the unveiling of artifacts Lord Garnett had brought back from the steamy, far-off jungle. Specifically a net containing four smoke-blackened skulls collected from a Borneo longhouse, trophies of that distant land's savage head-hunters. Apparently

Lord Garnett intended to author a paper concerning the display and could not resist the opportunity to announce his upcoming publication to those who would envy such an achievement. The following day Lord Garnett locked the drawing room containing the bones, assuring the grisly artifacts were safe from those who might covet his gruesome souvenirs. When Lord Garnett returned four days later and unlocked the drawing room he discovered his net of skulls missing.

"According to Cambers the room had not been tampered with," I completed my recitation. "The doors had been locked and the windows securely fastened from the inside."

"Quite true," Holmes agreed. "It was, after all, for that very reason Cambers sought my assistance."

"Yes," I admitted. "So why are we rushing to Lord Garnett's? You provided Cambers a written list of questions to ask, you seemed quite confident it was all the detective would need to solve the matter."

"This morning I received a message from Cambers," Holmes explained. "It seems another of the skulls in Lord Garnett's possession was taken."

"Another one? Good heavens! How many skulls did Lord Garnett bring back from the jungle?"

"It's worse than you know Watson," Holmes assured me. "This particular skull was still in use by Lord Garnett's son."

"What?" I exclaimed. "You mean the boy was kidnapped?"

"It is too early to make that assessment," Holmes insisted. "All we know for certain is that the boy disappeared sometime last night. Cambers returned to Lord Garnett's residence early this morning with the intention of putting answers to my list of questions. He was present when the child's absence was discovered."

"Well, Cambers seems a talented detective," I offered my opinion.

"You think so?" Holmes asked.

"You said he'd done well with that matter back in—where was it?—Bedford?" I reminded Holmes. "He seems quite an ambitious fellow."

"In my experience the mere presence of ambition is not indicative of talent," Holmes argued. "I should also point out that crimes occurring in Bedford are markedly different than the crimes of London."

"Surely crime is crime, wherever it happens," I suggested, earning a long-suffering look from my friend.

"Not so Watson," Holmes argued. "Regrettably we do not have time to debate the point. There is Lord Garnett's. Ah, and here comes your rising star." Holmes leaned forward and, in a conspiratorial whisper, added, "I will admit this detective shows some promise."

"Oh?" I said, somewhat surprised.

"He knows enough to call for me," Holmes explained.

§

Cambers waited anxiously as the cabbie brought his horse to a stop. Detective Sergeant Cambers' open face was twisted into an expression of calamity, his eyes darted to and fro, reminding me of a frightened rabbit. Holmes dismissed the cabbie and turned to the Scotland Yard man.

"You've completed a search of the grounds?"

"I have Mr. Holmes," Cambers answered. "We've found nothing, nothing at all. I was just on my way in to inform Lord Garnett."

"How many constables are with you?" Holmes asked.

"Four," Cambers reported. "They're good men."

"And my list?" Holmes asked pointedly. "Have you managed to gain the answers I instructed you to seek?"

Cambers looked surprised by the question but, seeing

Holmes' unfaltering expression, the young man grimaced and confessed. "I'd just begun, Mr. Holmes, when the kidnapping—"

"Kidnapping?" Holmes interrupted the Scotland Yard detective. "Has that been determined?"

"Well," Cambers prevaricated. "The boy is only seven years of age. It seems unlikely he'd just wander off alone in the night."

"Seems unlikely." Holmes shook his head. "I trust we're able to do better than that Mr. Cambers."

The young detective's expression rearranged itself into a guarded look. "Of course, Mr. Holmes, any help you can provide will be appreciated."

Holmes nodded, indifferent to whether his assistance would be appreciated or not. "How many of my questions were you able to answer before abandoning them?"

"I'd been speaking to the chief cook, Mr. Holmes," Cambers explained. "She'd just completed the questions on your list when the alarm went up. As you might imagine Lady Garnett is hysterical. Her physician has visited and I believe her Ladyship has been sedated."

"Have you the cook's answers?" Holmes asked.

Cambers dug in his pocket and removed the sheet of questions Holmes had written out for him the previous evening and another sheet of paper, presumably from the chief cook.

"Very well." Holmes examined the cook's list. "And the other question you were to ask her?"

"She says she had no idea as to the nature of his Lordship's stolen foreign treasure," Cambers said.

"Was that the phrase she used?" Holmes asked. "Foreign treasure?"

"I think it was, yes," Cambers answered. Shuffling his feet impatiently, he added, "I should really report to Lord Garnett. He's most insistent that he be kept informed."

"You must proceed as you think best," Holmes declared. "Watson and I shall make some inquiries of our own. I assume the head butler waits inside?"

"I believe so," Cambers said without conviction.

"Then we shall gather answers for your neglected list." Holmes gestured for the Detective Sergeant to lead the way into the house.

"If you discover anything—"

"I will keep you informed," Holmes assured the detective. We hurried up the stairs and into Lord Garnett's grand house. Detective Sergeant Cambers, anxious to make his report, waved us towards the kitchen where the household staff might be found before hurrying away in search of Lord Garnett. In short order Holmes was questioning the head butler, a white-haired elderly gentleman with a timid but impeccable appearance.

"I wish you to write a list naming everyone who visited this house during the two days before Lord Garnett's dinner party," Holmes requested.

"Of course, sir," the butler replied. "Anything to assist the young master's return."

"You are aware of the other matter?" Holmes asked the butler.

"The theft?" The butler shook his head. "I'm afraid his Lordship has not seen fit to inform me of it."

"Even so, you know of it. Surely the police spoke to you? Asked you if you'd seen anything suspicious?"

"No sir, they did not." The butler's formal demeanour and neutral expression still managed to quietly express his disapproval.

Holmes scowled in a manner that, to my eyes, seemed somewhat theatrical. The detective complained, "I was hoping you could tell me what was stolen."

"Well, sir." The butler looked left and right before leaning forward and conspiratorially lowering his voice. "I believe it was some object he brought back from his Borneo holdings. Although I don't know the item's exact nature I did see the trunk in which it arrived. If you care to examine the trunk I believe it is still in the drawing room."

"Indeed," Holmes said. "The drawing room is down this hallway?"

"By the stairs sir," the butler agreed.

"Once you've completed your list please bring it to us there."

The drawing room fitted Cambers' description perfectly. A large, elegant space filled with an assortment of seats scattered around a small fireplace. Two doors opened to the interior of the room and four large windows looked outside. Holmes inspected the lock on the door through which we entered.

"Well, Watson," Holmes mused as he examined the door. "Does it seem strange to you that neither the chief cook nor the butler are aware of the nature of Lord Garnett's stolen items?"

"It is a large home," I reasoned. "Likely the kitchen staff don't normally have access to the drawing room."

"And the butler?" Holmes asked, shifting his attention to the first of the windows.

Frowning, I considered the problem. "No doubt a busy man—"

"No doubt," Holmes agreed, moving to the next window. "However that explains nothing. If neither head of staff were aware of the skulls' presence it follows that none of the staff knew of them."

"Can you be certain of that?" I asked.

"Gossip, Watson, is as much a force of nature as sunlight or sea tides," Holmes explained. "If any of the staff had seen the skulls they would have spoken of it and, once uttered, word surely would have reached the ears of one of the household chiefs. Imagine if I placed a skull on my mantle in Baker Street, how long do you think it would be before Mrs. Hudson informed you of the addition?"

Chuckling, I conceded the point. "But what does it mean Holmes?"

"Only that Detective Cambers has been shockingly misled as to the nature of the thefts. He believes a net of skulls has been taken when in fact a mysterious foreign treasure has gone missing." Holmes finished his examination of the last window and turned his attention to the remaining door. I moved to follow when something outside the window caught my eye. A branch of one of the rose bushes had been recently broken, a few dark threads were tangled in its thorns and at the edge of the garden a partial footprint was visible in the soft soil.

"Well-spotted Watson," Holmes commented as he examined the door. I continued to look out the window.

"You saw it too." It wasn't a question, I knew Holmes' methods too well to believe he had missed such evidence. "Why didn't you tell me?"

"Because it is meaningless," Holmes declared. "It has nothing to do with the theft of the skulls or the missing child. As I'm sure you'll agree, the matter of the missing boy is too urgent to allow us to loiter over such trivia. However else he was misled, Cambers was correct when he stated the doors and windows had not been tampered with. Meaning the thief had a key or found another way in and out of this room."

Turning his attention upward, Holmes surveyed the high ceilings. "Now Watson, never having visited a Borneo longhouse, I must confess to a degree of uncertainty regarding how best to display a net full of skulls. However, I suspect that hook in the ceiling would serve, don't you agree?"

"It seems secure enough," I answered.

"And it is a recent addition you can see a handprint where the workman braced himself as he put it in. And yet—" Holmes turned around, his eager eyes searching for something by the fireplace. "Ah! There it is!" Striding over to the small fireplace Holmes recovered a long, slender pole with a metal catch on the end. Holding the pole aloft, he retraced his steps to the ceiling hook. The pole easily reached the hook, leaving no doubt it had been constructed for just that purpose.

"And here is the trunk the butler mentioned," Holmes observed, resting the pole between the mantle and a green trunk lying open on the floor. Holmes bent to examine the trunk with his lens. For a moment Holmes was silent, then he stood suddenly upright with an alarmed expression on his normally reserved features.

Holmes turned to me, putting away his lens, and began to speak. "Watson, I fear—"

Fate deemed I would have to wait to discover what had wrought so sudden a change in my friend's demeanour as the butler chose that moment to enter the room. He announced his presence with a deferential "Sir?"

"Quickly man, quickly!" Holmes exclaimed, rushing towards the servant. "You have the list?"

"Yes sir," the butler replied, holding a folded sheet of paper in his gloved hand. "I only just completed it. I thought, perhaps, you—"

But Holmes snatched the list from the servant's hand and unfolded it quickly. As he did so I saw Detective Cambers approaching, no doubt reacting to the urgency in Holmes' loud voice.

Behind Cambers came another figure. From the stout man's harried expression I knew it must be Lord Garnett. The strain of his situation showed clearly on the strong features

159

of his face. Beneath dark brows his Lordship's brown eyes seemed wary, as if cringing in anticipation of the morning's next blow. Yet even in the midst of these troubles a ghost of the old adventurer remained. Thick, dark hair and a moustache he had not yet attended to, a tan darkening his face and the back of his strong hands. There was doggedness to his movements, as if his every step was an act of determination and anyone who dared hamper his way had best be prepared to pay a steep cost for their insolence. Yet even as he approached my reaction towards his Lordship was not one of intimidation or respect but was, rather, one of sympathy. It was plain to my senses Lord Garnett was very close to being overwhelmed by the unexplained disappearance of his son.

Such were my impressions of Lord Garnett. Holmes seemed to take no notice of his Lordship's approach. Holmes' formidable powers of concentration were focussed on the butler's list and, in his other hand, the chief cook's list he'd pulled from his pocket.

Detective Cambers and Lord Garnett entered the room together. His Lordship, seeing his butler waiting, raised his hand and started to give instructions to his servant. "Ah, I wonder if you might see to—"

"I have not yet finished with this man." Holmes interrupted firmly, though he did not look up from the lists he was examining.

"I beg your pardon?" Lord Garnett asked, blinking in surprise. Apparently his Lordship was not accustomed to being interrupted while addressing his servants.

"I have further need of this man," Holmes insisted.

Turning to acknowledge his employer, the butler seemed intent on ignoring Holmes and letting the matter drop. Whatever else he had endured, it seemed Lord Garnett was not willing to suffer impertinence such as Holmes was displaying.

"And who, sir, are you?" Lord Garnett asked, his voice a threatening rumble.

"My name is Sherlock Holmes." Pulling the butler's coat until the man was forced to turn and acknowledge him, Holmes pointed to a name on the list. "I require an address for this man."

"I regret, sir, that I do not know the address offhand."

"Then find someone who does!" Holmes demanded forcefully. "And hurry!"

Shocked by Holmes' insistence, the butler turned pleadingly to Lord Garnett. His Lordship seemed quite taken aback by Holmes' manner and was about to voice his displeasure when Holmes spoke first.

"Lord Garnett, your son's life may depend on the speedy resolution of your butler's errand. If you value your child's life, I suggest you give him leave to go."

"Of course," Lord Garnett nodded to his servant, who promptly left the room at a pace seeming, for one so dignified, a run. "Now then, Mr. Holmes is it? I fail to—"

But Holmes had turned his attention to Detective Sergeant Cambers. "I will require two of your uniformed officers, those you judge to be most capable, and I require them now."

Cambers, his face clouded with displeasure at being addressed so in front of his Lordship, frowned. "Now see here Mr. Holmes—"

"Now!" Holmes repeated. "We must act quickly if we are to capture this villain."

Cambers opened his mouth to argue but snapped it shut when he noticed Lord Garnett's formidable attention on him. With an uncertain shrug, Cambers hurried from the room much as the butler had before him.

"Now then Mr. Holmes," Lord Garnett started but, to the surprise of both his Lordship and myself, Holmes set off down the hallway at a quick run. For a moment Lord Garnett seemed at a complete loss. I had the impression it had been quite a long time since his Lordship had met anyone as insolent as Holmes. His Lordship watched Holmes' slender figure disappear beyond the doorway and then he turned to me in a manner reminiscent of heavy artillery.

"And you are?" Lord Garnett asked me.

"Doctor John Watson," I said, offering my hand. Lord Garnett shook it firmly, apparently relieved to be dealing with someone familiar with the concept of courtesy.

"Are you with the police?"

"No," I answered, somewhat embarrassed. "I'm here with Sherlock Holmes."

"Ah," Lord Garnett nodded. "Then perhaps you can tell me: Who is this Sherlock Holmes? Is he a policeman?"

"No," I admitted. "He is a detective, a consulting detective. Cambers came to seek his advice last evening and sent word this morning of your misfortune. Naturally we came to offer what assistance we could."

"Assistance?" Lord Garnett repeated in surprise. "Is that what he was doing?"

"I assure you, Lord Garnett, my friend's methods may seem odd but he is a remarkable detective." Yet I had barely finished uttering these words of confidence when Holmes rushed back into the room bearing a large basin of water. Ignoring both Lord Garnett and myself, Holmes hurried to the fireplace and, upturning the heavy basin, doused the burning coals. An enormous plume of smoke and steam spilled from the fireplace and when it cleared Holmes was standing surprisingly close to Lord Garnett.

"Lord Garnett," Holmes addressed the missing child's father directly for the first time. "Can you tell me when this room was last cleaned?"

"Have you lost your mind?" Lord Garnett sputtered, waving away the last of the steam.

"It was cleaned before you locked the room, was it not?" Holmes asked, refusing to be distracted by Lord Garnett's outrage.

"Of course," Lord Garnett answered.

"Naturally." Holmes turned to me and explained. "It would make little sense to lock the servants out of the drawing room if it had not already been tidied. And as the staff was unaware of the nature of his Lordship's souvenirs it follows the skulls were closed up in that trunk. Correct?"

Lord Garnett's complexion changed to an unhealthy ruddy colour as he replied to Holmes. "Who the devil do you think you are, coming into my house and—"

"Oh, I am sorry," Holmes apologised, much to Lord Garnett's surprise. "I thought I had introduced myself. My name is Sherlock Holmes and your son's life depends on me."

Holmes' reply had a profound effect on Lord Garnett. The man's bluster seemed to disappear, his ruddy complexion paled in horror and he reached for a nearby chair to steady himself.

"The skulls were closed up in that trunk, correct?" Holmes repeated his question.

"Yes," Lord Garnett answered meekly.

"I see no evidence of the trunk having been locked," Holmes mused. "Yet it seems likely the skulls were not simply laid inside. There must have been something more."

"There was," Lord Garnett agreed. "A bag, I purchased it from a sailor. It was—"

"Forgive me your Lordship," Holmes interrupted Lord Garnett dismissively. "I hear your man approaching."

Just as Holmes predicted the butler appeared in the room, a slip of paper in his hand.

"You have the address I requested?" Holmes asked.

"I do sir."

Detective Sergeant Cambers, with two of his constables in tow, followed on the butler's heels. The expression on Cambers' open face made it clear he intended to regain control of the situation. Holmes, however, completely ignored the detective.

"Give the address to the constables here," Holmes instructed the butler. "Gentlemen, you are to go to this address and search the premises for Lord Garnett's missing skulls. Take note of all you see there, with a special eye towards any children you might observe. Find the man and ask to see his certificate. I doubt he has one, despite the law concerning his trade. Regardless of what excuse he provides take him to Scotland Yard for questioning. If he has the temerity to ask what he is to be charged with inform him the charge is murder."

"Murder?" Lord Garnett whispered, his face paling even more. His Lordship staggered against a seat and fell into it.

"Courage, Lord Garnett," Holmes instructed the missing child's father. "There is still hope. You were about to describe the bag you purchased from the sailor, the one you used to store your net of skulls. If you would be so kind as to share your description with the constables?"

"What?" For a moment Lord Garnett looked confused and I feared the events of the dreadful day had overtaken his reason. After a moment however, sensing the rapt attention of the constables, Lord Garnett managed to speak in a curiously disconnected, uncharacteristically soft voice.

"The bag? Oh yes, I purchased it from a sailor. It fit quite neatly into the trunk and was made of sealskin. Waterproof you see, very handy. It opened at one end and I threaded a chain through the grommets so I could lock it with a padlock. I didn't want anyone to look inside. It could give someone quite a fright and I was planning to write a paper. I didn't want to give any of my rivals a chance to examine them. Of course, I lined the inside of the bag with wool; you cannot allow the skulls to get cold you know, or else the souls of their owners will come back and haunt you."

Lord Garnett's eyes had grown quite wide as he uttered the last part of this speech, weaving a macabre spell which held the constables, Cambers, the butler and myself captivated.

Breaking the spell, Holmes proved himself immune to the fascination gripping us. "How charming. Constables, you know your duty. See to it!"

The constables started off, completely oblivious to the hand Detective Sergeant Cambers' raised to stop them. Or perhaps the constables merely reacted to the more forceful nature of Holmes' authority.

Cambers was, by this time, glaring at Holmes and I feared a confrontation between the two men was imminent. Holmes must have sensed the Detective Sergeant's hostility as he suddenly spoke. "Watson, why don't you show the Detective Constable what you discovered at the window?"

Suddenly I found myself the focus of Cambers and Lord Garnett. "Of course Holmes," I replied, remembering how Holmes had dismissed the apparent clues as trivial. "I was over here when I noticed—"

"A footprint!" Cambers exclaimed.

"Yes," I agreed. "And you see there, some dark threads tangled among the rose bushes."

"They certainly weren't there yesterday," Cambers proclaimed. "Obviously the footprint was made by the kidnappers."

"Whoever made the footprint didn't gain entrance into the drawing room," I observed. "The windows were still secure and there's no trace of mud in here."

"Likely they tried the windows and found some other way in," Cambers judged. "We'll need a closer look."

Cambers left the room, presumably to go out to the garden and examine the footprint. I turned and was surprised to discover I was once again alone in the room with Lord Garnett. Holmes and the butler had disappeared while I was distracted by Cambers.

"They've gone upstairs," Lord Garnett informed me. "Your friend said he urgently needed to examine the roof."

"Whatever for?" I asked.

Lord Garnett simply shrugged, he seemed utterly drained by the experiences of the day. I suspected Holmes' use of the word murder had deeply frightened the man. Wishing I had some comfort to offer, I stood and said simply, "I think I'll join them."

"Yes," Lord Garnett agreed. "Perhaps I'll come as well."

"It might be best if you were to rest." It was, I reflected, not a very helpful suggestion but the urge to prescribe rest is deeply ingrained in all physicians.

Lord Garnett shook his head. "I know you mean well," he said, "but I couldn't rest. What if they found something and I was asleep? No, it would be best if I went somewhere in case I was needed."

"Then perhaps, before we go, you'll join me for a brandy?" It was all I could think to offer.

"Yes," Lord Garnett agreed. He stood and went to fetch the drinks from one of the cabinets along the wall. Returning, he passed me a glass with a generous measure of amber liquid in it.

"And to think yesterday my most pressing concern was the missing skulls." Lord Garnett shook his head and grimaced. "And now your friend seems to think he has found them."

"Likely he has," I said. "As I said, he is an extraordinary detective."

"Do you believe he can find my son?" Lord Garnett asked, unable to look me in the eye as he voiced his deepest wish.

"He will find him," I assured the man. "Of that I have no doubt."

Lord Garnett nodded sadly, hearing the unspoken fear in my voice. In truth I had no doubt at all regarding Holmes' ability to locate the child but there was no way of knowing in what condition we would find the boy.

"Henry is often a difficult child," Lord Garnett confessed. "Headstrong and quite independent despite his young age. We've often quarrelled but I am extremely proud of him. Do you think I will have the chance to tell him so?"

"Honestly, I don't know," I admitted. "But if anyone can find the boy, it's Sherlock Holmes."

Nodding, Lord Garnett drained his brandy and set the empty glass on a nearby table. Though I had barely tasted mine, I set my glass next to his. The brandy had done Lord Garnett a world of good, returning some colour to his complexion and easing some of the strain in his determined features.

"Let's find Holmes, shall we?" I suggested.

"Yes," Lord Garnett agreed, leading the way out of the room. I caught a glimpse of Cambers and his remaining constables through the windows as we passed.

Apparently Lord Garnett saw them as well. "Your friend tricked them. He saw Cambers was spoiling for a fight so he had you point out the footprint in the garden. He only did it to keep them out of his way, didn't he?"

"I believe so," I admitted, following Lord Garnett up the stairs. "When I first noticed the footprint in the garden Holmes told me it meant nothing. He seems to be in a dreadful hurry but I don't understand why."

"Well," Lord Garnett said, "I suppose that's a hopeful sign."

§

We found the butler on the uppermost floor of the house, standing on a small balcony and clutching a precariously perched ladder which Holmes climbed down with a fearlessness that bordered on the reckless.

"Watson! I trust Cambers is occupied in the garden?"

"He is," I agreed. "But Holmes, why—"

"Sorry Watson, time is short," Holmes forestalled my question. "Lord Garnett, could you show me to your son's room?"

"Of course," Lord Garnett nodded. "This way."

"Lord Garnett," Holmes said as he followed his Lordship out to the stairs. "Your son came to see you late last night."

"How on Earth did you know that?" Lord Garnett asked.

"He must have had some complaint," Holmes observed. "What did he say?"

Lord Garnett lead the way down the flight of stairs. "It sounded so childish at the time but it chills me to think of it now. He claimed he'd heard a ghost Mr. Holmes, a ghost moaning in agony."

"You did not believe him?" Holmes asked with perfect sincerity.

"No, I didn't," Lord Garnett admitted.

"That is your son's room there?" Holmes asked, not waiting for Lord Garnett's direction.

"It is," Lord Garnett confirmed, again startled by Holmes seemingly supernatural abilities.

Holmes turned and addressed Lord Garnett and the butler who had followed us downstairs.

"Go to the garden shed," Holmes instructed them. "Bring me a pick, a pry bar, a lantern, some rope, whatever you can lay hands on. Quickly! Bring them to me here!"

To my surprise both the butler and Lord Garnett hurried

away to fulfil Holmes' command. Holmes turned and looked at me with weary eyes. "I will say this for the headhunters of Borneo, they are honest enough to display their sins in plain view. It is an example we could learn from."

"Holmes, whatever do you mean?" I asked.

"Bones, Watson," Holmes admitted, walking into the missing child's room and pulling a pocketknife. "My knowledge of the subject is not as extensive as Lord Garnett's but it is enough to confirm my observation. Headhunters display the fruits of their savagery proudly rather than hiding them inside walls. You didn't, by any chance, bring your stethoscope with you?"

"No." Holmes had stopped me on the street, between home and my Kensington practice, before I'd reached the tools of my profession.

"Pity," Holmes observed as he unfolded his pocketknife and inserted the blade into the wall

"Holmes?" I asked, watching in mute horror as Holmes dragged the blade through the wall. He was making a dreadful mess but, after carving a gouge more than two feet long in the wall, he seemed to find what he was searching for. He withdrew the blade, folded it and put it back in his pocket.

From outside came the sounds of men running up the stairs. Lord Garnett rushed into the room, a large pick in his hand. The butler had found a pry bar, a hammer and a lantern, which he dropped onto the child's unmade bed with obvious relief.

"Some water would not go amiss," Holmes observed as he took hold of the pick Lord Garnett had brought. The butler, his refinement stretched somewhat thin, observed Holmes with a cool look but left to fulfil the detective's request.

"This must be done with some care," Holmes told me

as I picked up the pry bar. "The trick is to pull the bricks outward, not to let them fall inside."

"Bricks?" I asked.

In answer Holmes swung his pick into the wall and, in a shower of lath and plaster, uncovered a section of chimney. Such destruction caused me a measure of surprise but Lord Garnett, sitting on the edge of his son's bed, simply watched without expression.

"Hurry, Watson." Holmes swung the axe again, knocking one of the chimney bricks inward at an angle. Hurrying to help, though not at all certain the purpose behind this extravagant destruction, I reached in with my pry bar and attempted to pull the brick outwards.

"Back in the hallway you were going to ask about Cambers and the footprint in the garden," Holmes explained as I worked. When the brick fell out he swung the pick once more, loosening more bricks. "No doubt by now you've reached the obvious conclusion, the footprint and remnant of cloth were left by one of the police constables as they searched the grounds this morning."

Hearing this, Lord Garnett was unable to contain a bleak chuckle.

"Can you be certain of that?" I asked.

"Of course," Holmes said as he swung the pick again. "You saw the footprint, the distinctive pattern of a hobnail boot. And the colour of the threads match the police constable's uniform precisely. While I do not wish to mention the constable's name, I have matched the evidence to the subject. If his name was mentioned I fear the poor man would suffer Cambers' displeasure. It is a peculiar conceit of Scotland Yard investigators; they seem convinced all the footprints in the world belong to someone else."

"And the skulls?" I asked. "What makes you believe you know where they are?"

"Believe?" Holmes swung the pick again. "Watson, your lack of confidence is astounding. The man whose address the butler found is the chimneysweep who finished tending to Lord Garnett's chimneys the morning of the party."

"A chimneysweep?" I shook my head. "Holmes, there's no possible way a grown man could fit down that chimney."

"No?" Holmes asked. "It would, of course, depend upon the man but you are most likely correct. Unfortunately, and to our nation's great shame, chimneysweeps discovered a method of overcoming such obstacles centuries ago. There are laws against the practise now, a system of certification designed specifically to bring an end to the dreadful practise. Surely you see it now, Watson? Lord Garnett?"

At that moment I was prying out bricks, enlarging the hole Holmes had knocked in the chimney.

"Lord Garnett, if you would be so kind as to light that lamp," Holmes asked. "The boy's complaint of spirits moaning in the night, that must clarify matters? This is, after all, the same chimney we saw in the drawing room, one floor beneath us."

"Are you suggesting something is trapped in the chimney?" I asked.

"Something?" Holmes shook his head. "No Watson, someone. The evidence is clear although the crime itself is obviously based on a series of misunderstandings and random chance. Start with the assumption the chimneysweep is a villain. He comes to Lord Garnett's to practise his trade and hears the servants talking about their Master's return and the strange trunk he has taken such care to bring back with him. Surely, the servants gossip, it must contain a great treasure! The chimneysweep, being a villain, listens carefully and constructs a plan. He apologises for not being able to complete his work that day but promises to return early the next morning to finish."

The hole in the chimney was now large enough I could insert my head through it but Holmes urged me to continue widening it. "Early next morning the sweep returns, carrying the brushes of his trade with him. Hidden in among his tools is the means by which he hopes to accomplish his theft. A climbing boy."

"A climbing boy?" I stopped my task.

"Not so long ago the city was teeming with them," Holmes explained as he gestured for me to continue my efforts. "It is entirely likely this sweep was once a wretched boy earning his living as a sweep's apprentice. The legislation forbidding the use of climbing boys is quite recent but the sweep, having survived his apprenticeship, feels the law unjust. After all, what is his crime? Teaching children a trade? And if nine of his ten young apprentices perish, well, London is filled with orphans after all. A child trapped within a chimney brings no harm to anyone, even saving his master the cost of a burial. And those that fall to the fumes or the diseases arising from breathing smoke and eating soot can easily and inexpensively be disposed of."

"Holmes?" I asked.

"Slightly wider Watson," Holmes said, taking the lit lantern from Lord Garnett. "My fears were first stirred in the drawing room when I discovered a smudge of soot on the lid of the empty chest. They were confirmed when I saw the sweep's name and occupation on the list of visitors the butler prepared. You recall my next action?"

"You fetched water to put out the fire in the grate," Lord Garnett recalled.

"Then proceeded to the roof hoping to find the boys up near the opening of the chimney," Holmes explained. "Unfortunately all I found there was a trail of blood."

"Boys?" Lord Garnett asked. "How does my son's disappearance figure into this?"

"The role of the climbing boy was quite straightforward," Holmes explained. "He was to wait in the chimney, enduring the smoke and fumes of the fire below, until nightfall. Then, putting out the fire with water brought for that purpose, he was to climb down, remove the exotic treasure from its case and bring it to the roof where the sweep waited. Unfortunately for the boy, the sweep betrayed him. Rather than take the child and the treasure the sweep opted to take only the treasure. He struck the boy, leaving a trail of blood inside of the chimney. The climbing boy fell, becoming entangled in the flue. Whatever his injuries, he still had the water he'd brought to douse the fire. Somehow he clung to life until your return."

"The ghost Lord Garnett's son complained of?" I asked.

"The climbing boy," Holmes agreed. "Finding no one willing to believe his night time tale, your son acted on his own. Quite bravely too, if I may be permitted to observe. He crawled up the chimney himself. Unfortunately, it appears he also became entangled in the dark. There Watson, that should be large enough."

Holmes hurried in, sticking his arm with the lantern and his head into the opening we had made. He quickly pulled his head out again. I couldn't help but notice the soot staining his cheek.

"They are there!" Holmes announced. Holmes took off his coat and tied a large loop in the thin rope from the garden shed. Lord Garnett was up and running to the stairs, yelling in commanding tones for assistance.

"Are they—" I couldn't bring myself to finish the sentence.

"They're not moving," Holmes observed, "and they are black as night. Beyond that I cannot say."

§

Lord Garnett returned with Cambers and the constables in tow. The butler reappeared, bearing a full glass of water in each hand. It was a tight fit but Holmes was able to reach into the darkness and loop the rope around the trapped boys. He pulled out the first blackened form, then the other. The two small children were indistinguishable under the soot they wore.

One of the boys coughed and gratefully accepted water from the butler. As the child's face was cleaned I witnessed the joyful reunion of Lord Garnett and his son. The climbing boy was, I am saddened to say, already dead when we pulled his small, broken form from the darkness.

"He'll hang for this," Detective Sergeant Cambers vowed as Holmes explained the nature of the crime. When the two constables returned from their errand they reported finding everything as Holmes predicted. A sealskin bag containing the darkened skulls, its lock broken, was found in the sweep's home as was evidence of several orphans. The sweep had no certificate and had been practising his trade with no license

As we took a cab from Lord Garnett's, his Lordship's profuse thanks still ringing in our ears, Holmes expounded on the point he'd been trying to make when we arrived at the manor. "As a rule the crimes of the countryside are crimes of honest malice, acts of base motive, and Cambers is well-suited to such offences. London, on the other hand, offers its denizens crimes of opportunity. Misdeeds requiring little or no planning, acts of indifference, and Cambers is ill-prepared for such random villainy. I would also point out that it is not enough for a detective to simply ask the correct question. After all Cambers did ask Lord Garnett for a list of everyone who visited the manor the day of the theft, yet how was his Lordship to know which trades-people had visited? No, a detective must match the right question to the right person, a lesson young Cambers has yet to learn."

The Oba's Voice

s my friend, Sherlock Holmes often observed, my pen tends to favour tales in which the great detective plays an active role. Such cases were more the exception than the rule. For most investigations Holmes acted as a consulting detective, offering insight into different matters brought to him by private investigators, members of the constabulary, and other parties desirous of a riddle's solution. Upon this field, time and again, Holmes proved the worth of his convictions in reason and deduction. In defense of my literary efforts, two men talking within the comfort of the Baker Street lodgings would take more skill than I possess to spin into a gripping yarn. Still, I do recall one of our most otherworldly cases beginning in such commonplace circumstances.

I arrived at the lodgings and, having just stepped in from Baker Street, found myself shoved rudely to the side by a tall, bearded fellow as he strode outdoors. I had time only for a glance at the departing visitor but his expression was composed of equal parts annoyance and anger. From atop the stairs I heard Holmes' voice call out, "Unsworth!" but it was too late, the man was through the front door and lost in the traffic beyond.

Looking up, I saw Holmes looking down to the landing. His lean features were arranged in an annoyance as profound as the man who had fled but also betraying a sense of confusion.

I closed the front door and made my way up the seventeen steps, joining Holmes as he retreated into his rooms. The detective made for the small reserve of alcohol we kept on hand. He poured two good, stiff measures and offered me one as he imbibed the other.

"What was all that about?" I asked, taking a sip.

"I'm not certain," Holmes admitted. "Detective Sergeant Unsworth came to me two days ago with a small problem; we discussed the matter and came to what I believed was a solution satisfactory to both logic and the state of my finances. He returned just now to explain how mistaken I was, while offering not a shred of logic to defend his conviction."

"Were you cross with him?"

"I don't believe so," Holmes admitted. "To be honest, I was somewhat taken aback by the man's insistence on our suspect's absolute innocence. Upon our first meeting Unsworth struck me as a promising detective. Though he had not concluded his investigation with a suitable suspect, he had gathered his evidence in a thoughtful and methodical manner that spoke well of his abilities. He seemed quite willing, I would say eager, to discuss the case and accept what assistance I could offer. His actions then were completely at odds with the officer who just left. Very odd."

"Perhaps if you could share the specifics of the case with me?"

"Of course," Holmes agreed. We settled into our accustomed chairs and Holmes continued. "Though, to be frank, it was not a matter of much interest. A simple robbery. Unsworth's failure to identify the culprit was not due to lack of skill or diligence but rather due to the common failing of disregarding scandalous gossip. Items were reported stolen from the home of Jeremy Claverhouse, some items of silver and a small amount of cash removed from the office he kept in his home. There was no sign of forced entry, it being a large household the staff were constantly engaged in various tasks. A number of visitors had been in and out of the home, any of whom could easily have taken the items in question. Suspicion immediately fell upon the household staff but, obviously, they were not involved."

"No?" I prodded.

"Perhaps a newly-hired staff member might make off with the trifling bit of silver found in the office but anyone who spent more than a couple of days in the home would be aware of items worth far more in other areas of the house. No, clearly the staff would not have risked so much for so little. Narrowing our list of suspects to visitors brought us to a manageable number; seven guests entered the house on the day in question. As the office was next to the main entrance, it was Unsworth's hypothesis that the thief had not been granted unsupervised entry further into the home. A logical assumption based on the facts. Our list was then reduced to three, two senior tradesmen and a young delivery boy."

I considered the matter. "None of whom, I imagine, figure in the gossip you have been listening to."

"That is a shockingly irrational basis for eliminating them as suspects," Holmes chided me. "Unfortunately for logical principles, you are correct. What Unsworth failed to account for was the homeowner's current situation as I learned it from sources of high society gossip I have cultivated. Jeremy Claverhouse was, until recently, engaged to be wed to a Miss Ellen Beldon, daughter of the wealthy industrialist Franklin Beldon. Theirs was, by all accounts, a love match, however the marriage had been postponed due to Miss Beldon's father's poor health. To the delight of the gossips, however, the forthcoming marriage was canceled entirely due to Miss Beldon being wed to Lewis Tallowfield, recently retired from the Royal Marines. By all accounts, Claverhouse was left bewildered and heartbroken by the affair. Even more curious was his confession to one of the agony gossips that he had received a letter from Mrs. Tallowfield, Beldon, confessing she was as confused and bewildered by the sudden turn of events as he was. You see how this changes matters."

"I do not." A small confession made familiar by my long association with Holmes.

"Unsworth assumed, not without cause, that the theft at the Claverhouse home was a crime of opportunity rather than intent. Given the current happenings with young Claverhouse, that reasonable assumption could no longer be relied on. During my consultation, I informed Unsworth of this possibility. I asked if there was a safe in the office; he told me there was but that it showed no signs of having been tampered with. I instructed the Detective Sergeant to ask Claverhouse where he kept the letter from Mrs. Tallowfield and to confirm it was still in his possession. We then reviewed the list of visitors to the home on the day in question and quickly found one matching the description of a former Royal Marine. Though not Lewis Tallowfield himself, it seemed likely to be a known associate and someone willing to carry out a task for a comrade."

I considered the matter, finishing my drink. "Why would this confederate take anything but the letter?"

"In case he was discovered in the office," Holmes argued. "Particularly if he was found by the safe. The discovery of trifling amounts of silver on him would reveal him to be a thief but conceal the true aim of his endeavour. And I was correct. Unsworth informed me yesterday that Claverhouse checked his safe and confirmed the letter was missing, though the thief had left the empty envelope in the safe. A well-conceived gambit, if trivial in nature. Unsworth informed me he was planning to confront Lewis Tallowfield this morning, though in truth I did not expect much to come of it. If Tallowfield was clever, as leaving the envelope behind indicates he was, he need simply burn the letter to deprive the Yard of any connection between him and the crime. Likewise his associate need simply sell the silver and pocket the cash and there will be no way for a court to convict him. Unsworth and I were certain of what had happened and who was responsible but, alas, the chances of proving it in court seemed questionable."

"How would the thief open the safe?"

"Oh, simple enough. He knew the combination, as Ellen Tallowfield could provide it to him. She was aware of the combination and Claverhouse had not changed it since their estrangement."

"Fascinating," I admitted. Though I had experienced Holmes' deductive abilities on many occasions, they never failed to impress. "And today?"

"Well," Holmes frowned. "Unsworth came over, I knew he was intent on confronting Tallowfield this morning but, as I said, had little hope of obtaining any useful evidence from the visit. He was concerned about the state of the wife, who reportedly wrote the letter to Claverhouse claiming to be held against her will. Still, the hand must be played out. Apparently Unsworth made the visit and confronted Tallowfield. He returned to me in order to declare the man innocent of all charges and – what was his phrase? – incapable of any wrong-doing."

"That seems strange," I admitted.

"I offered the Detective Sergeant the opportunity to explain his conclusion but he just kept repeating that Tallowfield was innocent of this, or, indeed, of any crime. It was most frustrating, the man seemed incapable of hearing reason and unwilling to explain how he arrived at his conclusion. You saw him when he left, my impression was he was as annoyed at me as I was with him. As I said, our earlier interactions convinced me he was a promising and talented detective. Nor do I offer such praise lightly. Now, I confess, I am at a loss. I don't know what to make of the Detective Sergeant's behaviour."

"What will you do?" I asked.

"I'd not considered it," Holmes said, cradling his drink. "You understand, it's not that I am unwilling to hear arguments for Tallowfield's innocence. I am more than willing, anxious even, to hear such a case made. Unsworth simply offered no argument at all. I suppose if Unsworth cannot explain what changed his mind regarding Tallowfield, I must go to the source. It is a small, unprofitable matter but, as things stand, I'm unable to dismiss the possibility that Tallowfield is holding his wife against her will. That, and my initial evaluation of Unsworth, will nag at my thoughts until I resolve them. I will present my card to Lewis Tallowfield, confront him with my suspicions and tally my findings against the Detective Sergeant's. I am certain it is nothing, a mere annoyance, a trifle at best."

§

We left the topic and went on to discuss other matters. By the time I left, Holmes' humour had been restored. Likely, I would never have recalled the case again had I not read in the paper of the passing of Franklin Beldon, Lewis Tallowfield's father-in-law. In the absence of any male heirs, the fortune was left to his only daughter, Ellen. I wondered, as I read the news, if Holmes had interviewed Tallowfield before the unfortunate passing. Naturally, when I next returned to Baker Street, I asked my friend of it.

"Oh," Holmes seemed to bat away my question with a wave of his hand. "It was nothing, less than a trifle. Tallowfield was completely blameless, quite an amiable fellow."

I waited for my friend to continue but he offered no further explanation, seemingly content to relax in his seat. "I'm relieved to hear it," I offered, "Though I am curious. Your reasoning implicating Tallowfield seemed constructed on firm ground; how did he convince you of his innocence?"

Frowning, Holmes leaned forward. "Well, it's simply inconceivable that Tallowfield would be involved in such a matter. He is quite incapable of any wrong-doing."

This, I admit, startled me. I had never heard Holmes offer such a glowing evaluation of anyone. Sherlock Holmes was always willing to consider the worst of any man, woman or child. Given the necessary, dire circumstances, he often assured me, anyone was capable of illegality. I'd never heard Holmes offer such a general endorsement regarding any person, living or dead.

"What sort of man was Tallowfield?" I asked. "He seems to have impressed you."

"Amiable," Holmes offered. He then sat in silence, apparently unable or unwilling to continue his curt description.

"Holmes?" I asked, thoroughly bewildered at my friend's response. "Are you well?"

"Quite well," Holmes assured me. "Why do you ask?"

I shifted in my seat, suddenly uncomfortable. "Is this one of Mycroft's schemes? Something I should not be inquiring about? If so, you need only tell me to drop the matter and I will. There's no need for such games between friends."

Holmes frowned, his eyes narrowing as he examined me in a genuine show of confusion. "My dear Watson, I have no idea what you are talking about."

"Really, Holmes." I was, I admit, peeved. The irritation which Holmes experienced with Detective Sergeant Unsworth seemed to settle on my shoulders like a yoke. "Do you not? Tell me, did you take a cab to Tallowfield's?" Holmes nodded. "And the cabbie, what did you make of him?"

"Young fellow, I'd say no more than twenty-two but a dab hand with horses. Short in stature, but his beasts followed his lead as if he were a giant. Newly married, the tokens of his new bride were almost too numerable to mention. His clean shaven features, horse sense, and familiarity with the city and curious formality all spoke to him being the son of a coachman for one of the more prominent families in London. In fact, looking at the manner in which his trousers were pressed—"

"Enough," I interrupted. "And Tallowfield, what do you make of Beldon's son-in-law?"

"An amiable fellow," Holmes answered. "He seems quite incapable—"

"—of any wrongdoing." I finished the thought. "Do you honestly not hear the difference?"

Holmes sat motionless, save for the occasional blink. "I don't think—"

"Look," I said, reaching for the pencil and paper Holmes kept on a table. "I will list all the details you told me of the cabbie before I cut you off. Young man, short, recently wed, talent with his horses, odd sense of formality, recently pressed trousers. Correct?"

"Clean shaven and son of a local coachman," Holmes added. I dutifully jotted down the extra points.

"Quite so, and now, Tallowfield: Amiable, incapable of wrongdoing ... have I missed anything?"

Holmes stiffened in his seat, a puzzlement creasing his brow. He held out his hand and I passed the paper over to him. His frown deepened as he looked at my handwriting.

The hour was late and my humour was, I admit, somewhat soured by our discussion. "Really, Holmes, if you don't wish to discuss Tallowfield, I will not compel you to do so. If there is some matter not for my ears, that is all you need say. I've no wish to press you. If you feel you cannot trust to my discretion, well, I admit I am somewhat stung by that, but I understand your business often involves delicate matters. You need not feign ignorance on such basic questions. Friends owe each other nothing but honesty. Now, if you'll forgive me, it's been a trying day and I should be getting home. Good evening."

§

I was, I confess, somewhat curt with my friend but not, I felt, without cause. It was with some surprise then that I received a message from Holmes the next day, shortly after lunch. The missive was delivered by one of the Irregulars, the street children who were Holmes' most trusted envoys, but one he rarely employed to deliver simple correspondence to me. Yet the message could not have been simpler, it consisted of a single word scrawled in his own hand, a word I never expected to receive from Holmes: Please.

I returned to the lodgings as soon as I could. Holmes was waiting inside, dressed for departure but seated and clutching some sealed envelopes and a set of field glasses. Holmes often allowed himself to go for days without sleep when a case had a hold on him but it was immediately clear to me this sleepless night had not been a hurdle the detective nimbly leapt but a mountain he had dragged himself over.

I hurried towards my friend but he raised a hand to stop me. His eyes had a haunted aspect to them as he fixed his gaze on mine. "I require your assistance, Watson, but I cannot explain. I don't understand it myself but I require you do exactly as I ask. I am returning to Tallowfield's. I must speak to him again. I know how much you deplore peering through windows but I have no choice but to ask you to observe our discussion. There is a restaurant across the street, you can use the field glasses. Watch, observe, but under no circumstances are you to enter. When we have spoken, I will come to you and you must hand me the envelope labelled 'one'. I must read this letter in your presence. Do you understand?"

"Not at all," I answered, "but I will do as you ask. Why don't you simply read the letter now?"

"There's no need," Holmes said. "I know what it says. I wrote it."

"You wrote yourself a letter?"

"I cannot explain," Holmes admitted, not without some cost to his dignity. "Once I read it, well, if I raise my voice to you or act in any way unlike myself, you must give me the envelope labelled 'two'."

"There are three envelopes here," I noted.

"The third is for you," Holmes answered. "If all goes well, I will ask for it back unread. If I do not do so by noon tomorrow, you are to open it, read it and act as you feel best. I know this is unorthodox but it is critically important. Believe me when I say: I would explain all were I capable of doing so. My hope is that soon we shall be able to reason out this puzzle together. My fear is that my reason has fled. I am sorry to ask this of you Watson, you deserve better of me, but—"

"Of course Holmes," I interrupted. "If it's that important, I will do as you ask."

I placed the letters in the inner pocket of my jacket but Holmes insisted I remove the third envelope and place it in a different pocket. He seemed himself but as anxious as I'd ever seen him. An odd occurrence as Holmes was usually quite unflappable once he had decided on a course of action. We went down the stairs and out onto the street where we hailed a cab. In short order we were being carried through the streets of London.

"Now Watson, it is of the utmost importance you do not enter the Tallowfield home. It would be better if Lewis Tallowfield mounted my head on a spike rather than you reveal yourself to him. Understand?"

"No," I admitted.

"Nor I, Watson, but I assure you it is so. I expect I will be shown into his office, I need you to observe every detail that occurs during our discussion as precisely as you can. You must write it down, all of it, and when I return you must give the description to me. Whatever my state, I must receive the list of your observations. Then you are to give me the first envelope, especially if I do not ask for it."

"And the second envelope if you raise your voice or do not seem yourself."

"Just so, Watson, just so. You know the situation at the Tallowfield home, if you see any sign of Mrs. Tallowfield make what observations you can but the priority is to record every detail of my interaction with Lewis Tallowfield. Are you able to do this?"

"Naturally," I answered. "And if you do not return for me, I shall follow you and give you the first envelope."

"Watson, I do not have the words to express my gratitude. Or my trepidation."

§

When the cab stopped, Holmes showed me to a restaurant across the street. I sat at a booth by the window and, with the magnification offered by the field glasses, was able to peer into Tallowfield's office unhampered. Holmes had arranged with the restaurant owner and staff that my strange, and frankly unforgivable, eavesdropping would not be disturbed. Before Holmes left, he had me list the contents of the office as best I could observe them. There was, to my eye, nothing remarkable. A painting of a merchant ship hung in a gilt frame on a yellow wall, a large desk of dark wood with a green blotter on it. There was an absence of decorative items on the desk save a bronze bust of someone I could not make out, three pens, one ink well, and four neatly piled ledgers.

As I watched, Lewis Tallowfield himself wandered into my line of sight. He was a man of average height and slight build, dark hair, a handlebar mustache of modest size. Perhaps it was a holdover of the annoyance I had felt towards Holmes the previous night but, to my eye, the man did not seem at all amiable. His movements seemed brisk, the sneer of his lips and squint of his eyes seemed to radiate unfriendliness. He gathered some sheets of paper and moved to the desk to compose a missive of some sort. I could not identify exactly why I felt distrustful of the figure brought close to my eyes by the field glasses' lens, but I did not like the man.

I swept my gaze across the other windows of the house but did not discover any sign of Mrs. Tallowfield. Black cloth hung on many of the windows, no doubt a sign of mourning for the late Franklin Beldon. Holmes clapped me on the shoulder as he left. Feeling somewhat foolish but determined to do all I could, I jotted down the time of Holmes' departure.

After all of the instructions, after witnessing Holmes anxious demeanor, the actual meeting between Tallowfield and Holmes was remarkably brief. Holmes was shown into the office. Tallowfield rose from his seat, setting aside the sheet of paper he had been writing on and placing the pen carefully on the desk. Holmes spoke. Tallowfield listened. It was clear to me Holmes was deeply uncomfortable as he spoke to the frowning Tallowfield. Tallowfield nodded, then reached to the bronze bust atop his desk. He spoke a short sentence, lifted his hand from the bust and sat down. Tallowfield returned to his correspondence. Holmes was out of the office before the man picked up his pen. I jotted down the time the interview ended.

Part of me expected Tallowfield to hurry to a secret compartment or open a safe. He did no such thing, simply finished writing, set aside his pen and unhurriedly left the office for a part of the house I could not observe.

I completed my notes, picked up the field glasses again and searched the empty office. Nothing of note stood out, though I found my attention drawn to the bronze bust on the man's desk. I focused as tightly on the object as I was able. It was difficult to be certain but I thought the bust was of an African man, a crown of some sort upon his head.

Seeing the bronze, knowing Tallowfield had been a Royal Marine, I was put in mind of recent stories from the kingdom of Benin. Holmes was not normally interested in international affairs except on those occasions when they intersected with his obsession with all things criminal. When the Royal Marines, under the command of Admiral Harry Rawson, attacked the city of Benin in retaliation for the murder of the British vice consul general and his travelling party, Holmes set aside his customary apathy for international politics to condemn the exercise as simple theft on a grand scale. The Benin royal palace was looted during the punitive expedition, its treasures hauled off by the marines while the King of Benin, referred to as the Oba, was exiled from his realm. I wondered if Tallowfield had been in western Africa during those events and if the bust on his desk was a reminder of his time in the service. It seemed likely, at least the timing seemed to fit.

§

Behind me, I heard the sound of Holmes' voice. Setting down my field glasses, I scribbled a quick note regarding my speculation about the bronze bust, wrote the time of Holmes' return and turned to greet my friend.

"Watson?" Holmes said, his gaze falling on me. "Oh, of course, we were supposed to meet here, were we not?"

"That's correct." I assured him, watching his manner carefully. He seemed less anxious than he had been before going to meet Tallowfield. My first impression was that the short meeting must have gone quite well. Yet, doubt is a terrible curse, there seemed a vagueness to my friend that was not at all in his customary nature. I held out the list of observations I had compiled.

Holmes stared at the folded sheet of paper. "What is this?"

"My observations of your meeting with Tallowfield," I explained. Holmes looked at me politely but bewildered, as if he had forgotten the solemn instructions he had so forcefully given to me.

"Oh," Holmes waved his hand. "That won't be necessary, I am convinced Tallowfield is not involved in any matter requiring my attention."

"Holmes, I must insist."

Reluctantly, Holmes took the list. He read it over quickly. "I don't see how this will help," the detective complained.

"Yet you must keep it." I instructed my friend, feeling somewhat bewildered myself. Reaching into my pocket, I withdrew the first envelope. Holmes betrayed no sign of recognition as I handed it to him.

"And this is?" Holmes asked.

"Holmes, are you well? Surely you recognise the letter, written by your hand, that you instructed me to give to you."

Yet it was clear by his troubled expression that he did not. Holmes sat in the booth and tore open the envelope. He read a few lines, then glanced up from the page with an angry expression. "Is this some sort of joke?"

I blinked in surprise, uncertain what to make of Holmes' display. Fortunately, I was in no doubt as to what I should do next. I drew the second envelope from my pocket. Holmes snatched it from my hand, tore it open and began to read. I must admit, seeing the colour drain from my friend's face was disturbing. A palsy seemed to travel up his arms, shaking the paper as he held it.

"Perhaps a brandy before we continue with our day," I suggested.

Holmes glanced up from his letter, his expression grateful. I ordered the drinks. We drank in silence. Holmes seemed to have no words. He assumed a posture of profound thought and deep discomfort. Though I offered my assistance with whatever was troubling him, for clearly something seemed to be distressing the detective, Holmes simply ignored my concern and spoke as little as he was able. We took a cab back to Baker Street, where I saw him safely to the door before continuing home.

Holmes had not asked for the return of the third letter.

§

It would be an interminable wait, I knew, yet I pressed through the remainder of the day with the letter close to hand and a resolution not to succumb to the anxiety I felt.

Night fell. Both my medical training and military service had instilled in me a high regard for sleep taken before action. Dawn broke over the city; I took the unopened envelope and went about my daily routine. When the messenger finally arrived, at a quarter of noon, I was pulling on my coat and donning my hat in preparation for the journey to Baker Street.

Climbing the steps, I found Holmes waiting at the door. He looked utterly drained, pale, with dark bags under bloodshot eyes. Another difficult night and, although I had seen my friend in the throes of withdrawal and under the emotional extremes his work inflicted upon his soul, he looked to me on the brink of a shattering breakdown. I entered the rooms and Holmes quickly closed the door after me, turning the key in the lock and kicking a shim under the door to secure it in place.

"Is that necessary?" I asked. Holmes replied with a breath of laughter as he collapsed sidewise into his chair. He wore his robe, its color spilling about his paleness like a bloodstain.

"Did you open it?" Holmes asked, his arm thrown over his eyes as he faced the ceiling. Pulling the letter from my pocket, I held the sealed envelope out for his inspection. Lifting his arm, turning his head, a ghost of a smile tugged at his lips.

"Watson, you truly are a most remarkable man."

"I've always believed so," I agreed. "Holmes, what the devil is—"

Holmes held up his hand. Wearily, he rolled from the chair and walked across the room before stopping to pull on a pair of gloves. That done, Holmes disappeared into his bedroom and returned with an object wrapped in a thick blanket. Placing the weighty object on the floor before me, Holmes looked up and found my gaze.

"Under no circumstances are you to touch this," Holmes warned. I nodded and he unwrapped the object. From beneath the blanket emerged the regal features of one of the Obas of Benin, rendered exquisitely in bronze. Up close it was a stunning work, remarkable for its detail and for the air of authority the sculpted metal face seemed to radiate.

"Is this the bronze from Tallowfield's desk?"

Holmes winced at the name, visibly recoiling from the utterance. It took him a moment to regain himself. When he did, he said, "We will not be using ... that name. I will explain as best I am able but we will be referring to that person as 'the marine'."

"If you insist."

"I do, and yes, that is the bronze bust described in your notes from yesterday."

"It really is quite amazing. I feel as if it might command me back to war. I assume you had a good reason for stealing it."

"Indeed. I stole it to save Britain, the Empire, and every person within it from unspeakable tyranny." Holmes stated, paused, then added, "Or, at least, to preserve the lesser tyranny of the existing arrangement."

"Well," I replied. "As long as you had a good reason."

Holmes managed a chuckle, the expression restoring my hope and confidence in my friend's ability to endure whatever affliction he was suffering. "You recall our conversation regarding ... the marine? It was — dear Lord, was it only two nights ago? It feels as if months have passed. I was troubled by your reaction to the descriptions I offered but, after you left—"

"I was annoyed, Holmes, for which I must apologize. I had no intention of causing you distress."

"No, Watson," Holmes insisted, leaning forward in his seat and grasping my forearm with a desperate strength. "You behaved entirely correctly, though I did not understand in the moment. Had you reacted in any other way, I shudder to think what might have occurred. I looked at your notes, the description of the cabbie and the marine, confronted the variance between the two descriptions you brought to my attention. I could not deny the obvious when it was laid out so plainly but I did not – could not – explain the cause. Yet it seemed so little a thing, a small, nearly imperceptible flaw. I set out to correct my error, putting pencil to paper and writing a full description of the marine. You know what I wrote?"

"An amiable fellow, incapable of wrong-doing?"

"Exactly!" Holmes barked. Regaining his composure, he repeated himself in a calmer tone. "Exactly. Had I not written it out, I would never have observed the difference but, looking down on the meager spill of words I could not deny the description was lacking. Admittedly the fault still did not appear as ghastly as it shortly would. A small thing, I assured myself as I repeated the exercise, confident even as I was writing that I was performing my task as fully as I was capable. This was, in my mind, still a small, insignificant failure. Then again, you know my axiom concerning little things."

"I do, they are infinitely the most important."

"Correct. When I looked at what I had written, found it identical to what I had written previously, I felt the first stirrings of unease. Logically, there was a simple explanation but it chilled me as no other deduction has before. The fault may lie in my reason. A test was necessary. I filled pages with descriptions of those I had encountered before and after my meeting with the marine. Having performed these exercises adequately, I felt somewhat reassured and returned to my original task. Though I felt no different completing the marine's description as when I was completing the others, the results returned the same two damnable points as before. My reaction, I admit, was not to my credit. I experienced a panic I have never known before, a doubt in my abilities which very nearly unmanned me. If I could no longer rely on the authority of my reason, what would become of me?"

"It was at this point I recalled the example of Detective Sergeant Unsworth," Holmes continued. "A thought occurred to me; I was behaving exactly as he had. The annoyance you expressed when I offered my description of the marine was precisely the irritation I had shown when he described the very same man. His inability to describe the marine was exactly the inability I now suffered. It seemed a flimsy chain of logic but I clutched it like a drowning man. What if something had occurred to us during our confrontation with the marine? I could not imagine what would cause us to behave as we had, but I could not deny the similarity of our circumstances."

"Is that when you called for me?"

"Not at that moment, it was still the dead of night. I was not idle however, I can assure you of that. With this new direction to investigate, I set to work. And because I was unable to trust to my own abilities, I documented everything as completely as I was able. It was possible, perhaps inevitable, that I would suffer another incident which would compromise my ability to conduct a proper investigation. Therefore it was imperative to leave myself a trail to follow, a chain of unassailable logic that could not be shaken by even the most hostile of minds. I dispatched correspondence which would result in as complete a description of the marine's activities and character as possible. I worked as a consultant to myself, composing lists of observations which would advance my case should I risk another encounter. In short, I arranged as complete an investigation as my not inconsiderable resources allowed."

"And, as I did so, I discovered truths regarding my own compromised reason. Quickly I discovered that when I referred to the suspect by name I was utterly unable to believe him capable of any crime, no matter how small. Even writing his name caused my entire investigation to tremble. Yet when I referred to the man as 'X', such as one would do with a math problem, my logic remained crystal clear. It was curious, like a wound across my reason, one which I was unable to resist probing despite the pain resulting from the exploration. It was draining in a way no other case has been. Even in the darkest of circumstances, I have always been able to trust to my reason. Until now; it was a difficult night."

"I imagine so," I sympathised.

"Before the dawn, I had set the whole affair in motion. I learned a great deal regarding the marine's history and ambitions yet, despite the unimpeachable sources of the information, very little of it seemed sensible. The marine was recently discharged from service and, despite not having completed his full term, received a full pension. Despite his record showing no particular deeds of gallantry, the recommendations he obtained upon his discharge were universally glowing and, more curiously, rather repetitive in the wording of their endorsements. Though they came from several different officers, spread out over a wide enough geography to deny any collusion, they all used the same turns of phrase. Tracing through his record I was able to pinpoint when his superiors changed their opinions of the young man. February Nineteenth, Eighteen Ninety-Seven. Prior to this date every record detailed an undisciplined soldier with little regard for authority, afterwards every entry praises his abilities despite a lack of specific action to inspire such testaments."

I pondered the situation. "Where was he stationed?"

Holmes glanced to the bronze face on the floor between us. "West Africa. Benin. The marine was part of the punitive expedition that captured the African city and sacked the royal palace."

"Perhaps he distinguished himself during the action there," I suggested.

"A possibility," Holmes admitted. "If so, it was not recorded in his record, nor in the official dispatches. Benin was a bloody, terrible thing. I believe we discussed it at the time. My opinion has not changed."

I recalled the conversation, having followed the event in the papers. By all reports the Benin massacre had been a nasty business indeed. Holmes had called the affair theft on an international scale, an unconscionable act by Her Majesty's Empire. Future generations, he insisted, would pay the price for today's arrogant crimes.

"More curious still, the marine's situation following his return to London was a tale of remarkable fortune. Having received his full pension and the glowing recommendations of his superiors, the marine quickly made the acquaintance of the wealthy industrialist Franklin Beldon, and his daughter Ellen who was at that time engaged to be married to Jeremy Claverhouse. There were, apparently, no witnesses to this introduction. No one knows how they met, it is entirely possible the marine simply walked up to the grand Beldon home and introduced himself. With alarming speed, however, the marine listed the Beldon house as his primary address and Jeremy Claverhouse found himself bereft of his betrothed. The marine was announced as a vice president of Beldon's companies and Ellen Beldon was married, all with unseemly haste."

"From the cramped hold of a ship off the coast of West Africa to the vistas of London high society," I observed. "That is an extraordinary change in circumstance, nearly too fantastic to believe. I recall Claverhouse spoke of a letter from Ellen Beldon suggesting she was being held against her will. I looked for her at the home but I saw no trace of her."

"So dramatic a change of station is bound to cause gossip," Holmes allowed. "What is remarkable is how little of it attached itself to the Beldons or to the marine."

"You discovered all this before summoning me? That was a productive morning." Seeing my friend's expression, I hastened to add, "Was there more?"

"Two other facts which seemed relevant," Holmes admitted. "And a conclusion, which you know. The first was this: Since making the Beldon house his residence, the marine had not been seen outside the dwelling. Apparently, as near as I could tell, he has not set a foot outside the door since entering. Unsworth found that, he reported it to me when we discussed the Claverhouse burglary. The second fact was that the marine had a confederate, another former marine who had been discharged earlier. This was the suspect seen at the Claverhouse home the day of the theft. He has also been seen at the Beldon places of business acting as the marine's liaison. It all appeared a very peculiar arrangement to me, significant in ways I did not then understand."

"And your conclusion?"

"While I had more information before me, I lacked the insight to string the pearls together. Obviously, I needed more data. Yet, with my own reason compromised, I could not risk returning to the Beldon's residence without certain safeguards in place. Adopting a disguise, I returned and scouted the location, found a place from which a third party could observe the marine's office undetected. I learned what I could from a safe distance but it was still maddeningly insufficient. Despite the danger, I knew I had no choice but to return and confront the marine again. My belief at the time, having learned all that I had, was that knowing what had apparently occurred previously would prevent me from succumbing a second time. Utter vanity, pure stupidity. Thank goodness I took the precautions I did, despite my doubts. And thank goodness you were there, Watson. Without you I … well, I shudder to think what might have happened."

"Holmes, I saw the whole meeting. Nothing remarkable occurred during your encounter with the marine. At least, nothing I could see."

"But you did see it! It wasn't something visible but it was no less impossible for that," Holmes explained. "You saw me walk into the marine's office, saw him as he spoke to me – no more than a couple of sentences – and bore witness as I turned and left. You must understand, when I entered that room I was full of suspicion and when I left, scant seconds later, I was completely convinced he was utterly blameless. I believed my preparation would prevent events playing out as they had before. I could not have been more mistaken."

Holmes released a long sigh, one echoing with regret and broken pride. Leaning back in his seat, composing himself, his gaze met mine fully. "You must have wondered, Watson, what was in the letters I gave you."

"I did."

"The first letter was simply a summary," Holmes explained. "A note informing me that I might be suffering from an aberration in my reason, advising me to return to Baker Street and review the information I had gathered. It was not strongly worded. I was convinced it would not be necessary, that all I had discovered would still be with me when I read it. I was wrong."

"The second letter was worded more strongly. Although I naively thought it would not be required, I wrote that under no circumstances was I to express anger with you, Watson. I wrote, in terms I knew I would be forced to accept, of the great debt I owed you, not just in this case but across my career. I told myself that, regardless of how irritating I found you in that moment, I was certain your behaviour was not at fault. The letter repeated that my own reason might be compromised and not for the first time. It urged me, as if I were a simpleton incapable of instruction, to return to Baker Street and the files waiting for me there. Files I had forgotten, though I had written them only hours before. It was, I admit, a blow to my pride and I cautioned myself not to lash out at those dear to me. Here I was, Watson, returning to a scene I had already examined. Replaying an interview I could no longer recall. These things are simply not in my nature. Having to do so was a blow, not just to my professional pride but to my very identity. The despair threatening me was intolerable."

"And this letter?" I asked, holding up the third sealed envelope. "The one meant for me?"

"The most dire scenario, my worst fears given form. I had forgotten I wrote it until this morning, it did not occur to me until I retraced the logic resulting in the first two letters. At that point I knew I must have written a third. You may keep it, if you like."

"What did you write in it?"

"I don't recall the wording, Watson, but I expect it lists events to be alert to and, should a number of them occur, to urge you to leave Britain with those dearest to you. It predicts the fall of the Empire and the end of British democracy."

"Holmes?"

"Authority, Watson," Holmes explained. "It is at the heart of the entire affair, from the petty theft at the Claverhouse residence to the potential collapse of the nation. The string that lines the pearls together. Consider the marine, his relationship to authority is straightforward enough. The officer commands it, he performs it. How grand it would be for the marine to give commands and watch while the world performed his bidding."

"Every soldier has daydreams," I chuckled. "Life doesn't work that way."

"But what if it did?" Holmes continued, his voice charged with a fervour that was unlike his normal aspect but, at the same time, completely like the inner fervour he concealed. "What if you were a Royal Marine who had just looted the royal palace of Benin and found, in your share of spoils, an object that allowed you to command anyone? What would you do? How much would you dare?"

This remark gave me pause, I saw the first outlines of what Holmes was proposing. "Leave the service, acquire sufficient wealth to live in comfort, find a wife. I see how it fits the pattern."

"I cannot explain how such an object came to be," Holmes continued, a gleam in his eye bordering on maniacal. "Such a history is unavailable to us here and now. If there is such a thing as a loving God, it will remain unknown. If someone used such an influence to become the King of Benin, can you imagine the struggle required to wrest him from the seat of power? Afterwards, a new King, what would he do with such an object? Destroy it? Would it not be safer to hide it away within the palace, keep it safe should such power ever again be required? There is a tale here which we can only imagine. How appropriate that this object, this talisman of complete authority, should fall into the hands of a soldier seeking plunder to carry back to his distant kingdom. A poison pill among the stolen feast, a curse destined to topple the oppressors."

"Holmes—"

The detective raised his hands, palms turned outward. "I am getting ahead of myself but consider the facts. After Benin, the marine hurriedly leaves the service and returns to London. He quickly establishes himself in a new address, a new situation, gains himself a new wife. Yet he knows his authority is the result of the talisman, he dares not leave it unguarded. He finds himself an agent, willing or otherwise. He arranges matters to his benefit. There are difficulties he does not anticipate, Claverhouse for one. If only the man would come to him the whole problem could be made to disappear but he refuses all his invitations. The theft takes care of the matter and when the Detective Sergeant arrives he is easily handled with a simple command. Unexpectedly another detective appears, but what of it? He is dealt with as easily as the previous. And if he stubbornly returns once more? Every power has limits and it is clear the detective is struggling, barely able to utter a word against the marine. A command is repeated and, tail between his legs, the accuser slinks away.

"It was your notes, Watson, that led me to the truth. You described the marine laying his hand on the bust and speaking – briefly – to me, as well as the meek manner in which I retreated. Even so, I was slow to believe. I am indebted to you."

"Holmes," I said slowly, not yet convinced of all he had said.

Holmes nodded. "In the small hours of last night, I returned to the marine's home. After confirming the notes from my previous reconnoiter, I entered the home and sought the bust. I found it in the safe. Knowing the marine had only recently taken up residence, I was able to find the combination written on an envelope tucked under the desk blotter. I took all precautions available to me. My knowledge of burglary is considerable if only theoretical in nature. Even so, such an enterprise is prone to discovery by a sleepless man."

"You were discovered?"

"By the marine himself. In a panic, he lunged for the bust. Desperately he barked at me to return the effigy to him. I dodged him and, with the bust in my grip, told him to remain still and silent. He did so. Immediately. It was unnerving, to say the least. He stood there in his bed clothes, waiting for instruction."

"Dear lord."

"He had no reason to cease his attack. I was clearly in the wrong, trespassing in his home, taking what, by English law, was his. I stared at him in shock and, even in that dark moment, I found I could not believe him capable of any wrong-doing. He was, in my view, such an amiable fellow."

"What happened next?"

"I asked him how he had come by this bronze. He answered, holding back nothing. He explained all he had discovered about its remarkable ability to control others. Everything he had done since coming into possession of it, everything he planned to do. He held nothing back. I heard the entire tale from his own lips and I was horrified."

"How did you get away?"

"Simplicity itself Watson. I instructed the marine to forget my intrusion. If only I had left it there, said no more, but I also told him he must make right the wrongs he has committed. It was an ill-conceived command but, as I am sure you comprehend, I had little time to consider my words. For his part, the marine simply nodded an acknowledgement of my instruction. I left with the bronze, encountering no further obstacles. The remainder of the night was spent waiting for Scotland Yard to knock on my door and arrest me."

"But, clearly, they did not."

"Oh, they knocked on the door shortly after dawn. Inspector Gregson. I had spoken to him yesterday, he aided me in my inquiries regarding the marine. I answered, resigned to my fate. Gregson asked me if I was aware of the marine's suicide hours earlier. I informed him I was not. Gregson wanted to know if I had any suspicions regarding the man, seeing as I had been so desperate for information about him the day before. I told him I had harboured some doubts regarding the death of Franklin Beldon but that I was unable to attach any wrong-doing to the marine. It seemed unlikely any crime had been committed. The marine's suicide might be attributed to the horrors he had encountered in Africa but I was not certain. Gregson and I shared tea as we spoke, it was all very cordial. Within the privacy of my thoughts however, I experienced a deeper fear than I have yet known. Gregson thanked me for my help and bade me to look after my health as I seemed somewhat drawn. I thanked him and wished him well in his investigation."

Holmes rose from his seat and went to fix something for us to drink. I remained seated, attempting to make sense of all I had heard while staring at the face, rendered in bronze, of the Oba.

When Holmes returned, handing me a drink, I asked him. "Do you really think the marine could have threatened the entire Empire? I mean—"

"Oh yes," Holmes said with confidence. "The marine would inevitably have become our sovereign. How could anyone resist such a lure? Perhaps he would have been a reasonable monarch, but perhaps not. What is clear is that he would not have been bound by any reasonable counsel. It is not something he would have considered necessary. And, this is the galling thing of it, such a fate would not be undeserved. There is a certain justice to it, all things considered."

"What will you do now?" I asked.

"Are you asking if I plan to rule this green and pleasant land myself? The idea is not without temptation. Think of the reforms I could enact, the good my unquestioned authority could accomplish. Don't look so startled, Watson, all men have daydreams. No. I will not attempt any such thing. I feel I have an obligation to Detective Sergeant Unsworth to ascertain if the commands given to him by the marine resulted in any lasting damage and, if so, to do my best to make right the wrongs inflicted on him. Then there is the matter of Ellen Beldon, the undoubted victim of the marine's authority. If I feel I can undo some of the harm done to her, I will attempt it. I am loathe to touch the thing however, I abhor the thought of giving instruction with an authority not my own. Once I have done what I can for the unfortunates affected by this tragedy, I will take myself to the seaside. I will consign the bust, splendid as it is, to the ocean floor. Far from the affairs of men."

Contaminated Sample

he bespectacled man entered as so many did, with a drawn, downtrodden expression and the furtive fidgeting marking those who had exhausted all options, save for Sherlock Holmes. The client moved less like a ship on a friendly wind and more as a soldier on a march against terrible odds. The gentleman's round face was set in a grimace until he caught sight of Holmes' chemical equipment. In an instant the grim countenance was transformed into one of cherubic delight. His hands reached out and gently tested the arrangement of glass and the quality of the tools. From his widening grin, it was clear our visitor approved of all he found. Fortunately for the lodging's atmosphere, none of Holmes' noxious experiments were currently in progress. The flames were extinguished, the fluids drained and the equipment cleaned and ready for the next endeavour. After a moment, the visitor nodded in satisfaction.

"I say, this is quite a well-done arrangement. Efficient, given the limited space, well-maintained and well-stocked, capable of quite a range of experiments. Even so, I suspect ventilation would be a problem in a room of this size."

"You have no idea," I commented. Holmes winced as my barb found its mark.

"It serves my needs," Holmes told the visitor. "This is my associate, Doctor Watson, you may trust to his discretion. Please, have a seat. Your letter stated the matter was urgent but, beyond that, was frustratingly vague. In fact, Mr. Plaskett, after reading it I was not inclined to grant you the appointment you requested."

"Oh," Mr. Plaskett said, taking his seat. He was a man of no great height, somewhat stout, with a greying hairline retreating across the battlefield slope of his head. Behind his round spectacles, bright eyes seemed to look upon the world with delighted surprise and no small amount of wonder. Even so, I saw marks of strain in the corners of his eyes and the dark hollows under them. "May I ask what changed your mind?"

"A note sent from a mutual acquaintance, Sir Norman Lockyer, who spoke highly of your character and urged me to offer whatever assistance I can, at his expense. When I asked him as to the nature of your problem, he replied that he had absolutely no idea, nor did he care to know, but he was certain you were incapable of dishonor. It is rare to find an academic offer such unreserved praise, particularly for a fellow academic."

"Oh, I'm not really an academic," Plaskett insisted. "Not anymore. Sir Lockyer flatters me."

"Perhaps, but the chalk dust on your jacket informs me you still hold a place in the halls of academia," Holmes observed. "Based on the chalk, I would conclude your field of study to be mathematics or physics, as the chalk dust texture suggests calcium rather than gypsum. Of course, the copy of *Annalen der Physik* in your jacket pocket makes such observations unnecessary, it marks you a physicist as plainly as a crown marks a king."

"Well spotted, sir!" Plaskett congratulated Holmes.

"Your letter was straightforward enough, revealing you as

one accustomed to describing complex matters. You wish me to accompany you to Cheshire on a matter both urgent and important but you fail to describe the problem inspiring such concern. Rest assured that whatever you tell us will be held in the strictest confidence. Whatever difficulty brings you here, I urge you to be frank and forthright about it. Watson and I have investigated all manner of scandals, both great and small. Your tale, no matter how sordid, will not shock us."

"I understand your frustration regarding my secrecy," Plaskett admitted, his voice unapologetic. "There are, I assure you, valid reasons for my silence. Doctor Watson, will you also be involved in this matter?"

"Should Holmes accept the case, I'm happy to offer whatever assistance I can."

"Of course," Plaskett nodded, taking a deep breath as he considered his situation before continuing. "Gentlemen, I am in desperate need of help yet, bound by circumstances beyond my control, unable to simply and plainly ask for assistance. Here is what I suggest, if you'll indulge me, I will tell you a story. My story. For reasons which will soon be obvious, I've never told this tale. And I caution you, if you repeat any of it, I shall be bound by oath to deny it. Such deception is hurtful to my nature but I am bound by oath, both to a higher cause and to a dear friend. When I have told as much as I can, I will describe the conditions allowing me to accept your assistance in the critical matter which plagues me now. When my story is finished, I will leave so you may discuss the matter among yourselves, and will return tomorrow to hear your verdict. If you cannot accept these conditions, I will bear you no ill will and will seek help elsewhere. If you are willing to burden yourself with my case, and agree to my terms, only then can I fully explain my problem. Does this seem acceptable to you both?"

209

I agreed readily, eager to hear Plaskett's tale. It was obvious from the emotion in his eyes and the way his restless hands twitched that the poor fellow was under strain. Holmes, on the other hand, was reluctant. "A great deal of bother," Holmes remarked. "I assure you, Mr. Plaskett, Watson and I have heard all sorts of confessions, some of which would shock you to your very core. You may rely on our discretion, as so many others, including Sir Lockyer, have. There seems no point to your elaborate precautions, save for the wasting of my time."

"I beg you, Mr. Holmes," Plaskett pleaded to the detective. "Indulge me."

"Very well," Holmes reluctantly agreed. "Though, you should be aware, I am doing so only because of Sir Lockyer's sincere recommendation of your character. Tell us as much as you are able."

Plaskett appeared relieved. Leaning back in his chair, drawing a deep breath through his nostrils, he spoke. "How strange, I have clutched these secrets so tightly and so long that I almost do not know how to begin. Twenty years ago, I was a young man seeking my doctorate in physics. I burned with a desire to place my name next to the great minds in my field, to earn a place among the worthy minds pressing back the shadows of ignorance. I was devoted to the study of physics with a near religious fervor and my ambition, my desire for personal glory, drove me far more than I understood in my youth. Despite the failings apparent to my aged eye now, I still feel a fondness for the young and desperate fool I once was.

"The subject of my doctorate concerned the study of magnetism. I devised a clever series of experiments hoping to reveal some of the mysteries that swing the compass point. Perhaps later, if you're interested, I can describe those experiments in more detail. What is relevant is that

I had suspended a quantity of iron fillings, dust really, in a solution to better observe the lines of force of various magnetic arrangements and intensities. The hour was late, I was alone in my laboratory and had just completed, verified and recorded a series of difficult observations. As I recall, I was quite exhausted in body though my mind was overly alert and enjoying the satisfaction of having completed a challenging task. I decided to indulge myself. Since the equipment was still active, I was able to manipulate the magnets such that the iron fillings danced as if borne upon unseen ocean waves. A sight few men have seen and I found the spectacle oddly soothing.

"I had not been playing with the equipment long before duty again intruded on my relaxation. Standing, I put away my notebook. When I turned my attention back to the iron fillings, I beheld the impossible. The metal, still under the influence of the magnets, had abandoned the lines of force I left them in and rearranged themselves into a series of letters, clear as any written by the hand of man. They spelled out my name. I was aghast.

"Examining the sight, a blatant violation of the second law of thermodynamics, I was surprised to see more letters forming. They were instructions, bidding me to increase the magnetic intensity if I wished to learn more, to decrease the intensity should to avoid further communication. Rather than commit to either of these options, I set about checking my equipment for signs of tampering."

"A reasonable action," Holmes agreed.

"The results of which, I'm afraid, were entirely unreasonable. I had built the equipment myself, I knew each detail of its construction, yet I found nothing amiss. It is difficult to describe how I felt in that moment, my heart was pounding madly, as if I stood with my toes extended over a great chasm, but my mind struggled to accept the reality of the letters waiting so patiently in the solution. Part of me was certain I was being made to look a fool; another part of my thoughts urged me to simply switch everything off and carry on as if nothing had happened. Yet, whether it was a trick or not, I wished to understand what I was seeing. With the dials I increased the magnetic intensity. The fillings swam apart and reformed—"

"What did they say?" I asked, somewhat breathlessly.

"Firstly, they offered an apology," Plaskett said. "I have always remembered that, the kindness of it. I spent all that night in my laboratory. Indeed, I spent the next two weeks alone in there, refusing to admit any of my colleagues. Together with the unseen hand arranging the iron dust into readable letters, we established the beginnings of a vocabulary based not on modulated sound waves but on variations in magnetic intensities. My friend, whose nature I did not then understanding, apologised for daring to contact me. Through our communication I was becoming – how shall I describe it? A chemical term seems most apt – a contaminated sample. You see, my friend – and, really, I have no better term to describe the intelligence I converse with – holds a comprehension of the universe far beyond what mankind has achieved. As a result of our exchanges, my understanding of the universe has been advanced beyond anything my ambitious younger self could have dreamt. There is, naturally, a cost to such knowledge. I've been tainted with insights I have not earned, understandings none on our globe could formulate. I am a contaminated sample, one which must be discarded lest it spoil the experiment. In exchange for all I have learned from my unseen friend I swore an oath not to publish any scientific papers, or to promote any of my own scientific theories, as they all come from a contaminated source."

"You are employed by the university," Holmes observed.

"Where I help other men advance science," Plaskett

explained. "Science remains my great love, how could it not? I fancy I know more of the secrets and extraordinary grace of the universe than any man ever has, more than any man will for generations. Yet any contribution I would make to the great cause would be tainted by friend's insight, comprehensions as yet unearned."

"Surely the truth, particularly scientific truth," Holmes argued, "remains true regardless of who makes the discovery. Whether or not it is earned seems irrelevant to me. Whether you measure the freezing point of water in the Celsius or Imperial scale, the water itself freezes at the same temperature."

Plaskett smiled, pleased with Holmes objections. "Ah, yes, Mr. Holmes," Plaskett nodded. "I once thought as you do. However—forgive me for saying so—you are very wrong. Take it from one who has struggled under this burden for longer and more diligently than you've been able to. How shall I explain it? You see, on the surface, any two experiments yielding the same result reveals a truth of the universe. To take your example, something as basic as the freezing point of water, how it has been determined appears to make no difference. However to a scientifically advanced intelligence, the study of the two separate experiments yields insight. A man in the frozen Arctic's experiment to determine the freezing point will be wildly different to the method conducted in a vast, African desert which has never known the cold touch of frost. To truly understand the scientific process, valuable insights can be obtained from the comparison of the experiments. No such insight can be gathered from a man who simply states the freezing point of water as a rote, memorized fact without any scientific process attached. My friend and his people are keenly interested in how science works, gaining insights from the experiments of those whose manner of thinking is wildly different than their own. Applying perspectives gained from our attempts to unlock basic truths, they apply them to the complicated problems they struggle with. Have I explained myself, Mr. Holmes? While our discoveries are ancient knowledge to them, they observe and delight in the methods by which we achieve our progress."

"An interesting arrangement," Holmes replied. "Your explanation gives me food for thought. Still, it does not explain why – your friend – was compelled to contact you. Nor does it offer any insight into why he chose such an unusual and laborious method of correspondence."

"Ah, you are suspicious," Plaskett observed. "And rightly so! You are a detective, after all, accustomed to the falsehoods and treachery men inflict on one another. As to our method of communication, it is simply the most efficient and non-disruptive available. Why he was compelled to reach out in the first place: He needed my help, to protect our reality, to save our world."

"Save the world?" I repeated, somewhat taken aback by the ordinary manner in which Plaskett muttered so extraordinary a claim.

"Quite so," Plaskett admitted. "Now, after conversing for a span of more than twenty years, my unseen friend asks for my help once more. Yet, with the stakes so high, I find myself in need of assistance. I cannot, in good faith, proceed alone. I am no longer a young man, nor as fearless as I once was. I have become more aware of the consequences of failure and I do not wish my shortcomings to jeopardize the fate of our planet. Thus, I seek your help Mr. Holmes, and yours as well, Dr. Watson, but before I do I must insist on the following condition.

"Upon your honour, you must promise as I have: Not to publish, or share what you learn from our experience together. Not in a scientific publication, not even in any of the more common literature. All I have thus far revealed is as nothing and, as I have said, I will be forced to deny it in any event. However, if we proceed together you will become, like me, contaminated samples and, as such, forced to isolate yourselves from the great scientific struggle that defines mankind. It may not, at first, seem much to ask but, I assure you, I do not make this request lightly. It is possible my concerns are nothing, that together we'll discover only a mundane set of coincidences waiting in Cheshire. However, there is a chance you'll experience something extraordinary, revealing truths you feel need to be shared with the world. You may come to curse this day, the day which we first met, as I have occasionally cursed the day I read the first letters in my laboratory. Yet I must hold you to your word."

Holmes stirred uncomfortably in his chair. I saw his hand twitch towards the pipe on the side table, but he resisted the urge to take it. "I have published some monographs—"

"And I have read them," Plaskett replied. "Matters regarding the solving of crime are not included in this promise, though I should like to review them before publication for my piece of mind. Likewise, should Dr. Watson discover a cure for a disease or a surgical technique that may improve the lot of men, he is free to publish under the same conditions. I am, however, quite insistent that none of what I reveal to you may be released to the wider world. To do so would, in the end, reduce the glory of mankind's intellect and spoil the efforts of future scientists across the globe."

"Well," I leaned forward, entranced by the story I had just heard. "I do not need to think any further, I am ready to give you my word now."

"Yet I am not ready to accept it, not until you've considered your promise thoroughly. I shall return tomorrow morning, after you have had time to discuss my request. Should you accept my terms, I would advise you to bring supplies sufficient for a journey to Cheshire. I've no doubt you've many questions—how could you not?—I regret I cannot say more at this time. Until tomorrow, gentlemen, and know that regardless of what you decide, I appreciate you listening to my story."

Having spoken all he would, the scientist made his way out to the street. By the time he had hailed a cab, Holmes was drawing heavily from his cherished cherrywood. Holmes and I discussed the matter, our conversation returning again and again to the implausible details of Plaskett's story and the condition of the man's reason. Holmes allowed that he had observed no sign of mental imbalance in our visitor, beyond the words he had spoken, and I could tell he was deeply intrigued by the possibility of learning more. For my part, having no scientific ambitions to speak of, I was quite willing to offer my pledge. It seemed I was giving up nothing.

When I tried to engage Holmes in speculation regarding the nature of Plaskett's unseen friend, he was frustratingly unwilling to consider the matter. He scoffed at my suggestion of ghosts, Holmes sneered at any opinion which verged on Spiritualism, and laughed out loud at the idea of intelligences from other worlds. I felt he was being rather unfair but, sensing his willingness to commit his aid, I suffered his amusement with what good humor I could muster.

§

The next morning found us dressed for travel. Plaskett, the signs of another restless night clear on his face, arrived with a rucksack over his shoulder. Holmes subjected the man to a barrage of questions regarding possible future publications involving his obsessions: logic, chemistry and methods of crime solving. It was with chemistry Plaskett was most concerned. As a result of these negotiations, we nearly missed our train to Cheshire. Once we had settled in our seats, Plaskett at last took us into his confidence.

His tale was unlike anything I'd expected. Holmes leaned forward in his seat, reminding me of a great cat perched in a jungle tree, eager for prey and ready to pounce.

"Where shall I begin?" Plaskett asked in an unhurried voice I was certain endeared him to the students who attended his lectures. "Yes, Mr. Holmes, I can see you are anxious to focus on the practical tasks waiting in Cheshire. If you will indulge me a moment, I feel I must suggest a concept which – I promise – has a bearing on all that lies ahead."

Holmes grimaced but nodded.

"I would like to suggest to you a useful definition of reality, an understanding of the universe we occupy. My proposition is that reality is defined by the three dimensions: height, length and width, as well as a fourth we call time."

"While I see your argument," Holmes objected, "I don't consider time a dimension. However, in the interest of learning why we are travelling to Cheshire,—"

"Let us set aside the matter of time for now," Plaskett conceded. I had the impression he enjoyed the arguments Holmes threw his way, as one might enjoy an evenly matched game of rugby. "No objections, Dr. Watson? Very well, for our discussion we will accept three dimensions as being equal to one reality."

After pausing to give Holmes a chance to object, Plaskett continued. "Yesterday I told you of the first messages I received from my unseen friend and our struggle to find a method of communication between us. No doubt you wondered as to my friend's nature. Having received your promise, I can tell you that my friend exists in another reality."

Holmes frowned, then shook his head. "That does not make sense."

"Oh, but it does," Plaskett argued. "Believe me, gentlemen,

given the state I was in upon receiving my first message, I would have much preferred my friend to reveal himself as a ghost, or something divine. Let me remind you of what defines a reality—"

"Three dimensions!" I interrupted. "But, setting aside the question of time, only three dimensions exist, so there can only be one reality."

"An obvious fact," Plaskett agreed. "I recently read a monograph stating nothing is as deceptive as an obvious fact. Are there only three dimensions? There is no mathematical reason we need confine ourselves to such. Our senses perceive three dimensions but our maths can imagine a great deal more."

Holmes gave a grunt of reluctant agreement. I was, I admit, not as quick at grasping the concept.

"Let me explain it this way," Plaskett said, taking pity on a former army doctor. "I saw a violin in Holmes' place yesterday. Imagine such an instrument but instead of four separate strings, imagine only one string traveling from the tailpiece to loop around the nut. Each time the string is looped it shifts to another reality, another set of dimensions. At the waist, the strings appear quite separate but if you follow any of them you'll find there is only a single string. Now imagine our reality is one of those strings. We cannot perceive the others, they appear quite separate from our own, but they are in fact the same string. Does this help?"

I nodded uncertainly.

"My unseen friend exists on a different string, a different set of dimensions, than our own." Plaskett explained. "Now imagine we wanted to produce a pleasant note on one string and we do not care what happens to the others. Rather than drawing a bow across their string, they could produce the same note by plucking at another. Do you follow?"

Holmes was quick to leap on the inference. "You are

suggesting your 'unseen friend' contacted you because another reality threatens our own?"

"Just so," Plaskett nodded. "My unseen friend and his people enjoy a very advanced, very peaceful civilization that has thrived for eons. They study their universe, just as we study ours, and long ago discovered the existence of additional dimensions and how they combine to make distinct realities. They've studied these realities, the strings on our imagined violin, and found cultures living there more aggressive than their own. Some of these realities seek to cross dimensions, hoping to improve their reality to the detriment of others. Plucking one string to make a pleasant note in another."

"Why you?" Holmes asked. "Why, specifically, were you chosen?"

Plaskett chuckled at the question. "I wish I could say it was because I possessed special qualities my unseen friend recognised as invaluable, but that would be a lie. The incursion which my unseen friend detected was in London and, due to my experiments, I happened to be in the most magnetically active area of the city. They were able to manipulate the magnetic lines of force at far less energy cost than transferring actual matter between dimensions. They required an agent in our reality to investigate the possible incursion and I accepted the task. In exchange for my service, I have been rewarded with an understanding of the universe I could not have achieved without them."

"While being unable to contribute to science yourself," Holmes observed.

"There was a heavy cost to my actions," Plaskett admitted. "I do not regret it."

Holmes watched Plaskett carefully, examining his reactions. "What did your investigation reveal?"

"A warehouse down by the Thames, filled with intelligent creatures from another reality. I tried to communicate with them but they attacked me. If my unseen friend had not insisted I construct devices for my defense, I would surely have perished."

"Hmm," Holmes replied, his tone suggesting skepticism.

Plaskett grinned. "You still think I'm mad, don't you, Mr. Holmes?"

"It is a possibility I've not eliminated," Holmes admitted. "However, you are not my first client to suffer such an affliction, and your madness is intriguing. I take it your unseen friend has detected another incursion into our dimensions?"

"I'm afraid so," Plaskett confessed. "This time in Cheshire, specifically the town of Winsford. As soon as I learned of it I hurried there but, arriving at the specified location, I found nothing save an empty field. Given the nature of what I seek, that does not eliminate the possibility of an incursion. Investigating further would require putting myself at risk and, as I am the only person on the planet aware of the danger, I felt it prudent to seek assistance."

"A logical precaution," Holmes agreed. "I look forward to discovering what awaits us in Winsford."

"Just outside Winsford actually," Plaskett said. "But I am looking forward to it as well, Mr. Holmes. And I am glad you gentlemen are with me. Together we will unlock this riddle."

§

We arrived at our destination. It was exactly as Plaskett described, an empty field of grass.

"This is the spot?" Holmes frowned.

"It is, as near as I can calculate it," Plaskett said. "Rather disappointing, I'm afraid. I walked in a circle around the area but saw nothing amiss. However, if the incursion is only in two dimensions, or just a single one, it may be impossible to see. Therefore this is what I propose: You gentlemen remain here while I walk across this field. Should something ghastly happen to me, you must not approach me but remain distant."

"Something ghastly?" I asked. It was difficult to imagine such a thing, on such a bright morning in such a pleasant field.

"Yes. If there is an object existing in two, or even a single, dimension, and I walk into it, well, the results could be quite disturbing. You see, existing in less than three dimensions the edge of the incursion could pass through a three-dimensional object without any friction whatsoever."

Holmes nodded his understanding. "If it lacks a dimension any object could pass through without resistance. You'd be sliced by the sharpest, thinnest blade imaginable. It would make a sharpest razor seem blunt."

"Exactly," Plaskett agreed cheerfully, pleased with Holmes' reasoning. "If that happens, you must return to London. In my laboratory you will find my notes and equipment. Contact my unseen friend and ask him how to proceed. You'll find the address and instructions in here." Saying so, he handed his heavy rucksack to Holmes, who promptly handed it to me.

"Is there no other way?" I asked, shouldering the heavy burden.

"None that I can think of," And having admitted this, Plaskett left us and started to march across the field, his arms held out like a dowser searching for water.

"Good luck!" I called after him as he strode away.

"An interesting choice of words," Holmes mused at my side. "What would be considered better luck? Slicing yourself in two, or proving yourself mad?"

I didn't answer, my eyes fixed on the scientist striding bravely across the field. When Plaskett judged he had travelled far enough, he turned back to us, took three steps to his left and crossed the field again. The morning passed slowly, with

221

the professor traversing the field in a careful grid pattern without result. Once he'd completed his grid, he rejoined us.

"I don't understand," Plaskett complained. "This is the correct place, I am certain of it. I've no idea what to do next."

"I propose we return to town," Holmes said. "I saw an establishment there where we might refresh ourselves while deciding on a course of action. You've done your part, it is time to let me do mine."

Having no better suggestion, Plaskett agreed. Once the pub came into sight, Holmes went his own way, promising to meet up with us after making some inquiries.

§

"My calculations were correct." Plaskett complained as he finished his meal. "I don't see where I could have gone wrong."

It was at that moment that Holmes rejoined us. "You understand, Mr. Plaskett," Holmes said as he joined us at our table. "It would prove something of a relief to me to brand you a madman and move on to my next case. However, I'm afraid we cannot, in good faith, do so just yet. There is an ironic possibility which requires further investigation before washing my hands of this matter."

"What have you found?" Plaskett asked, but Holmes was engaged with the publican, ordering his lunch, forcing Plaskett to wait for his answer. Turning back to the scientist, Holmes asked, "What is Winsford famous for?"

The scientist blinked at the unexpected question, clearly having no idea what Holmes was driving at. Being more accustomed with the detective's ways, I offered a tentative answer. "Salt?"

"Well done, Watson," Holmes said. "Winsford is, in fact, home to sixty-six different salt operations."

"Salt operations?" Plaskett asked.

"Salt mines," I explained, gratified to see understanding brighten Plaskett's expression.

"One of the operations was recently abandoned," Holmes continued, accepting his lunch from the publican. "It is empty, though the mines themselves still exist. Before we can dismiss this affair as folly, I suggest we investigate the abandoned mine for signs of recent activity. We will need some supplies, and some calculation, if we are to find the area beneath the field you crossed so diligently this morning. Ideally we could hire a local guide, someone familiar with the mine—"

"Absolutely not!" Plaskett shook his head.

"I assumed you would object," Holmes admitted. "So I took the liberty of finding the mine entrance and found some maps of the caverns, but we must be properly outfitted. Even empty, the deeps are not without danger. The irony of this, the notion that your calculations failed to account for the dimension of depth, amuses me. Three-dimensional thinking was required."

If Holmes expected his barb to sting, he was disappointed. Plaskett laughed aloud at Holmes' observation.

§

So it was that I found myself some fifty feet or more beneath the surface of the earth, my path illuminated by a dim lamp mounted on a recently purchased helmet. The passages were dark and silent but, much to Holmes' irritation, a scuttling, clattering sort of noise echoed up from the lower levels. The sound grew stronger as we approached the tunnel Plaskett's calculations suggested we visit first.

"There's no good reason for anyone to be down here," I whispered to Holmes, unnerved by the noise.

"True," Holmes agreed. "Yet here we are."

Plaskett held up his hand in the dim light. "Before we go any further, I should give you these."

He handed me three round objects, each about the size of a cricket ball. Holmes received the same. "You see here?" Plaskett pointed the weak helmet-light at one of the spheres, illuminating an electrical toggle switch. "Before you throw these, you must flip the switch."

"Is it an explosive?" I asked, uncomfortably considering the weight of the earth above us.

"No, nothing like that," Plaskett shook his head. "It is a device designed to interfere with cross-dimensional signals."

"Well," Holmes said without confidence. "That's reassuring. Watson, did you bring your revolver?"

"I did," I answered. "Do you think—"

"No, gentlemen," Plaskett interrupted. "You have, despite your doubts, trusted me this far. Let us play the hand out. A revolver must be our very last resort."

I saw Holmes shrug in the weak light. Having no wish to argue, I conceded the point. I had no desire to shoot anyone, regardless of their dimensions of origin, but I also nursed a fierce hope of ascending from this vast crypt and stepping back into the sunlight. Plaskett led us into the tunnel, Holmes and I followed. The distant walls were white, the chambers through which we passed were large enough that our feeble lights often did not reach the walls. I had an impression of immense spaces but the air surrounding us was unnervingly still. Despite the lack of a breeze, the air carried a salty taste. At intervals we came across great stone pillars carved from the earth around us. It was an eerie place, still as a grave, dry as a desert, tasting of the sea.

Another tunnel appeared before us, Plaskett unfolded the crude map Holmes had obtained. The scientist turned to face us, seemingly about to speak, when something in the tunnel scuttled into view. Whatever the scientist was about to say was lost, as Holmes and I gasped in amazement.

Some distance away there appeared a blue, glowing spider, tall as a horse. The clattering sounds we'd been following were the tips of its many legs on the stone floor as the unearthly thing propelled itself through the tunnels. It shone with an uncanny, flickering blue light, as if glowing rain splashed on the arachnid from all directions at once. Most remarkably, the uncertain, blue light failed to illuminate any of the stone around the monster. The beast turned what I assumed to be its head towards us, fixing on our party with an unnerving number of eyes, and leapt towards us.

My reaction, I confess, will not be recorded in the annals of British chivalry. Startled, I stepped backwards, lost my footing, and fell in a heap. Holmes seemed frozen in place, a reaction I well understood. While his intellect had been amused by Plaskett's fantastic tale, he made no secret of his doubt. Yet the sight before us defied any other explanation. Holmes flipped the toggle on his sphere and drew back his arm, but it seemed too late. The beast was almost upon us.

And then, it was not. As might be expected, Plaskett's reaction to the multi-legged monstrosity was quicker than ours. With a calm demeanor, he watched and, as the horror closed within a certain distance, he flipped the toggle switch and, with an underhand throw, tossed it towards the creature.

From my vantage point on the ground, I saw it quite clearly. The ball never made contact with the charging blue terror, rather, as it approached, the monster simply disappeared. The ball continued on its uninterrupted trajectory. I distinctly heard it land on the stone floor. The nightmare beast was gone. It had vanished completely.

"I begin to understand your disdain for Watson's revolver," Holmes commented as I regained my feet. Quickly checking my jacket pockets, I was relieved to find my three spheres. I pulled one out, clutching it in my hand as if I were a drowning man thrown a line from a passing ship.

"It doesn't harm them," Plaskett assured Holmes. "They do not belong in this reality. The device emits a signal which interferes with the forces allowing them to exist here. It returns them to the dimensions composing their reality."

"How many of those monsters do you think there will be?" I asked, pleased to find my voice functioning again.

Plaskett frowned as he heard my question. "They are intelligences, Doctor, quite equal to our own. Their science is clearly more advanced than ours. Keep in mind that they are creatures of Earth, just as we are. They are not monsters."

Taking a calming breath, Plaskett continued his answer. "I don't know how many of them might be waiting for us. If incursion is their goal, and their presence suggests it is, they will be building a gateway mechanism. We must find this mechanism and dismantle it. You've seen how my devices work? They use electrical batteries, and have a limited charge. Take care not to engage them too soon. If you find one that has been thrown, flip the switch to off immediately to conserve the charge. However, if necessary, they can be used more than once. Now, if you gentlemen are ready, I suggest we follow this tunnel as quickly as we can. They know we are here."

Having spoken his piece, Plaskett hurried down the dark tunnel at a jog. I had time to exchange a quick glance with Holmes, an expression of commiseration, before following the scientist.

§

It was a scene which haunted my nightmares for months, running through the darkness and coming upon the blue monsters wrapped in their strange glow. It gave us an advantage, however, for our targets were revealed plainly. Plaskett had dispatched three before I tossed my first ball at an enemy scuttling in retreat. I retrieved some of the spheres so, as I came around the final column, my pockets were filled with at least half a dozen of the devices.

There, at the tunnel's end, was the mechanism Plaskett told us to look for. It appeared as a series of archways arranged in a circle, each lit with an internal emerald light. Fortunately, this emerald brightness acted as proper light did, bathing the white walls and columns of the tunnel with its illumination. Plaskett ran to the closest archway and stopped. Reaching into his rucksack, he discovered he had exhausted his supply of devices. One of the creatures charged towards him, rearing up on its hind-legs before a ball tossed by Holmes caused the creature to vanish. I tossed some of my supply to Plaskett. He caught the spheres and offered a grateful nod.

Looking around, I could not see the blue glow of any further creatures. I reached into my pocket, retrieved one of the devices and was about to offer it to Holmes when he spotted one of our foes within the archways. Curiously, it did not glow as the others had. It was crouched over an open panel, short mandibles, around what I assumed to be its mouth, working on the mechanism's interior.

"There!" Holmes barked, charging through the archway.

"Nooo!" Plaskett shouted desperately at Holmes. I could see Holmes try, too late, to stop. He had passed through the gateway and disappeared as completely as our foes had. The creature within the gateway scuttled quickly out of view, disappearing from within the gateway and from our dimensions completely. It did not appear anywhere in the cavern.

"Confound it!" Plaskett said, pounding his fist against the archway. His quick fingers scrambled to discover a way into the mechanism's interior.

"Where is Holmes?" I asked.

"I do not know," Plaskett answered. "Hopefully he finds himself in their reality, if so, I may be able to return him. Wait, where are you going?"

I did not answer. I hurried through the archway, one of Plaskett's spheres clutched in my throwing hand. Wherever Holmes was, it was clear he was alone and in peril. Praying I was not too late, I charged after him.

§

I hit a stone floor with a thud. My stomach immediately released its contents, splashing foreign dimensions with a wasted meal from Winsford. Rolling on my back, I found Holmes at my side. Around us –

It seemed we lay at the bottom of a pit made of foes, completely surrounded by solid walls of huge spider creatures. They no longer glowed, having traded their garish livery for shades of brown, black and grey. Seemingly stacked atop each other, they formed walls of mandibles, legs and eyes. They shrieked as one, their outrage a deafening thunder.

My hand still held one of Plaskett's spheres. I flipped the toggle switch, intending to hurl the device into the midst of our overwhelming foes. Instead I found myself immersed in the white light once more, pain screaming along every nerve. I felt completely sickened, yet unexpectedly eager to experience the marvels I had felt before. I desired nothing so much as to be immersed, once again, in the incredible, indescribable music of existence.

§

I woke on the stone floor of the salt mine. Plaskett was crouched above me, a look of deep concern on his round features. His eyeglasses reflected the emerald light of the archways.

"That was the bravest, yet most foolish, thing I have ever seen," Plaskett told me in tones of conviction that allowed no argument. "Charging across dimensions to save your friend. I thought you were both lost. However did you return?"

Feebly, I raised the sphere clutched in my hand. I attempted speech but found, for the moment, awe had rendered me mute.

"Oh, very clever!" Plaskett exclaimed. "A sharp bit of reasoning, Doctor. Just as the spheres banished our foes to their dimensions, it returned you and Holmes to yours."

In all humility, I must confess I'd entertained no such thought. In my hand was a weapon which defeated our foes before and I'd sought to use it again. It worked better than I intended.

Plaskett checked on Holmes, who was stirring. Satisfied, the scientist returned to the removed panel where the last of our foes had been working. Reaching in, Plaskett yanked out objects not crafted by the hands of men. The green light flickered out immediately. On the floor were our helmets, scattered during our attack, their dim lights welcome beacons. After all I had experienced, I found my mind embraced the comfort of the darkness.

"I feel as if I have fallen from the highest mountain," Holmes announced as he returned to wakefulness. "Where did we go?"

"A difficult question, Mr. Holmes," Plaskett answered. "In one sense, you did not travel anywhere. You simply left this reality for another. The truths of multiple dimensions do not fit easily into our thoughts. Tell me, gentlemen, what did you see?"

"Impossible things," I answered, sitting up and accepting the helmet and lantern Plaskett offered me.

"Miracles," Holmes released the word like a gasp of wonder.

"You've been given a rare insight into the nature of reality," Plaskett told us. "It may take some time to reconcile the experience to your thoughts. The danger has passed, it is safe to rest. Give me some time to dismantle this gateway and then we can return to the surface. Soon, I fear, you'll understand why I was so firm in the conditions regarding scientific publications. No doubt, someday in the future mankind will discover the truths you've experienced today. It would be a shame to rob them of that privilege. We stand at the beginning of the great adventure that is science, gentlemen, and though the three of us can no longer be a part of it, we can enjoy watching it unfold."

Grimoire

he public house was across the street from the chapel, down the slope of the hill. Sherlock Holmes paused, examining the arrangement of the nearby buildings with a keen eye. This village was old, its streets and avenues laid down long ago without thought to modern requirements and, yet, it served well enough. Given its age, the chapel was larger than would have been considered normal but not remarkably so. The structure sported a bell tower, presumably with a bell hidden within its summit, though a smaller brass bell made one wonder if its larger ancestor had suffered some manner of disability. What was most remarkable, Holmes noted, was what was missing rather than what the chapel showed. There were no graves, either old or new. No doubt there was a rational explanation, though the churchyard offered little in the way of clues.

And the public house, *The Black Horse*, nothing special in name or its presentation. Like the church, the building appeared very old but with none of the fussiness or trappings which local pride often affixed to such elderly structures. No plaques or notices declaring its uniqueness, no special care taken to preserve the old glory of the place revealed in the recent repairs or modifications. Like the rest of the small village, it was old but functioned well enough.

The sun had just set but the street was empty, another curious absence. Given the season, a visitor might expect some traffic in and out of the public house. The hour was not late, even by rural standards, and Holmes sensed the presence of local eyes tracking his movements. It was a pressure, the unseen weight of hidden attention, pressing him towards his appointment. Unlike the streets of London, where any manner of strange, investigatory activities would scarcely be noted, a stranger's mere presence was unusual enough to draw interest.

Pushing open the doors of *The Black Horse*, noting the unusual weight and thickness, Holmes was somewhat surprised to find the interior empty, save for the seated proprietor. A pint of dark, three-quarters full, sat before the man. As Holmes stepped inside, the man, dressed in a formal waistcoat and tie, stood to greet him.

"Mr. Sherlock Holmes?"

"Indeed," Holmes answered, doffing his cap. "Do I have the pleasure of acknowledging Mr. Trefor Morgan?"

"Pleased to meet you." The man was of average height, his hair dark and curly. He was well-built, solid in appearance. There was an air of authority about him, though Holmes could observe none of the tell-tales of military service in his bearing. He shook the detective's hand with a firm grip before stepping away and retreating behind the bar. "You've travelled quite a distance. What will you have?"

"A pint of bitter," Holmes said, placing coins on the bar. "I am surprised to find your establishment so empty. I trust your business is not normally so slow."

"Well, you understand," Morgan answered with an affectionate tone, "when a detective travels all the way from London to visit you, a man gets somewhat apprehensive.

I arranged for the place to be clear for this evening, so we might enjoy our conversation discreetly."

Ignoring the coins on the bar, Morgan carried the drink to his table and invited Holmes to sit with a nod. Holmes did, taking his seat and, following his host's lead, took a sip of his pint. Finding the taste of it surprisingly excellent, Holmes took another sip.

"Now, sir," Morgan said, "I received your letter but I must admit I've no idea why you would be interested in traveling so far west to speak to me."

"I was asked to consult on a matter in Oxford, a murder attempt—"

"How ghastly!" Morgan interrupted.

Holmes dismissed the man's concern with a wave and continued. "An elderly professor at the University apparently lost his reason and attempted violence on those nearby. Several of his colleagues were forced to restrain him but not, unfortunately, before he was able to inflict a fatal wound upon himself. I was not far away, investigating another matter, but the sudden and unexpected nature of the crime caused the local constabulary to contact me for assistance. An overreaction, I'm afraid, the facts of the investigation were established quickly and have not been disputed. All that remains, I'm afraid, is a question more for philosophers than detectives. To wit: What made the Professor lose his reason?"

Pausing, Holmes took another pull of his drink.

"I fear you have travelled a long way for nothing, Mr. Holmes. I've heard nothing of any of this."

Holmes nodded, reached into his jacket and pulled out an envelope stuffed thick with papers and laid it on the table before Morgan. Uncertain, Morgan took the envelope and looked at it.

"The postmark isn't from here, it's—"

"From the village down the road," Holmes agreed. "Yet I have reason to believe the letter was composed in this village. It was found, as you may have deduced, on the desk of the Oxford Professor. According to his associates, he was working on a translation when his reason abandoned him. The placing of the letter supports their assertion. Feel free to look inside, Mr. Morgan, I think you'll find the contents of interest."

With obvious reluctance, Morgan pulled the pages from the envelope. A number of photographs spilled from the folded paper of the letter. Eyes widening, he arranged the images in a line, orientating them so that they formed a series. That task finished, he opened the letter and read it in a slow, deliberate way. When he came to the end, he reached for his pint and took a long pull.

"Do you see why I consider this village to be the letter's point of origin?"

"No, I can't say I do." Morgan answered, a streak of Celtic stubbornness in his voice.

Holmes' expression twitched into an approving grin, gone as quickly as it appeared. "Can we agree that the photographs show a book which is filled with old Welsh? Based on the distance between the book and camera, it is apparent the pedestal on which the book rests is set in a long but oddly narrow room, perhaps a tunnel. The shadows from the flash-powder indicate the walls are not straight but curved and, you'll note, oddly textured. All of this suggests the photographs were taken underground, a tunnel or a cave.'"

"Wales is full of caves," Morgan noted.

"None of which are located in the village corresponding to the postmark. The next logical step is to see which nearby villages could have such caves, based on publically available geological surveys. Would you care to guess which village that would be?"

"Well," Morgan said, "As you're here, I'll be guessing it's this one."

"Correct," Holmes nodded. "Such a fact is suggestive but hardly conclusive. The photographs offer further insight, given the description in the letter, and it is likely whoever took the photographs developed them himself. It was not difficult to contact the closest supplier of the chemicals required and discover where such products have been delivered. The answer is, interestingly, the chapel across the road. Then there is the letter itself. People mistakenly believe a typewritten letter to be anonymous but, I assure you, such is not the case. I have written a monograph on the distinctive features of various typewriters and how to trace a letter back to the machine that produced it. In this case the typewriter is consistent with a type issued to various local parish offices."

Morgan shook his head. "Sounds to me as if you need to visit the chapel, not the pub."

"An interesting observation," Holmes remarked. "What makes you think I have not?"

The Welshman opened his mouth to speak but closed it again, shaking his head.

"As it happens, an actual visit to the chapel was not required," Holmes explained. "A courteous letter with a reasonable inquiry inspired the chapel secretary to reply with a typewritten letter delivered by mail. From this sample I was able to match the typewriter to both letters. I also noted the stationery on which both letters were written are from the same supplier, manufactured at the same time. So, as should be obvious by now, I am confident the letter and the photographs originated from this village and that chapel. I see you wish to argue the point, and I am willing to hear your arguments."

Morgan shook his head again. "Are you suggesting this

Oxford Professor went mad reading a book? That's clean off."

"Perhaps," Homes agreed. "Nevertheless, I am here to tie up a loose end of my investigation. Provided I find the answers to my questions, I see no reason to involve anyone further in this matter. It is, as you say, unlikely the letter and photographs have anything to do with the Oxford violence. Once I've confirmed the letter's origin, there will be no reason why I, or Scotland Yard, need explore the matter further."

Morgan's broad features settled into an expression of frustrated concentration under his mop of curly, black hair. His pint lay forgotten at his elbow. "Why," the publican asked, "are you asking me? Why aren't you going to the chapel?"

Holmes managed a chuckle. "If it wasn't apparent to me before I arrived, everything I've observed since entering your establishment convinces me you are the man most likely to provide the answers I seek. A pub emptied of locals for a private meeting? A man who is fully aware I have yet to visit the chapel? Someone confident enough to meet with a detective completely alone? I must admit, I expected to hear the footsteps of men in one of the adjacent rooms but I have heard nothing. Whatever is happening in this village, it is clear you are at the centre of it. At the very least, you are aware of it. Is the book here, Mr. Morgan? I have travelled far to examine it."

Morgan's frown of concentration deepened, a building storm cloud that must eventually find violent release.

"There's no need for this to be difficult," Holmes assured the man. "I understand you are reluctant to speak of these matters to an outsider, however I am a detective. Part of my profession involves the keeping of confidences. Whatever you tell me, no matter how fantastic, will be treated as confidential. A matter not to be discussed."

"Easy enough to say," Morgan answered. "I know who you are, Mr. Holmes. You are not the only one who can find things out. London may be distant but we're not so backwards out here we can't read newspapers or send letters of our own. You're somewhat famous, in a queer way. Out here, we don't trust secrets to famous people. They're too eager to tell stories, do anything to increase their fame. Maybe I'm not clever enough to know it, but for all your bluster about bringing in the law, I don't understand what crime's been committed. Not against the law to take a photograph of a book, nor to write to professors up in their ivory towers. Seems to me, you're the one being bold, coming out here all alone and trying to nose out other people's business. I can see how threatening folk who've broken the law might work but, as that's not what happened here, I don't see why I ought to tell you anything."

"A fair point," Holmes admitted, raising his hands palms out, as if in surrender. "Yet, if you've researched me, you've likely learned that I have dealt with sensitive situations in the past. Despite pressure from a variety of sources, I do not betray confidences shared with me."

"Unless there's some bugger to slap in prison."

"Agreed, I rate justice above confidentiality. It is, after all, my profession. However, as you say, no laws appear to have been broken here. I applaud you for preparing for our meeting, Mr. Morgan, I believe I can be of assistance to you if you will take me into your confidence. I will find my answers, one way or another."

"What can you do for me?" Morgan asked doubtfully.

"You understand this is supposition," Holmes said. "I know nothing about the book in question, nor is my knowledge of this village extensive. Feel free to correct me if my theory strays from the truth. From my perspective, it all begins with this letter. There is the matter of the postmark, obviously it would have been simpler to post it from here. Yet, it was not. There are many reasons why someone might post an envelope from a distant village but everything about this letter is quite deliberate in nature. The care taken with the address, the typewritten pages, the effort taken with the photographs, both in their staging and in their development. The letter is deliberately unsigned, no address provided for the courtesy of return correspondence. All of this suggests the writer wished to remain anonymous. Why? After all, the letter hopes the photographs will be enough to allow for a translation of the ancient text, surely after all this effort the writer wishes to learn what is written there? Most suggestive of all, no further correspondence from the writer has been received by the university."

"How's that suggestive?" Morgan wondered.

"It indicates that the sender is aware that writing to the professor will not generate a reply. It suggests the writer has been keeping a watch on the professor, as if alert to the possibility of harm befalling him.'

Nodding an acknowledgement, Morgan waited for the detective to continue.

"My suspicion, not yet proven, is that the letter-writer's anonymity was not to prevent the professor from learning the source of the photographs but to prevent those of his village, this village, from learning who wrote the letter even if they happened on it. Of course, when I say 'the village', I mean, specifically, you."

"Me?" Morgan asked.

"The man whose whim empties the pub, who knows all visitors to the village, have we not discussed this previously?"

"Suppose we have," Morgan admitted. "But—"

"I would prefer not to hear more denials," Holmes insisted. "Why would a man take such elaborate measures to have a book translated? Why go to such lengths to conceal his identity? Obviously, the book is not his property or there would be no need for such effort. The apparent age of the book in question, as confirmed by the Professor's notes before he suffered his break with reality, suggests the book may not belong to any one person. Items of such antiquity are often valued by –how shall I describe them? – secret societies. I don't suppose it will come as a surprise to learn your neighboring villages suspect such an organization exists here, given the way this establishment is closed to outsiders on the nights when a full moon occurs. It's gossip, of course, and of no matter to me. I have no interest in stripping a law-abiding society of its secrecy. I notice you have not corrected my theory yet, so I shall continue."

Morgan leaned forward, speaking to Holmes. "I notice you've not said how you plan on helping me. Nothing you've said so far offers me anything."

"If my theory is correct, a member of the clandestine society who revealed one of the secrets of the organization to an outsider would undoubtedly find themselves in breach of the group's regulations. Hence the need for the letter-writer's anonymity. I am prepared to give you the letter and photographs so you can offer proof to the society that a violation of the rules has occurred."

"I have the letter and the photographs," Morgan said, an unmistakable threat in his tone.

"Of course," Holmes admitted. "I have also presented you the logic connecting these exhibits to the chapel. Such logic, though correct, often is not emotionally powerful enough to convince those who wish to deny the truth before them. I have reason to suppose that you are the head of this secret order, would you like me to explain how I deduced that?"

"No."

"Pity. As the head of the society, I have no doubt you know who has betrayed the order. Of course, I know as well. Yet you will need to convince the others and, naturally, they may be reluctant to take action against one of their own. I have further proof, proof which comes with the letter writer's signature."

"Give it to me," Morgan said, standing.

"I did not bring them with me. A measure of caution, in case you saw fit to take items—" Holmes' gaze fell on the letter and the photographs on the table "—without permission."

Morgan shook his head. "What sort of proof?"

"A receipt for camera equipment," Holmes explained. "And another for an order of photographic chemicals. Both are signed by the same hand."

Morgan considered, then asked, "Ephraim?"

Holmes nodded.

"Gods damn the old fool!" Morgan brought his fist down on the table. Letting out a long sigh, he shook his head. "I knew it would be him but I didn't want to believe it. He's my uncle."

"I trust this information will not place him in danger," Holmes replied.

"No," Morgan admitted, raising his hand to his forehead to better contain his runaway thoughts. "Though he's like to tell you death would be kinder. He'll be, well, exiled. It'll sting, no doubt, but he knew well what he was risking and he went ahead and did it all in spite of the danger. He's an old fool, who has betrayed his brothers, but there was no malice in it. He never believed, not really, not like the rest of us. And you'll give me those paper bits, with his sign."

"In exchange for answers, yes."

"Well, I don't like it," Morgan admitted, setting his hands on the table. Remembering his pint, he drained it in a long pull. Once finished he set his hands back on the table, his expression one of a man resigned to an unpleasant but necessary task. "Ask your questions, though it seems you know as much as I about it."

"The book in the photograph," Holmes leaned forward, intent on observing the publican's expression as he answered. "Do you believe it caused the mayhem in Oxford?"

"There's no doubt in my mind," Morgan admitted. "Not in my mind, nor my heart. I know it's not a fashionable way to think in these modern times, but we were warned the words in the Grimoire must be kept unknown. Our task is to keep the Grimoire secret and safe, a task bestowed by the one true King. Ephraim, that old fool, how will he live with what he's done?"

Holmes, normally so controlled, couldn't hold his question in."The one true King?"

Shifting in his seat, Morgan met Holmes' gaze. "Laugh if you like, all I know is what I've been told by my father, told to him by his father before and so on through the centuries. The book was entrusted to us by the one true king, the Lord of Summer, the once and future."

"Arthur?" Holmes said. "That seems unlikely, though the professor's notes speculated the book was compiled at the time of the Roman withdrawal. Forgive me, I've drifted from my line of inquiry. You know where the book is currently?"

"I do. It is safe. There will be no further incidents, such a dreadful thing will not happen again. We've protected the Grimoire for more than a thousand years, Mr. Holmes, and we'll protect it for ten thousand more if need be."

Holmes nodded, considering. "Do you expect me to believe that over the course of a thousand years, the book has never been read?"

"Well, I wish I could," Morgan confessed. "There have been incidents, long ago the Grimoire was taken out of the village. More often someone finds a way to read from it, with the same results as your Oxford man. Madness and death. I can promise you the book has not been taken from us since Edward III sat on the throne."

"Remarkable," Holmes admitted. "Yet, given the danger, I feel I need to inspect its hiding place."

"That is not wise," Morgan warned. "Your concern is understandable but, I warn you, the book affects people. It calls to them, some burn with a desire to learn what is written there."

"Why not simply destroy it?"

"That would be straightforward, wouldn't it? But there's a prophecy. Some day there'll come one who requires the knowledge Myrddin laid down so long ago. Though we are tasked with its protection, ultimately our duty will end in failure, the one who needs the knowledge will read the Grimoire and retain their wits. They'll thank us for our service and our duty to the true King will be fulfilled."

"I could argue the logic of—"

"You could but logic has little to do with any of this," Morgan countered. "All this is a remnant of a time past, an age having naught to do with logic or science."

"I must insist on knowing the book is safe. You understand, a danger such as this ..."

"Were I you, I would feel the same. Yet I must have your word before I can agree. You must promise to obey me, must promise to never return to this village, and must promise to never speak of what you see or what I've told you with any but me."

"I agree to the terms," Holmes answered easily.

"For me, this is a chance to learn," Morgan explained. "Tell me, Mr. Holmes, where do you think the book is? You seem clever enough, if you were to seek the book without my guidance, where would you go? What would you do?"

"Clearly I have the advantage of knowing the book is kept underground," Holmes noted. "My initial suspicion would be under the chapel. Simply put, it seems the oldest building in the village, indeed, in the whole cantref. And people expect such places to have underground structures. Crypts are common when chapels do not sport graveyards. I would expect the entry would be well-concealed and difficult to find. I would, forgive me for saying so, begin my search for the underground passage here, in this building. It is close enough to make a tunnel through the limestone feasible and there is less opportunity for it to be found. There may be other nearby buildings where entrances are concealed but I did not notice them being open to the public, so gaining entry there would require more planning."

Morgan nodded. "And where would you search here? Forgive me, but this is a singular opportunity for me. Most strangers don't even know we have defenses, the chance to ask an outsider about them is a rare treat. I'd value your opinion."

Holmes started to rise, then hesitated. "With your permission?"

"By all means," Morgan said, remaining seated as Holmes began a meticulous examination of the establishment. Morgan sat and observed as Holmes examined the public house's open area, then disappeared into the other rooms. When Holmes finally returned to the table, Morgan rose, walked behind the bar and pulled two more pints. Setting one in front of Holmes, he took a pull from the other, sat and asked, "Well?"

"The most obvious tunnel entrance is there," Holmes pointed to a bench seat by the window. "It is also placed where one would expect, given this establishment's position with regard to the chapel. For a moment, I confess, I considered my search over. Since I had time, however,

I continued searching and discovered a rather ingenious tunnel hidden in the kitchen. There is another in the cold room, well concealed though I admit the boxes piled before it gave away the secret. The kitchen tunnel is the one I would explore first, though obviously with a great deal of caution. How did I do?"

"Quite well, Mr. Holmes," Morgan admitted, offering the detective a congratulatory tip of his glass. "You would be right to avoid the most obvious tunnel over by there, it has a nasty drop in it. And you're correct about the boxes in the cold room, they were piled there to draw your attention. While that tunnel is not a trap in the way the other tunnel is, it does not lead to the Grimoire."

"So I chose correctly," Holmes proclaimed.

"No, the kitchen tunnel does not lead to the Grimoire. You've missed one, Mr. Holmes, and it's the one we need to take."

Holmes frowned. "Where?"

Shaking his head, Morgan held up a dark, cloth bag.

"You mean to blindfold me?" Holmes asked.

"I do." There was a hint of apology in Morgan's voice. "If you'd found it, I'd not have, but seeing as you didn't ..."

Holmes finished his drink. "Shall we?"

"We shall indeed," Morgan agreed. "Unless you've thought better of it?"

"I have not," Holmes replied. Morgan placed the bag over his head. Holmes was confident he knew where he was guided but, as he heard the sound of some manner of mechanism being released, he regretted allowing himself to be hooded. Following Morgan's guiding hand, Holmes moved carefully down the steps. When they had moved down several paces, Morgan reached up and took off the hood. The Welshman had a lantern which, though the light was weak, was sufficient to light the width of the narrow tunnel. They travelled through the tunnel, arriving at a small chamber from which separate tunnels were carved into the limestone. Morgan stepped forward, into the tunnel on his right.

"We seem to be heading in the wrong direction," Holmes noted.

"Aye, that's as it seems," Morgan answered. "These tunnels are the work of a different age, a more brutal time. When people think of the past they tend to think people were stupid compared to modern folk, since they know nothing of electricity or economics, but the people thinking so are wrong. Whoever made these tunnels know full well where you expect to go, so they fill that way with nasty surprises. Some of our own folk have run afoul of those, though they ought to know better. Them as made these passages meant to protect the Grimoire, weren't afraid of being bloody-minded about it either. You follow me, Mr. Holmes, I'll show you the Grimoire and bring you safe out again, long as you do as I say. 'Tis not a place for them as can't listen, understand?"

"I do, Mr. Morgan, I will follow."

§

As they ventured deeper underground, Morgan began to talk. It seemed to Holmes the man had a lifetime of knowledge, and speculation, regarding the limestone tunnels and those who built them but had enjoyed few opportunities to discuss them. "You see here, I've no idea how they made the stone so smooth. Grew up in these parts, I know these stones and I know I could never get such a finish on them. And here, see where the stone goes dark. Its blood, I'm sure of it, but when it was spilt I could not say. We've records, mind you, but I've not found anyone recording a fight in these parts of the tunnels. Perhaps it's animal blood, don't reckon there's any way to tell after so long."

Holmes followed, finding himself fascinated by the words of his guide and by the narrow tunnels themselves.

"Really, it's a labyrinth down here. How they managed to lay it all out, without modern survey tools, all down here in the dark. It's beyond me. Yet they did it."

Another bend in the tunnel and there was the book, seated on a pedestal carved from the stone of the floor. "There it stands," Morgan declared. "You stand here, Mr. Holmes, no need to get any closer."

Holmes stopped behind Morgan, a calculating gleam in his eye as he gazed at the leather covers. "I wish to hold it."

"No, Mr. Holmes, this is as close as you get. Best we turn around now."

"Don't you ever wonder?" Holmes asked, a strange passion infecting his normally composed voice. "After all these centuries, sitting there unread, it seems wrong not to touch it. I will hold it in my hands, the book of Merlin, just for a moment—"

"No, you shall not! Please Mr. Holmes, you seemed so reasonable, you must not!"

Holmes lurched forward, attempting to push past the Welshman. The tunnel did not leave enough room for the maneuver, and Morgan stood as unmovable as the tunnel wall. Seizing the detective, Morgan threw him back down the tunnel. Holmes sprawled on the tunnel floor.

"Stay down there!" Morgan barked at the fallen man, stepping backwards towards the book's pedestal. "I've no wish to hurt you, I don't, but think Mr. Holmes! We've protected this book for centuries! From all threats, not something we achieved only with kind words and friendly chatter. I don't wish to hurt you but I will if I must. You need to step away!"

Holmes regained his feet, his eyes fixed on the book behind Morgan. Morgan's eyes flared. Holmes, disregarding the threat, took a step forward.

"So be it!" Morgan cried as his hand went to the wall, disappearing behind a ledge and emerging with a sword in his right hand. Holmes hesitated but did not stop. Seeing Holmes step forward, Morgan yelled again, "On your head, it is!"

Holmes took another step forward. Morgan's left-hand disappeared into a gap in the tunnel wall. The Welshman, his eyes fierce, stood waiting, sword in hand.

Holmes took another step forward. A portcullis, the ancient metal slamming down with impressive force, crashed from a cavity in the tunnel ceiling. Holmes pushed against it, found its strength undiminished by age. As his hands wrapped themselves around the flat metal of the fallen gate, Holmes heard another gate slam down behind him.

"A stalemate," Holmes observed, his eyes on Morgan.

"Think that, do you?" Morgan shook his head. "I trusted you, Mr. Holmes. Broke your promise. You brought this on yourself, you did." His hand reached for something behind the ledge, making repeated pulling motions. He could not hear the peal but Holmes reasoned the small bell on the chapel's tower was ringing.

"You forced me to do this, Mr. Holmes," Morgan stated. "I'd no wish to harm you but you left me no choice. Why'd you not listen to me?"

Holmes' keen ears heard sounds approaching from the tunnel behind him, light glowed along the limestone walls of the tunnel. In short order Holmes found himself facing a dozen Welshmen, all carrying torches, all armed with a variety of medieval weapons.

"Raise the portcullis," Morgan ordered. "Take this man,

bind him and blindfold him. Take him to the chapel for trial. Make sure uncle Ephraim is there. I fear it'll be a long night, one full of tears."

§

Holmes did not resist. When the hood was removed, he found himself in the chapel, surrounded by thirty men, all armed with swords. The space had been neatly converted from a place of worship into a court. Trefor Morgan sat behind a table set on a stage, directly in front of the bound Holmes. Holmes' hands were bound together before him, arms held by large men. They shoved him down into a wooden chair before Morgan. Holmes glanced around, on the stage to Morgan's left stood half a dozen quiet Welshmen, the others filled the chapel. All were armed and, save for Morgan and Holmes, were standing.

Holmes turned to his left and, in a polite voice, spoke to the guard there. "In my left sock you'll find an envelope. If you would be so kind as to take it to Mr. Morgan, I would be grateful."

The guard glared down at him but looked to the man on Holmes' other side for direction. After a quick nod, the man bent down and felt Holmes sock, found the envelope and showed it to his partner. Quickly he walked to the stage, handing the envelope to Morgan. The publican opened it, looked at Holmes and, reluctant and confused, nodded his thanks to the detective as he held the receipts with his uncle's signature in his hand.

"You deserve an explanation," Morgan addressed the crowd. The murmur of conversation stilled, Holmes was once again impressed with the apparent authority the man held over the village. "This man is a detective, a famous one at that, mind what we say here for he's proper clever, he is."

"Clever or no, won't matter where he's going," a voice observed. "He tried to steal the Grimoire."

For a moment it seemed Morgan would argue but, in the end, he didn't. "You should know, I took him down the tunnels myself. I agreed to show him the Grimoire. I trusted him and I was wrong. He gave his word to do as I said but, once we got there he tried to push past me and reach the Grimoire. I had no choice but to pull the gates and sound the alarm. You all did as you should and I thank you for it."

One of the half dozen men standing on the stage answered. "This seems straightforward enough. We are to pass judgement."

Morgan looked to Holmes. "Anything to say in your defense, Mr. Holmes?"

"No," Holmes admitted, resignation in his voice. "I regret betraying your trust. I swear I will not speak of what I learned here. None shall hear of your secrets from me."

"No," the jury foreman announced. "That is not enough. You've shown your colours, we'd be fools to trust you again. Your fate rests with the Almighty now. The King's law is clear on what needs to be done."

The silent men around him nodded in agreement. The men standing next to Holmes reached down and grabbed him by the arms. Morgan's voice interrupted them, surprising all save the bound detective.

"There's more to discuss," Morgan said. "Ephraim, come forward."

An older man, his long hair snow white, walked forward with sword in hand. "Trefor?"

"This man came here because he had learned of the Grimoire. He'd seen pages of it in photographs. Any idea how that occurred, Ephraim? No? Do you want to know what happened to the man who received your letters? You know already, don't you? I'll tell you, exactly what we've always been told happens to those who try and read the Grimoire. He's dead Ephraim, a violent death, and that weight is on you alone."

"Trefor, we should talk—"

"We are talking! Here! Now! In front of all of us! You know the punishment for this. Do you deny it? We are your brothers in arms, we deserve to hear the truth from your own lips."

"I ... I don't know how to answer. Do you believe me capable of this? On the word of this thief? A man who tried to take the Grimoire?"

"Not just his word," Morgan said. "I will send two brothers to your place to search for the camera. Will they find it there? If you have such a device, why have you not shown it to any of us? Shall I send them?"

A calculating gleam came into Ephraim's eye. "They'll find nothing."

"Do not speak to me in riddles, Ephraim. Do you own such a device or not?"

"I do not," Ephraim said after some hesitation.

Morgan sighed heavily, hanging his head for a moment. When he raised it, his anger was as apparent as his determination. "Damn you Ephraim and damn your games. Every man here knows you longed to read the book, despite the danger. I know you have a camera. I know you took those pictures and mailed them to the Oxford man. And now you have lied to us. My fellow knights, I call for judgement."

"You've not proven your case!" Ephraim protested.

Pulling the receipts Holmes provided him, he passed them to the head of the jury. "This is a receipt for the purchase of a camera, signed by my uncle. These, I am told, are chemicals used to develop photographs, again signed for by Ephraim. You all know his hand."

"Before you judge him, let me plead for mercy. He is my uncle. He was our brother. There is blood on his hands, yes, and soon there will be blood on ours because of what he's done. For all that, while he may not be a worthy knight, I still believe him to be a good man."

The jury spoke in hushed, passionate whispers. The foreman nodded, turned to the others and announced, "Exile."

"No!" Ephraim cried out, his face stricken.

"And this man, his fate is in God's hands." The head juror intoned. A pall had descended over the room, sentencing one of their own had dulled their bloodlust. The old knight, Ephraim, stood befuddled in the aisle of the chapel, looking pleadingly at his neighbours who left without meeting his gaze. Holmes was hauled to his feet.

"Excuse me for asking," Holmes said politely. "What will happen to me now? Am I to be executed?"

"Well," the guard on his right said. "If you try to escape we'll have no choice but to end you. I'll not lie to you, some of the lads are spoiling for it. Should you come with us without a fight, you'll be out far from the eyes of men, where only God himself can see you. Perhaps he'll see fit to free you, there's no chance we will."

The other guard presented a hood. "Sorry," the guard grunted, the hood at the ready. Holmes tipped his head, making the task simpler for his captor. Allowing himself to be led by his guards, the detective offered no resistance. They stepped out of the chapel and onto the street. Unable to see, Holmes still had the impression he was being led out of the village on the main road. Remarkable, but no one stopped the procession, not even to ask what was happening. They marched into the night, the only sounds those of wildlife and the occasional clank of their metal weapons.

§

Once the hood was removed, Holmes found himself on a hilltop, their party hidden behind a screen of wild growth. They might have been standing here at any time in the history of the island, far from the modern world. Torchlight and metal weapons, a prisoner and a group of armed men atop a hillside, Holmes looked around but ignored the darkness of the pit open at his feet. The guards stepped in front of Holmes and cut the rope binding his hands. Another length of thick rope was brought out and tied around Holmes, under his arms, across his chest.

Morgan came forward, approaching Holmes. He checked the rope and spoke, in a low voice to Holmes. "I am sorry for this, Mr. Holmes, but I did warn you."

"You did indeed," Holmes acknowledged. "What happens now?"

"You'll be lowered into this cave," Morgan explained. "We will seal the opening and then leave. There is, as far as I know, no way out. There is no food down there, no water, no light. The thought is that, if you are meant to be free, God will free you. However, if you're meant to die, that will be considered God's will as well."

"A cruel death," Holmes noted. "But I understand the justice of it."

"If you prefer a clean death," Morgan said in a whisper. "I will see to it."

"No," Holmes answered.

"Here," Morgan said, passing Holmes a dagger. "Should you need to end your suffering."

"An unexpected kindness. Thank you."

Morgan stepped back. The guards guided Holmes to the edge of the void. Holmes sat on the lip, then eased himself into the darkness. The men holding the rope took the strain, lowering him gently to the ground below. Once he was on firm ground, they released the rope, its length falling around the forlorn figure in the darkness.

Morgan spoke into the cave at his feet, "May God have mercy on your soul, Mr. Holmes." He nodded to the men with him, who levered the stone back in place. Some remained, placing dirt over the cover, arranging the hilltop as if it had not been disturbed. Silently, they returned to their village.

Within the darkness, Holmes struck a match. Pulling a short candle from his pocket, he lit it and stuck it on a nearby rock. Sitting, Holmes pulled out a sheet of paper and a pencil and began writing a short note. When he finished it, he folded it and pulled an envelope from another pocket and addressed it.

§

Two days later, the stone cover was pulled away. Holmes had no sense of day or night in the darkness but, if it was who he expected, he reasoned it must be late in the evening. Holmes lit another match, brought the flame to the shortened stub of the candle. Looking around he gathered what he could.

"Watson," Holmes called up, when he saw the stars in the opening. "I am relieved to hear you. You are alone, I trust?"

"I am," the Doctor called down. "Did things go as expected?"

"More or less," Holmes admitted. "I must confess, those involved were generally more compassionate than I anticipated. Still, I am quite satisfied to conclude this matter. Have you enough rope with you? They threw some down with me."

Watson's face reappeared as he tossed a length a rope

down to the detective. In short order, Holmes was walking beside his friend, free under the stars. They moved from the hilltop and away from the village.

"Did you see the book?" Watson asked. "Was it the cause of the Professor's madness?"

"I did observe the book," Holmes admitted. "I was not allowed to read or touch it. I still have doubts as to the book being the cause of the madness but, in the end, it hardly matters. Even if the book does inspire insanity, it is well and safely guarded. We need not worry about it any longer, it is in good hands."

"And you were not recognized?"

"You doubt my disguises? No, my previous visit went undetected. It was fortunate there were no other caves in this area. The village concealed many more tunnels than I anticipated."

"Lucky they didn't just execute you on the spot."

Holmes shook his head. "Hardly chivalrous, not the way things work out here. Really, Watson, you would have been surprised with the courtesy I was shown at my execution. Anticipating your next question, let me assure you they will not seek to end my life once they learn of my escape. They will consider it God's will. As God created a mind capable of anticipating the murder pit's existence and discovering its location, they are not incorrect. I must admit the food and water I hid there, while sufficient, lacked taste. Let us find a place to eat before returning to London."

Mr. Trefor Morgan,

If this letter arrives by post, you will know I have escaped. If you find it on my person, I have not. In either case I feel I owe you an apology. You were honest and forthcoming with me and I feel I abused your trust. Given the stakes, I felt it necessary to test the defences around the item we discussed. If it could do as you believe, it must be kept separate from the world. My intention was to discover how the item was guarded. I admit I knew about the cave in which I have been placed some time before I presented myself at your public house, having scouted your village earlier. The bones I uncovered within revealed its purpose.

I trust my escape does not trouble you. In exchange, I will endeavour to not allow the Oxford matter to trouble me any further.

Sincerely,
Sherlock Holmes

Hero of Baker Street

 saw the smile spread across his reviled face like blood through linen, the sly expression spreading slowly over the doctor's features as he realized he had a predatory advantage over another. A trap, known only to him, had sprung and his unfortunate dinner companion had stumbled into it. He looked at me, a cruel gleam in his eye, and nodded subtly in the direction of his favoured small, private dining room. Bringing his long-fingered hand up, he brushed his ear, his attention focused on the unfortunate man seated across from him. I understood. My survival depended on reading such clues but, for all his self-proclaimed genius, the Doctor was not a difficult man to understand. He was cruel and enjoyed an audience to witness his cruelty. Once again, I was to be his audience. Tonight, in this grand room, with dinner guests, music and elegance all around, the Doctor would cull this man from the herd for reasons he would never deign to share. I didn't care to know his reasons, such knowledge could only burn. I was to listen. It gave me hope the exchange would not be too ghastly. Standing, I made my way from the other guests.

"Going someplace, Miss Dacosta?" The Doctor asked, voice dripping with a treacly innocence I doubted any of the others would note.

I nodded, offered a smile I did not feel. "A short errand, Doctor Chapman. I am expecting a message from Maude regarding a patient. Nothing to be concerned about."

Around the table the guests nodded, pleased to see a member of the asylum's staff show such concern for an inmate or, as they were called in the other wings of our institute, our guest. Tonight's grand affair was a celebration to welcome a new board member to the asylum, Doctor Douglas, a celebrated physician from across the sea whose brilliance and compassion was well established. Apparently, however, his medical genius did not extend to controlling the weather as a delay at sea prevented him from arriving in time to attend the dinner in his honour. Still, as a private organization, such events were a fundraising opportunity, too important to allow a tardy board member's absence to cancel.

Doctor Chapman noticed the others' approval of my apparent diligence and was pleased, then turned his attention back to the dinner guest he was cutting from the herd. I made my way across the room, found a waiter, and asked to have a plate delivered to the Ladies Waiting Lounge. The room would be closed to guests until dinner was finished. Of course, Doctor Chapman was a member of the club, the staff was naturally terrified of him, and such arrangements had been made on my behalf before. From the lounge I could overhear what was said in the private dining room without betraying my presence.

I waited, the meal arrived and I thanked the waiter who delivered it. Did I smile? Later it would seem important but I have difficulty remembering such small gestures. I try to smile to the staff. I am seen in this place in Chapman's company but I do not want anyone to think I share his nature. Kindness is an aspiration of mine, one it seems doubtful I shall ever achieve, but I do try.

Having finished my meal efficiently, I waited. Since making the acquaintance of Doctor Chapman a great deal of my time has been devoted to waiting. A practised skill though, I must confess, one which seems to be slipping from my anxious grasp. Eventually I heard the doctor escort his victim into the next room. By the sound I knew a waiter followed, pushing a dessert cart with some bottles rattling along. Drinks were ordered, desserts selected, cigars placed on the table.

"So," Chapman's voice, quite pleased with himself. "I know a secret."

"Do tell." A strong voice, with a somewhat nasal quality, eager to gain a confidence.

"I know who you are."

"Well," the guest replied, taking time to puff on a cigar. "That's not very impressive. I know as well. Who do you suppose I am?"

"We have an acquaintance in common," Chapman announced. "A departed professor. He told me once that, should he meet a premature end, I could expect a visit from a certain consulting detective. The professor warned me that it was pointless to try and identify this man by appearance as he had a gift for disguise. I would know if he was about though. If anyone made inquiries to me regarding him, I could be assured the detective would be present to hear the answers."

"I don't know what—"

Another voice then, chuckling. Who?

"Mind your place!" Chapman's sharp bark. The waiter then, the doctor was always a beast to staff. If the command was meant to stifle the laughter, it had the opposite effect. The chuckle grew into a genuine laugh. The waiter had cheek. I tried to imagine the doctor's expression at such impudence and found I could not. It seemed the poor waiter had no idea what sort of man he was dealing with, did not know enough to be afraid. I knew, but had no way to warn the unfortunate waiter.

"Perhaps it would be best if you left us alone," the waiter said. "The doctor and I appear to have private matters to discuss. I appreciate your assistance. Please inform the head waiter that I have enjoyed my service here but, regrettably, shall be unable to complete my shift."

"Are you certain?" Chapman's chosen victim asked.

"Quite."

I listened as the chair scraped the floor and the guest left through the door. The scrape of the chair again, a man— the waiter?—sitting. "And who," the waiter asked, "did you suppose that man was?"

Chapman's response rumbled like an impending apocalypse. "Now see here—"

"Sherlock Holmes?" The waiter asked, his steady voice somehow cutting through the doctor's bluster like a saber.

"How could you know that?"

"A simple deduction. If you are impressed by such straightforward logic I fear our conversation will be rather dull. Do try to keep your end up."

"How dare you! Who do you think you are?!"

"Sherlock Holmes," the waiter said, his voice calm and level. "And you are Doctor Fredric Chapman, director of research at the Belgrave Hall Asylum. Listening through the vent in the wall is, I believe, Cordeila Dacosta, a nurse also employed in the research department of the institute. I admit I do not understand why she is stationed there but I'm certain you've some reason for her presence. If you would like to invite her to join us, I have no objections."

I did not remember opening my mouth but, listening to the impudent waiter, I discovered my jaw had indeed fallen with surprise. How remarkable. Was he the same waiter who had brought me dinner? More remarkable, he knew who the doctor was, he'd known the professor, yet he did not sound afraid. He was either a fool or supremely confident. Discovering I was leaning closer to the vent, I straightened up. It would not do to be discovered eavesdropping, though in truth I no longer felt as if I could stop myself from listening.

"No? As you wish. Do you mind?" A clatter from the dessert cart. "The chef really does a remarkable job with these." A clatter of cutlery, a soft sigh of appreciation.

"You are Sherlock Holmes?"

"Do try to keep up, Doctor Chapman." Another mouthful. "I am Sherlock Holmes, the consulting detective of Baker Street." Another mouthful, then the sound of cutlery released. "You indicated Professor Moriarty mentioned me. I am, of course, flattered. And the professor's prediction turned out to be quite prescient, if not exactly in the manner you expected. I instructed my compatriot to make conversation regarding asteroid dynamics, and I was curious to see your reaction. Indeed, it revealed much. I assume you encountered Moriarty when you were at university together? Though, I must say, from what I've gathered, it does not seem a likely starting point for your association."

"James was a different man back then. He lacked vision. His pursuits were pedestrian. Academics, women, common things."

"Unlike yourself. My apologies, I have been rude. Would you care for one of these? They are really quite good."

"Simple chemistry." So dismissive, unwilling to enjoy anything so common, so like the doctor.

"Chemistry certainly, but hardly simple. So, if you don't mind me asking, how did you and Moriarty become partners? I assume it was after the accident which took the life of his wife."

"He came to me. We had never really got on but he knew of my studies, my ongoing research. He wondered if I could relieve him of his grief."

261

"He was your patient? Or, would it be more accurate to describe him as a subject of your research?"

"A bit of both, I would say." The doctor was settling in now, adjusting to the waiter who was more than what he seemed. Always eager to talk about his research, never missing the opportunity to show how clever he was. However wrong footed the conversation had started, Doctor Chapman was starting to enjoy himself.

"And did you? Relieve him of his grief, I mean."

"Oh yes."

"May I inquire how? Alienism? Chemistry? Surgery?"

"Some of each." I did not need to see the doctor's face to know the smile he wore as he answered. Smug, cruel, unpleasant, all blended on a loathsome face. "I doubt you'd understand."

"Perhaps not, our specialities overlap but they have decidedly different focuses. Your published papers offered little insight. According to those who knew him, the Professor was radically different after the accident. I had been willing to credit the change to emotional upheaval, the loss of his wife, but I wonder now if your treatment played some part. Interesting. When did your partnership begin?"

"Partnership seems too intimate a term. At most, ours was a business arrangement."

"Yet the terms of that unwritten contract have proven difficult to define. I know the professor supplied you with a startling amount of capital as well as staff, such as Miss Dacosta. Talented, educated, yet trapped in circumstances making them vulnerable to blackmail. There is a clear trail of evidence regarding the professor's obligations to you, however what the professor received in return is much more vague."

"Of course, if what the professor said about you is true, you must have some theories." Smugness in the Doctor's voice again.

"A few. Assassins, obviously, and other persons capable of a curious amount of intimidation. There are others whose skills seem unlikely, but—"

It was the doctor's turn to chuckle, the sound lacked humor but made up for it with arrogance. "Tell me, Mr. Holmes, do you believe in monsters?"

"My profession is centered on monsters, I have met several. Some I escorted to the gallows."

"Ahh," the doctor sighed, disappointed. "You fail to comprehend. Such a limited imagination. All those monsters were but men, given agency and soul by the Lord God. No, I mean monsters, genuine monsters, soulless and utterly reliant on others for direction. Creatures without pity or mercy, such concepts being as outside their understanding as they would be for a shark or tiger. True monsters, capable of greatness when given proper instruction."

There was a pause, how could there not be? The doctor spoke in generalities; I doubted the detective could fully grasp the horror being described. I could; of course, I had seen them and—God forgive me—played a part in their descent from humanity.

"There has been speculation regarding such possibilities." The waiter mused. "Of course, I considered it premature but when I presented some of the cases I'd investigated it was suggested the feats accomplished were beyond human limitations. I clung to less fantastic explanations."

The doctor spoke almost dreamily. "Oh, I could make such a monster from a mind like yours."

"No doubt. There have been inquiries, you know. From members of Her Majesty's government."

"What?" I did not have to see the doctor's face to see how firmly the hook was set in his mouth. For all his talk of advancing knowledge, the doctor thirsted for luxury and cash.

"My work often brings me in contact with agents of the government, though they are required to be discreet about their employment. Several have expressed interest in the possibilities suggested by your research. Inquiries have been made about securing your research."

"I would be amiable to such discussion, with the right gentlemen."

"Of course, but before I could make such introductions I would need to be convinced of its validity. I am unwilling to vouch for such research without further evidence. While my investigations have been remarkably suggestive, I have not seen any evidence directly pointing to anything fantastic. For example, if the professor requested, say, a vampire—"

"Vampires?" The doctor scoffed. "Vampires are simple, dull, almost common. I will admit that, early in my research, I followed examples drawn from superstition and folklore. Even then, vampires were not overly difficult. Tell me, Mr. Holmes, have you ever considered the matter of the wehr-wolf?"

"Actually, I have. When an unexpected death occurs, people seek comfort in assigning blame. A young person collapses in the woods, their body is subsequently savaged by wildlife; how simple it is to infer their death was due to some beastly attack. Simple, but faulty logic. Grief is not sated by assigning blame to woodland scavengers. There is always an outsider, someone not well-liked, someone the majority would be willing to sacrifice for relief following a tragedy. A belief in magic can plaster over any logic gaps the reasonable of the community might object to. The wehr-wolf is a symbol of misplaced justice and logic bending to convenience. Pure superstition."

"An interesting analysis, but you must admit it is a formidable superstition. Early in my career I constructed a wehr-wolf, and he still resides with us. Pure sentimentality to keep him, of course, but as one of my early successes I have not yet disposed of him. Perhaps, if it would ease your concerns regarding the making of introductions, you could come and see him for yourself."

"I rather expect examples of your research are scant, given how long you have lacked the financial support of the professor. Yes, I would be interested in viewing an example of your research."

"Such an appointment could be arranged. Forgive me for asking but I must seek assurances you would not bring those who, uh, wouldn't appreciate the science of my efforts."

A chuckle. "I take it you mean the police? No, of course not. You understand how my reputation would be affected were I to walk into Scotland Yard and started ranting about wehr-wolves. No, those I have spoken to regarding your work are more highly placed in the government. And after all, I cannot recall any legal statute you have broken. I will come alone. Well, my driver will come with me. He is a dangerous fellow and, should I fail to return at the proper time, he can be quite formidable."

"Shall we say Tuesday at midnight?"

Listening through the vent, my face felt like a slab of marble as I struggled to contain my despair. If the government was depraved enough to fund the doctor's research my nightmare might never end. Indeed, it would spread beyond the shores of our island kingdom and infect the whole world. I might never be free. Yet, even as my heart settled into shadows, the waiter's next words left me breathless with hope.

"Other matters demand my attention. Thursday?"

Thursday. My heart fluttered at the sound. I hardly dared to believe; hope was something I dared indulge in. An organ, dry and desiccated, brought to life by the man from Baker Street. Tears of hope clouded my vision as I brought my trembling hands to my lips. The realization of what I heard made my soul ring like a bell. The man, the waiter, surely he was an agent of the hero John Watson. The end of my nightmare might only be days away.

Quickly, I pulled a mirror from my clutch and checked my features. It would not do to allow my face to betray the man who placed such trust in me, the man who might deliver me from my suffering. Dabbing my eyes with a napkin, I slowed my breathing and composed myself. If the waiter walked by, he must not report to John Watson I'd looked shaken. I would not lose my nerve, not so close to the end. I imagined seeing Doctor Watson soon, his handsome, compassionate features, but—

"Miss Dacosta." The doctor's loathsome voice sounded from the other room. "We need to prepare our laboratory for a visitor."

§

As I'd predicted, I met John again on Wednesday morning. I had been dispatched on errands; the Doctor was anxious his laboratory appear as professional as possible and was willing to spend some of his horde in the effort. I was to make the necessary expenditures. Doctor Chapman seemed convinced Holmes' introductions to members of Her Majesty's government would result in funding for his terrible work. The thought sickened me. With the wealth of the Empire behind him, the horrors the cursed man could unleash upon the world were beyond imagining. John Watson was my only hope.

On this, our penultimate meeting, I knew better than to look for him. My eyes had eagerly sought him before but I never found him until he had already found me, appearing at my side, his warm eyes and slight grin tugging his lips as I noticed him there. As always, the threat of us being seen, or our conversations being overheard, was present but either he concealed his concern well or he was genuinely fearless because his sincere features never betrayed anxiety. On this day he met me on the train. A group of raucous, loud children emptied the carriage as riders fled to more sedate environs. Shortly after, the children were chased away by the conductor who, to my surprise, turned and revealed himself as John Watson. With the other travellers chased away, with the sound of wheels on the metals, he was able to sit across from me, close enough to touch had I been slightly more bold, and he spoke directly to me.

"The time has come." His voice was calm, his eyes kind, but a determination flavoured his words.

"At last," I answered. "That was your man, then? At the dinner, speaking to Chapman? I heard his conversation with Chapman. Tomorrow. Is ... is the child safe?"

"Yes. The house has been under surveillance all week and two trusted constables will be watching over it from noon Thursday until noon Saturday. We are, finally, ready."

"As am I," I agreed. "Doctor Chapman has been most concerned the laboratory appear as professional as possible. We have been scrubbing and cleaning continuously and now I am to return with fresh supplies. Appearances must be maintained for investors, even in Hell. The doctor is pinning a great deal of hope on your associate's promise of government funding. There's no chance of such a thing, I know it is a foolish fear, but Chapman is so convinced."

"Be assured, neither Holmes or I would allow such a thing. You remember what you need to do?"

"Oh yes, I know. You've no idea how long I've waited for this. The ward must be sealed from the rest of the institute. The delivery doors at the back of the ward must be the only way in or out. Cell number seven is to be kept empty, the door closed but unlatched. Before midnight, when your agent arrives, the ring of keys from the nurses' station should be replaced by the janitor's keys. When your agent appears with his driver, I am to place the key to the delivery doors in the driver's jacket pocket. All of which is quite sensible and simple; I don't understand why I am to place rubbing alcohol, cotton swabs, a basin of water and a towel in the closet by the stairs."

"I would not ask, were it not important," Watson said kindly. "And?"

"When I hear the whistle, I am to go to the nurse's station and lock myself in. I could help, you know, I am not helpless."

"I know, but you forgot the last and most important task."

"I've not forgotten. I am to take care not to reveal my part in this to Doctor Chapman. I still think I could do more. I fear death less than I fear being trapped in that awful place."

"I know," Watson assured me. "It should not be necessary, nor are we willing to take the risk."

"As I said, I am not some delicate—"

"It is not that, Miss Dacosta, I assure you. Doctor Chapman's research will end tomorrow but, should our plans fail and Doctor Chapman escapes, we cannot risk him knowing you helped us. He is a petty man, apt to seek revenge. We can protect the child for a time, weeks if necessary, but we cannot guard him forever. If he knows you've helped us, no, we will not risk the child's life."

Watson straightened then, I had not realised how close we had been huddled together, our faces nearly touching. He smiled, assuring me, "Nor will it be necessary. The plan will work."

"Will you be there?"

"Of course," he nodded. "You will not see me until events have played out. I look forward to introducing myself in my own clothing." He waved at the conductor's uniform he was wearing.

"You've had quite the change of costume for our small exchanges," I noted with some amusement. He had, in fact, donned the clothing of a clerk, a street sweeper, a tradesman and on one memorable occasion, a pastor during our secret encounters.

"An effort to evade detection," he explained. "Your jailer, Doctor Chapman, suffers a curious affliction. He seems unable to perceive men dressed below a certain station."

"He certainly underestimated your waiter the other night."

"As expected," Watson agreed. "Until tomorrow night, Miss Dacosta."

§

The asylum spread its architecture like a stern embrace, all straight lines and glassy reflections looming behind a well-tended stretch of lawn. From the large windows guests could be seen contemplating their wellness or talking pleasantly with others under similar treatments. This was a place where the wealthy came, checking themselves in and out as if it were a hotel, enjoying visits from talented physicians to discuss their well-being and making earnest plans to enjoy their privilege even more fully than they had previously. This was the front-facing asylum, pleasant, restful, peaceful.

There were two other wings extending from the rear of the building, in the shadows. The west wing housed staff and the east offered treatment of a different sort for inmates undeserving of the term guests. Certainly it wasn't how they viewed themselves, nor did Doctor Chapman consider them anything but captives upon whom he could perform his experiments. The world is cruel to those without voices raised in their defence. Doctor Chapman was many times crueler than someone indifferent could ever be.

Most of our wing was occupied by storage and disposal for

those poor souls unable to survive the procedures performed on them. Perhaps due to Doctor Chapman's aversion to exercise, most of the research was performed on the ground floor. Snuggled against the main building was the nurses' station, controlling access to those who might wander unknowingly from the tranquility of the asylum's public face. From there a long hallway, with doorways into inmate cells, numbered from one to seven. Between the nurses' station and Doctor Chapman's office, tucked into the stairwell was the narrow supply pantry. Further down the hallway was the laboratory, a cell rearranged as a viewing area, and the surgical theatre. The end of the hallway opened into a loading area where new inmates were marched up to their new lodgings or wheeled down for disposal.

§

My shift began with me watching helplessly as Doctor Chapman injected our patient, a wretched man I knew only as Lawrence, with chemicals necessary for tonight's demonstration. I did not allow any expression to betray me as I listened to Chapman soothe the wretched soul with false assurances. As if he believed this treatment to be the cure Chapman had been working towards for all the years of his imprisonment. Chapman lied so easily and with a sincerity Lawrence, whose reason had been deteriorating steadily each day of his captivity, absorbed with such a desperate hope it made me want to weep. I held myself still, allowing no flash of emotion to cross my eyes, no flinch as the doctor injected one cruel concoction after another into the ruined man. Once it was done, we left Lawrence and I followed the doctor downstairs to receive my keys from the departing nurse Augusta. When I first found myself ensnared in this hell, I had sought assistance from her but found nothing resembling compassion there. Part of me believed the woman was stone, as unfeeling as the moon. I struggled to understand what drove her but to no avail. For a time, I wondered if the Doctor had altered her in some way but her intellect remained formidable. Reduced intellect had always been the most distinct symptom of Chapman's research subjects. The doctor demanded three nurses serve in the research ward, no more and no less. Aside from Augusta and myself there was Maude, Doctor Chapman's favourite. It speaks to the conditions I endure that the stone-hearted, inexpressive and silent mystery of Augusta was more comfort to me than the constant whispering of Maude. Her eyes shone like a child who has found candy every time Doctor Chapman picked up a scalpel. Her slight but constant grin as she watched the suffering of those we imprisoned was as disturbing, albeit in a different way, as Chapman's direct cruelty.

After Maude handed off the keys, a token of authority within the ward, she left for her room. I found myself unaccompanied in the ward and went to the supply pantry and set out some cotton swabs, rubbing alcohol, a small basin of water and, after some consideration, a small linen. Having completed the smallest and most puzzling of John Watson's tasks I allowed myself to return to the routine which defined my miserable existence in this dreadful place. I toured the ward, observing the nature of the wretched and making notes in their files when appropriate. The cells were empty but I inspected them, as was my habit, closing the door to cell seven but leaving it unlatched. That task complete, I made my way into the main building as was my routine, and signed the necessary records there. I slipped the ward's private door key from the set of keys and tucked it into the string of my uniform's apron. Once back in the ward, I stepped into the janitorial closet and exchanged the set of keys there with the set from the nurses' station and returned to the daily minutia waiting for me at the nurses' station. No one, I believed, observed me as I completed tasks from the list John Watson had me memorise but, even if they had, I doubted my actions would have been noted. In dark moments of despair, I sometimes fancied Chapman, or one of his creations, could peer into my thoughts as if my skull was on a hinge. I took care not to permit myself any feeling of excitement or, indeed, hope as I completed these tasks. This was no time for emotion, allowing myself the luxury of hope could only betray me.

For so long I had denied myself to feel anything, I couldn't help but wonder if I would ever regain the capacity to do so again. Odd, how at the very times emotions are the most dangerous they rear up and strain at the reins. But my control was far too practised to allow anything to disturb the desolate calm of my thoughts.

§

Doctor Chapman returned an hour before our guest was scheduled to arrive. I noted the care he took regarding his appearance and attire, this night's appointment meant more to him than he was willing to say. The chance of continued funding was an opportunity he desperately wanted to seize. I wondered, not for the first time, what manner of life he enjoyed beyond the walls of this ward. There were hints, of course, in the rich manner of his clothing and the various scents of wine, good food and perfumes he carried in with him from the outside world. I had no existence outside these walls save for the errands I was tasked with and, until John Watson's unexpected appearance, these journeys provided little evidence of any possible place for me beyond the asylum; they were a cruel reminder that there existed an uncaring world beyond all this misery.

Chapman sent me to gather two attendants, in actuality two burly inmates whose mental abilities had been reduced to blind obedience by Doctor Chapman's handiwork. Often I wondered what these men had been like before Chapman had dimmed their minds and swollen their muscles, but there was less humanity in these two than Lawrence had retained. The doctor cared only for strength and obedience and he engineered them to suit his needs.

They were an obstacle I wasn't certain John Watson had fully anticipated.

So important was the evening for Doctor Chapman that he braved the stairs for the second time that day. With the attendants, trained as they were to respond to the Doctor's voice, Lawrence was fitted into a straitjacket and spit-hood before taking him downstairs to the observation area. Docile and pleading in his child-like voice, Lawrence allowed his restraints to be removed as he sat in the room's only feature, a much-battered metal chair. Lawrence waited, free within the locked room, eagerly awaiting his long promised cure.

Doctor Chapman led his attendants to delivery doors, within earshot should he summon them, instructing them to wait and attack anyone who attempted to enter. I tried not to worry for John Watson as I followed him back into the ward.

"You know what needs to be done," Chapman said in the hallway, his voice a study of impatient annoyance. "Do it. Why must you always wait for my instruction? You cling to your little rebellions, thinking they are without consequence, but you are mistaken. Have you forgotten the punishments for insolence?"

Silently, I set about arranging items for tonight's demonstration. He was quite correct. I knew all too well what was required and the knowledge shamed me. I felt the key dig into my side as I bent to my chores, providing a stab of hope I could not indulge in but which, I cannot deny, provided some comfort. When I finished, I went and toured the ward, ensuring that all the doors leading to or from the rest of the asylum were locked. Another item completed from John Watson's list. Chapman waited for me as I descended the stairs to the main floor.

"Here," Chapman handed me a case from his jacket pocket. "Fill it with this," he added, passing me a small, unlabeled bottle of clear fluid. Opening the case I discovered a syringe. Questions flooded my mind, but I knew better than to voice them. I filled the syringe and capped the sharp end of the needle with a piece of cork. Replacing the syringe in its case, I handed it back to the Doctor. He examined it with a glance and snapped the case shut. "Hopefully it will not be required," he muttered as he slipped the case back into his pocket, "but best to be prepared."

All was ready. Chapman surveyed the room like Wellington looking over Waterloo, nodding in approval, and instructed me to go to the institute's main entrance to wait for our guest, reminding me to show him all due courtesy. The manner in which he spoke promised suffering if his wishes were not completed to his satisfaction. I hurried to do as I was told.

§

At the reception area I offered my greetings to the staff on duty there, resisting the urge to check if the key was still tucked in my apron string. I wanted to offer the young nurse on duty a smile, to prove not everyone in the research section was a monster, but having schooled my emotions so tightly all day I found I was unable to form the simple gesture. I was too unsettled, my surface as calm as an eggshell. I waited with my hands folded in front of me, wishing I could turn off my mind and simply be inert until my presence was required.

Our guest walked in, dressed in a heavy overcoat and

striding with purpose to the reception desk. He looked somewhat like the waiter I remembered, and I wished I had looked closer when he brought me that meal. At this hour, it was unlikely to be anyone else. I crossed the floor and laid a hand on his forearm. "Mr. Holmes? I am to show you to Doctor Chapman. If you'll follow me, please?"

"Oh," the man stopped, somewhat surprised. "I should sign in, surely?"

"That's not necessary," I assured him. "Not for visitors to the research ward."

"I see," the man said. "Well, where is my driver? Oh, there you are." Another man, an older, bent figure sporting side whiskers and a cabbie's weather-beaten face, appeared beside us. "This young lady," Holmes offered a glance and a smile, "will show me to Doctor Chapman. Do you have the—"

The man held out a slim folder.

"Let me take that for you," I offered, reaching for the file. Quickly, I pulled the key from my apron and slid it into the driver's jacket pocket. I took the folder.

"Ta," the driver offered, before turning and disappearing through the doors.

"This way, Mr. Holmes."

As I escorted Mr. Holmes into the ward, I stopped and turned the final lock, sealing us from the rest of the asylum. For better or worse, there was no escape in that direction.

In the observation room, I had placed two plush chairs before the closed shutters of the cell in which Lawrence waited. A small table was placed between the chairs, brandy tumblers filled and some correspondence set there. The scene was almost domestic, and Doctor Chapman looked up as if in surprise at the guest's arrival. He set down the file he had been reading and hurried over, extending a hand in greeting. "Mr. Holmes, we're honoured you could join us."

Holmes grunted in response, shrugging himself out of his

overcoat. Setting down the file I was carrying, I hurried over to help him.

"Thank you," our guest said, his voice slightly different when not echoing through an air vent, though it still had the distinctive nasal quality I recognised. As I held the overcoat, Holmes made his way to the nearest of the seats. At a loss as to what to do with the heavy coat, I hung it on the doorknob, recovered the file I'd carried for Holmes and offered it to him.

"Thank you once more," Holmes said with a nod, drawing a pencil from the inner pocket of his jacket and opening the file. "You have no objection if I take notes, I assume?"

"None at all. As you know, Mr. Holmes, my research has been aided by certain discoveries from the dark continent, namely herbs from the coast of—"

"We can discuss specifics following your demonstration," Holmes interrupted. "Discussing your methods without providing results is a huckster's trick, Doctor Chapman. If you can prove your claim I shall be most interested in hearing of your methods but, until then, it seems a waste of time."

"Yes, of course," Chapman replied, flustered but still confident. He glanced at me before he sat beside our guest. I hurried to open the shutters to the viewing area while Doctor Chapman took up his brandy. "You understand this example is one of my older creations. He's been with us for several years now. We keep him for demonstrations such as these. More research has allowed us to fine-tune our processes, resulting in changes which are less dramatic but of more practical use. Even so, I believe you will be impressed."

With the shutters unlatched, through the metal lattice separating the rooms, Lawrence was revealed on his metal chair. He was a man collapsed in on himself, someone who took up little space and wished to occupy even less, a man whose dearest hope is to be overlooked. I had seen misery in his eyes before, I knew better than to meet his gaze now.

Our guest, however, had experienced no such warnings, he leaned forward in his seat, studying the poor soul beyond the wire mesh.

"For our more recent subjects, we can use a wide variety of stimuli to begin the transformation. For this patient, a chemical trigger is employed."

It was my cue. Walking in front of the lattice, I watched as Lawrence's eyes followed my motion. I pushed a lever to the left, opening a small recess which Lawrence could see under the window. He eyed the opening suspiciously, concerned now, his blood fizzing with the chemicals Chapman had injected into him earlier. Doctor Chapman expected me to encourage Lawrence to leave his chair, take the pill from the recess and, believing it to be a cure, to swallow it. I opened my mouth to speak but, not for the first time, I found myself unable to voice the lies.

"Come on Lawrence," Doctor Chapman said behind me. "Be a good chap. Take your medicine."

Lawrence's eyes darted from the doctor to me. I wanted to call to the poor lost soul, to let him know this would be the last time he had to endure this, that our liberty was at hand, if only he would suffer this one more time. No words emerged from me but I managed a small nod of reassurance. It was enough. Lawrence pulled himself from the chair, moving like a man two centuries old, and warily crossed the distance and took the offered pill. Holding it before him, he sniffed it.

"Smells like the last one." Lawrence complained, his soft, child-like voice tinged with suspicion.

"Be a good chap," Doctor Chapman urged him again. Lawrence looked at me, seemed to see the turmoil I was hiding within and hesitated. Thinking of the child, I met Lawrence's gaze and offered him another nod of reassurance. Such a small gesture, yet it seemed to tear the heart from me.

Beyond the metal lattice, Lawrence swallowed the pill. I

moved back, taking care to keep my face hidden from the two observers lest my despair betray me.

Lawrence turned and started back to the metal chair, falling before he crossed the short distance. Convulsing, he tried to form words but only short barks emerged. Twisting on the floor, his limbs seeming to shoot out in random directions, those barks escalated into screeches, then to moans. Then the howling began.

The change was beginning. His bones protested, the pops and cracking they made were horrible to hear. His spine seemed to arch in an impossible contortion.

"Good Lord!" The exclamation drew my attention. Our guest was out of his seat, stepping towards the metal lattice separating us from the—there was no other description— monster beyond. "What the devil is happening?"

Doctor Chapman sipped his brandy before answering. "His body is changing, from that of an ordinary man to something much more fearsome. I promised you a wehr-wolf, Mr. Holmes, did you doubt me? The result is not really all that related to a canine but it is certainly beastly. Observe his skin, you see how it is changing? The way it is puckering? It hardens, I believe it's a result of calcium shed as his arms and legs shorten. The hardness of the skin is, as I'm sure you understand, difficult to test but I believe it is strong enough to turn the blade of a knife or stop a small caliber bullet. The professor reported as much and I have no reason to doubt his report. The legs and arms, see how they change. You would think it a handicap, I did when I first witnessed it, but when he charges he uses all his limbs to propel himself. He's remarkably swift, and his claws—"

Holmes moved, fascinated and horrified, closer to the metal lattice."This man is dying. Stop this procedure. Now!"

"Quite impossible at this point," Chapman replied with theatrical regret. "He will likely survive, he has survived the transformation nearly a dozen times before. Mr. Holmes, I suggest you step back from the bars, the claws—"

The claws smashed into the lattice, bending the metal back, as long claws shot out to tear the throat from our guest. Holmes stumbled backwards, a thin gash along his jaw and throat welling with blood. He scrambled backwards, panicked. I dashed forward, helping him regain his feet as I pulled him away from the howling beast beyond.

"Impressive, isn't he?" Chapman said, an unmistakable pride in his stance as he watched the thrashing of the beast. "And you understand, this patient represents the least we can do. With proper funding we could effectively determine the full capabilities of each being we bring into existence. You understand the professor required specific capabilities which, generally, we were able to provide. The military applications are obvious, of course, but there are a whole range of possibilities in which this research could benefit Her Majesty and her government."

I was closer to Holmes than Chapman, my hands still on his arm. I could see the rage flush his features, the livid anger burning in his eyes as he turned to look at Chapman. Our guest was seized with rage, revolted by the inhumanity he'd witnessed. He pushed me away.

"Think of it, Mr. Holmes," Chapman continued, oblivious to our guest's rage. "A regiment of soldiers requiring neither weapons nor ammunition. They could stroll into a foreign city and, at our command, bring it to its knees. Nor is this the only variation to be explored. I have made a man quite capable of breathing for extended periods underwater, a sailor who requires no ship. I assure you such a subject is just as deadly as the one before you, though less—shall we say—animalistic in expression. I could make you an assassin, perfectly capable of finding employment in a royal household, who could be shaped into a weapon."

"Enough!" Holmes screamed, louder even than the monster in the next room. Blood stained his collar now, the dampness on the sleeve of his jacket. Chapman turned to Holmes, meeting his gaze, taking in our guest's stance. "Enough," Holmes continued."You have impressed me. You have managed a degree of cruelty and madness which I had no idea anyone was capable of. Your research, sir, is over. I will do everything in my power to bring this," our guest gestured beyond the lattice, "to an end. This madness must stop and you shall be punished for this depravity."

For a moment, Holmes and Chapman stood evaluating each other. A frown crossed Chapman's face, an expression of disappointment. He reached out with one hand, the other in his pocket. He seized Holmes' arm, looking with concern at the blood on the man's face, before the syringe emerged in his other hand. With practised skill, Chapman drove the barrel of the needle towards his opponent's upper arm, seeking the flesh beneath the fabric of his jacket and shirt.

§

Somewhere a whistle was blowing. It meant something but, even as I turned my head towards the door, I found I could not remember what. I walked to the door, out into the hallway which seemed full of the sound of stomping feet and the angry voices of men. No one else was supposed to be here, this was a secret place. Horrible and secret. A thousand of the Queen's Guard may have rushed past me, I was beyond noticing. Tears filled my eyes as I stumbled to the nurses' station. My carefully maintained indifference, the walls of the prison in which I locked away my emotions for so long, had burst at last. Weeping, I entered the nurses' station and locked myself inside. For a time, wracked with uncontrollable sobbing, I knew nothing beyond the tears obscuring my vision.

A frantic rattling of the doorknob brought me back into the world, someone pounding on the door caused it to shudder in the frame. A shout—Chapman?—then the sound of feet scurrying down the hallway. I could still hear the howling from the observation room, I suspected I always would. The thump of someone bouncing off a wall, the thud of a blow landing, convinced me a battle raged beyond my locked door. While I sat and wept.

John was out there. In danger. He didn't know about his friend, Holmes, being felled by Chapman's syringe. He didn't know about monsters who responded only to their master's voice. I stood, opened the door, stepping into the hallway.

It seemed empty. Blood along the wall indicated a battle had raged here but moved on. I walked on, unsure if my feet were reaching to the floor, moving towards the howling. I wondered if John was here, wondered if he'd found his friend or if Chapman had fed the poor man to his monster. Only one way to find out.

A shout, voices raised in alarm. "There he is!" and "Watch out!"

Chapman was there, hands around my throat as he threw me against the wall. His face had undergone a transformation, flushed with rage, eyes bulging. He was hissing something at me but I couldn't make it out. Spots appeared before me, separating me from my captor.

I thought I heard Watson's voice, shouting in alarm, and then something struck Chapman. The Doctor's grip loosened as he was slammed against the wall. Quick as a flash, a fist struck Chapman under his chin, knocking his head back and dazing him. Seizing him by the lapels, Chapman was pulled back into the hallway.

"Miss Dacosta? If you would, please."

Blinking, I looked over and saw cell number seven, the door closed but unlatched. I pulled it open. Chapman was thrown inside. He seemed to almost bounce off the far wall before slumping to the floor. My rescuer closed the door and locked it with a key of the set normally kept at the nurses' station.

"Well done, Holmes!"

Holmes? I turned but all I saw was the cabbie, standing straighter now, his eyes alert and calculating. He nodded, as if we were being introduced.

"Miss Dacosta, are you hurt?" John Watson's handsome face before me, his kind eyes filled with concern.

"She is fine," the driver—Holmes?—assured him. "And the Inspector? Doctor Douglas?"

"Doctor Douglas is fit to be tied, understandably, but he is well. The Inspector suffered a blow to the head but it doesn't seem serious. As for the other patient, well—"

"His name is Lawrence," I told him. "He will need water, lots of it, when the transformation starts to reverse."

"And when can we expect that to happen?" The driver asked.

"He remains a monster for about two hours," I reported. "Once he starts to change, it happens quickly."

"We've no choice then but to wait. Thanks to Miss Dacosta's timely assistance, we have the Doctor secured. The situation is under control. I shall inform Miss Dacosta of the next steps if you need to see to your patients."

"Of course," Watson nodded, offering me a tentative smile. "It's all over now. You did very well."

Then the driver was escorting me down to the supply pantry, while Watson disappeared into the observation room, where his friend, Holmes, no doubt lay. "John's friend, he's been poisoned."

"No," the cabbie assured me. He found a chair and guided me to it before pulling a box from the pantry to sit on himself. Upending the bottle of rubbing alcohol onto a cotton swab with practised ease, he began rubbing his whiskers. To my surprise, the whiskers, and some of the weathering on the driver's face, disappeared under the action. "Doctor James Douglas, formerly of the Beauport Asylum in Montreal, was the man you saw assaulted by Doctor Chapman. He was only pretending to be a detective."

"But, I thought—"

"A bit of disguise on our part. I am Sherlock Holmes," the cabbie said, continuing to remove the stubble and weathering from his face with cotton and alcohol. "When you saw me at the fundraising dinner, I was employed as a member of the wait staff. I had also altered my appearance to appear as Doctor Douglas, a double disguise. You may recall that Doctor Douglas was recently named a board member of this institute. The dinner was being held in his honour though he was unable to attend. In truth the good doctor had arrived in London in a timely manner but when Watson and I explained the irregularities in the institute's research department, he agreed to forgo the celebration and aid our investigation."

"Is he ... dead? I saw Doctor Chapman with the syringe—"

"Douglas is unharmed, though extremely angry. You are correct. Chapman did attempt to inject Douglas, believing as you did he was me, however it seems someone hammered out a number of biscuit tins and inserted them—not without some difficulty—into the sleeves of his jacket. Although the syringe remained stuck in the arm of his jacket which, while unexpected, certainly will make convincing testimony from the Scotland Yard Inspector who witnessed the aftermath of the attack."

"So Mr. Holmes, I mean Doctor Douglas, wasn't harmed?"

"There is a shallow wound along his jaw and throat," Holmes explained. "He certainly came close to danger this evening but Watson is tending to it. Douglas is also, as I mentioned, extremely angry that such outrageous experimentation occurred in a place of healing. He is vowing to have Chapman's credentials stripped from him, as well as pressing charges regarding the assault he suffered. While it was not my intention to expose our overseas companion to so much danger, I must admit the result is better than I could have anticipated. You understand that the laws pertaining to these types of experiments are not—how shall I put it?— robust. However the laws regarding assault and attempted murder are quite clear and Chapman will shortly find himself charged with both offenses. He will be imprisoned for a long time. Should he survive his incarceration, he will find himself unable to practise medicine and plagued by scandal. He deserves worse, I admit, but this is the best English law can deliver at the moment. I should also tell you this: The child is safe. Not just for this night, but always."

With his words an enormous burden seemed to lift from my soul. Had I not been sitting, I might have swooned. I felt as if I had been locked in a dark, sealed room for years and was now experiencing sunshine for the first time.

Holmes had stopped cleaning his face, leaving him looking like a man in the middle of one of Doctor Chapman's transformations himself. Part of his face was a weathered cabbie, the other half a dignified, clean-shaven gentleman. I realized he had been watching my reaction, a rather broad invasion of privacy, yet I found I had no objection to the intrusion. I found myself enjoying the first genuine smile I had known since my first meeting with Chapman.

"I must admit, Miss Dacosta, to being impressed with all you have endured for the sake of a child which—meaning no offense—you have never known nor are responsible for."

"I am the child's mother."

"Well, yes, a youthful indiscretion. The baby was taken from you immediately upon birth, was it not? Are you even aware of the child's gender?"

"It doesn't matter," I assured him. "It is not something I can explain logically. To do less would have made me a traitor to myself and to the child."

"A fact Doctor Chapman exploited ruthlessly," Holmes sighed. Tipping the alcohol bottle onto the cotton, he continued his transformation. "Watson and I are indebted to you for all you have done to end this madness. I can assure you the child is healthy, well cared for, and thriving. It has been a taxing evening. I have no intention of forcing more knowledge on you than you wish but, at your leisure, I am quite willing to share everything I know of the child."

My head was swimming with possibilities, more than I could accept at the moment. I pushed those possibilities aside for the moment. "What happens next?"

"There is a plan, one circumstances did not allow us to discuss with you. We intend to wait until the patient's transformation has reverted to his normal form before allowing further witnesses into the ward. It is our hope you might remain, a week, perhaps two, in London, to assist Doctor Douglas as he takes over the care of Chapman's patients—"

A bolt of panic seized me, I sat upright in my chair. "The attendants! I mean, they are patients, but Chapman has changed them! They—"

"No need for alarm," Holmes assured me, not pausing in his cleaning. "My understanding is they have been— conditioned—to respond to Doctor Chapman's voice. My purpose in attending the dinner where we first met was to hear the Doctor's voice. My imitation is not perfect, however it was sufficient to command Doctor Chapman's victims into the cells. They are locked in cells five and six; I used the keys you provided to secure them. Not before one of them landed a blow on the Inspector, unfortunately. Still, I suppose it would be wise to gag Chapman before he awakens. There is time."

His words calmed me. "It seems John Watson chose his friends well."

Holmes paused in his work. "That may be the most flattering compliment I have ever received. Thank you."

"I should see to the Inspector, and Doctor Douglas," I said, bracing myself to rise from my seat.

"Watson does have a gift for finding quality friends," Holmes observed. "He has the situation well in hand. You are aware that he is a doctor?"

"He is?" The information startled me.

"Oh yes," Holmes went on, having finished removing his disguise, and he placed his face in the towel I had set out what seemed a million years before. "Watson's use of disguise in this investigation was not typical and, really, was a simple matter of obtaining different uniforms, but it proved effective enough. If you are ready, will you allow me to make introductions? It seems past time you meet Watson, and the others, properly. I know he is concerned for you. Shall we?"

He stood and extended a hand. I was to be introduced to the hero of Baker Street, and the thought made my heart race with delight. I placed my hand in Holmes. "Thank you, Mr. Holmes."

About the Author

J.R. CAMPBELL is a writer and anthologist based in Calgary, Alberta, Canada. His fiction has appeared in a number of publications including *A Study in Lavender, Tesseracts 20: Compostela,* and *Challenger Unbound.* He has also contributed to Imagination Theater's *The Further Adventures of Sherlock Holmes.* Along with his brother in arms, Charles Prepolec, he has edited the anthologies *Gaslight Grimoire: Fantastical Tales of Sherlock Holmes, Gaslight Grotesque: Nightmare Tales of Sherlock Holmes, Gaslight Arcanum: Uncanny Tales of Sherlock Holmes, Professor Challenger: New Worlds, Lost Places, Gaslight Gothic: Strange Tales of Sherlock Holmes* and, with co-editor Shannon Allen, *By the Light of Camelot.* He has been nominated for Canada's Aurora award four times but, alas, has yet to win.

About the Artist

NICK GREENWOOD graduated from East Carolina University with a BFA in illustration. He has worked as an illustrator/concept artist/designer in the advertising, gaming, and publishing industries for over twenty years.

A brief list of clients include AT&T, Modiphius, Rubbermaid, Dias Ex Machina, Hardee's, IBM, Goodman Games, Green Ronin Publishing, Wyvern Gaming, and Poisoned Pen Press. Nick lives in Jamestown, NC, with his wife of 30 years and is the father of four daughters, two dogs and a cat.

www.ingramcontent.com/pod-product-compliance
Lightning Source LLC
Chambersburg PA
CBHW030346020726
47493CB00003B/702